The Assist

A Smart Jocks Novel

REBECCA JENSHAK

The Assist

Also by Rebecca Jenshak

prologue

Blair
Three Years Ago

"Who run the world?" Gabby and I scream the lyrics at the top of our lungs. Top down on her cherry-red convertible, music blaring, hair blowing across our faces, we pull out of the high school parking lot with the first day of classes behind us.

"One more year, Blair. One more freaking year, and we're out of this place," she says when Beyoncé stops singing.

"You don't think you'll miss it? Even a little bit?"

She shoots me a look that questions my sanity. "No. We're going to Valley U, we're going to study hard, party our asses off, and then, when we graduate, we're going to start some fabulous female only business and end up on the cover of *Forbes* or *Vanity Fair*. You and I are meant for more than Suck Hill."

Her enthusiasm is contagious. I want all those things, truly, but it's Gabby who is counting down the days until we can leave our small town of Succulent Hill, which Gabs lovingly renamed Suck Hill. I've always liked the community and friendliness of living in our hometown. Not Gabby. She's been dreaming of moving to Valley and attending the university there since we were in middle school.

Bringing the car to a halt at the four-way stop just outside of our neighborhood, she turns the radio down. There aren't any other cars as far as the eye can see, but we continue to idle in place. I meet her serious gaze. "What's wrong? Are we out of gas again or something?"

"Promise me we're getting out of this town."

I laugh off her words. "I promise."

She grabs my wrist and pulls on the friendship bracelet I made in eighth grade. The ratty thing made of purple thread from my mother's sewing kit still hangs on my arm. A matching one dons her wrist. It's become a symbol of our relationship and the promises we've made. "I mean it, Blair. You and I are getting out of this place. We're going to make something of ourselves. Run companies, have someone fetch us coffee, live in fabulous downtown apartments, and have brunch dates after Pilates on the weekends."

"I know. We've only been talking about it forever."

I don't understand the sudden urgency of her words. We should be enjoying our last year and planning what we'll wear to prom or what we'll put in the senior time capsule. College is a year away and there's so much to do before then.

"Swear it. Swear you're going to do it with me."

Gabby's perfectly styled blonde hair blows in the breeze like a commercial for Vidal Sassoon. It's easy for people to laugh off her ambitions as the rambling of a pretty girl whose been handed everything her entire life. She *is* beautiful, and she *has* been handed her share of privilege, but only I know how strong her desire to rule the world is. I don't believe in my own dreams nearly as much as I believe in hers.

I nudge her with my elbow. "I swear, Gabs."

My faith in myself is shaky, but I believe in Gabby, and with her by my side, I know we're capable of anything.

Dark clouds off in the distance warn of a monsoon storm rolling in just as Gabby parks in front of her house and closes the convertible top. "Sure you don't want to come with me tonight? Rachel's back to school pool party is going to be epic."

"Can't. We're going out to dinner to celebrate my dad's birthday."

Outside of the car, I breathe in the smell of rain in the distance. The wind has already picked up, and I'm looking forward to the heavy gusts and downpour that won't be far behind. When Gabby and I were little we'd talk on the phone through storms, anxiously waiting for the puddles that would be left behind so we could splash and play before the dry desert ground soaked up all the water. I shuffle toward my house, just three houses down from Gabby's. We've been neighbors our whole life, best friends too.

"You could sneak out after." Her sea-blue eyes light up with mischief.

"No thanks. I'm not risking getting grounded two weeks before the pep rally."

She kisses the air. "Fine, loser. I'll text you later."

"Later, Gabs."

I send her a wave over my shoulder and make my way home. Thirty minutes later, I'm sitting at my desk, watching the rain trickle down the window of my second story bedroom, when I see Gabby's car pull away from the curb. With a sigh, I pull out my history textbook and turn to the assigned reading.

If my best friend could see me now, she'd roll her eyes and call me an overachiever. I'm probably the only person sitting at home tonight instead of attending Rachel's party. Tomorrow everyone is going to be talking about it, and all I'll have to contribute to the conversation is the formation of the Provincial Congresses during the American Revolution.

I struggle to focus on the words as my brain tortures me with daydreams of how much fun everyone is having. Still, an hour passes and I'm almost done with the first chapter when my mom knocks on my door.

"Blair, honey."

I stand and stretch. "Come in."

I grab my purse, prepared to celebrate my dad's birthday. My brother and his new wife are meeting us. It should be fun. Although, it doesn't really compare to a pool party with all the coolest kids at SH High.

When I open the door, mother's face is not of happiness or celebration. My stomach drops, and my body tenses in preparation of receiving bad news.

"Mom, what's wrong?"

"Honey, it's Gabby."

The Assist

People talk around me. My brain catches and fixates on single words. Hydroplaned. Unconscious. Critical. Brain Trauma.

I don't care about any of it. I just want to see her. I want to march back there and see Gabby pop up out of bed and tell me it was all a big joke to get me out of the house for the night.

But it's two long days and nights of sleeping in the waiting room before they let me into her room in the intensive care unit. I've been warned about the trauma of the accident, internal and external, but when I see her lying in bed bruised and covered in bandages, I run to her side and grab her hand. It's only relief and happiness that brings the tears to my eyes as she tries to smile around the cuts on her face.

"Gabs."

She opens her mouth and then closes it, frowning. "I…"

"What is it?"

A single tear slides down her face. "I can't remember your name." More tears fall, and each one breaks my heart a little more. "I know you're important. I can feel it in here." She slowly lifts a casted arm to her chest and taps. "But I can't remember who you are."

A nurse in blue scrubs enters the room. "Gabriella, I need to take you downstairs for a scan."

The use of Gabby's full name opens the floodgates, and every emotion I've felt in the past forty-eight hours assaults me at once.

"I'll come back, Gabs." I squeeze her fingers lightly and then flee like a coward out of the room.

Tears blurring my vision, I stumble into the small sanctuary of the hospital and let the sobs wrack my body. I curse God and then apologize and send up a quick prayer. I'm not sure where I stand on God, but this doesn't feel like the right time to snub divine intercession.

A small head pops up in the front row, and I halt two rows back, leaving a respectable distance between us. A girl, no more than ten, turns and offers me a small smile. I wipe my face and nose and give her a half-hearted wave before settling into the pew. The wood creaks beneath me, and I gaze forward to the huge cross nailed to a cement block wall.

Little feet skip down the side of the room and a mass of blonde ringlets bounces beside me. "Hi, I'm Sunny."

Of course she is. She exudes light and cheer, which is saying something in this shitty excuse for a house of worship.

"Hi, Sunny. I'm Blair."

"I like your bracelets." Her eyes track my arm as she studies the colorful adornments with wide-eyed wonder.

"Thank you. Their friendship bracelets." My voice breaks and I swipe at new tears.

"It's okay to cry," she says with reassurance. "Momma says we gotta cry out all the sadness to make room for hope to grow. Positive thinking attracts miracles."

The door to the chapel opens and a woman looks in, finds Sunny and motions for her. "That's my mom. Gotta go." Sunny doesn't wait for my goodbye, she runs into the arms of her mom. I watch as the frail woman hangs her head low and clings to the bundle of sunshine.

It's too much, so I turn forward, giving them privacy and letting Sunny's words take root. Positive thinking attracts miracles, huh? I close my eyes and say another prayer because, devoted believer or not, I'm willing to call in favors just in case, and then I push away all negative outcomes and only allow myself to imagine the future with Gabby by my side.

one

Blair
Present Day

"*W*ell, that pretty much seals my fate." Vanessa flashes her test, showing off the red F at the top of the paper. "Wanna come with me to get a drop slip?"

"No. Don't leave me alone in here, V. It's only the first test. We can do this." My attempt at a pep talk fails miserably. Probably because I'm simultaneously suppressing a groan at my own hostile red letter. Circled and underlined for emphasis. As if I needed more than the large D staring up at me as an indication I hadn't done well on our first statistics test.

We wait for our classmates to filter out of the large auditorium, and judging by the grim expressions and mutterings about the evil professor, we aren't the only ones who did poorly. A small comfort, I suppose.

So much for my perfect GPA, and so much for winning over Professor O'Sean. He's the program coordinator for the accelerated MBA track that I'm applying to next year. It's just a hunch, but I don't think failing his class will help me get in. College hasn't been exactly what I envisioned when Gabby and I planned our futures all those years ago. Actually, that's too bland a statement. It hasn't been all bad, but so far, this semester royally sucks. I feel guilty for even thinking those words. It'll all work out. I just need to buckle down and study harder. Think positive.

Vanessa nudges me while we trudge up the stairs. She leans in to whisper, "My last chance to ogle the man candy."

I follow her slight head nod to the back row, which is occupied by three members of the university's basketball team. I'd like to think I would have noticed the trio, built like the nationally ranked athletes they are, even if Vanessa hadn't pointed them out each and every class. But the last month has been a haze of homework and studying. I'm not sure I would have noticed them even if they'd sat beside me. If it doesn't involve classes, caffeine, or sleep, I don't have time for it.

Their skin tone varies from light to dark, as does their hair color, but each one is tall and muscular. Decked out in athletic gear, they look like they walked off the set of a Nike commercial.

The one on the end closest to the aisle has his foot propped up on the seat in front of him, a black walking boot covering it completely from just below the knee on the right leg. His arms are crossed over his chest, and the blue Valley basketball shirt he's wearing is bunched up around his muscular arms and pecs. A baseball cap is pulled low so it's covering his eyes, but it doesn't matter—it's obvious whatever lurks below is as good as the rest.

"Why is the line moving so slow?" I step to the right to see what the holdup is. I have places to be, and it's lunchtime. What's the hold up?

"Slow down and appreciate the view with the rest of us," Vanessa retorts.

I glance ahead and behind, seeing nothing but necks careening and eyes darting to the back row. The line out of the class moves at rubberneck speed. Has this been going on since classes started three weeks ago? How had I not noticed the ovary explosion they caused? I'd assumed it was just Vanessa being well, Vanessa. Apparently, no one was immune to their beefy muscles and chiseled jaw lines. Except me.

I would be proud of that fact if my grade backed up the time I'd spent not noticing hot guys. I've actually been paying attention to the professor. I need this class. Correction. I need an A in this class. Now, I wish I'd used my time more wisely like V.

"Everyone is staring at them."

"Duh, look at them. They're the best part of this class," Vanessa says loud enough that the girl behind us snickers.

She's right about that. Each one of them is stop-and-stare worthy, but my eyes are pulled back to the guy on the end. The top half of his face is a mystery – always covered by a white university hat. But his lips are fantastic and full in a way that no lip injections could replicate.

I'm still starting at him when his teammate, the one sitting closest to him, reaches over and flips up the baseball hat, revealing a pair of heavy lids. He rights his hat and then reaches for the paper on his desk. My eyes follow his long fingers and bulge at the big red letter A that is underlined and circled just like mine. The underline and circle treatment of my D seems a lot less hostile now, so that's something.

But what the hell? This guy is sleeping during class and still gets an A?

"Why does he even bother coming to class if he's going to sleep through it? There's no way he earned that grade without help. How are the rest of us supposed to compete with the private tutors and special treatment that's afforded the student athletes?" The words spill from my mouth before I can censor and spin them in a more positive way.

We push out of Stanley Hall and join the rest of the students bustling between classes at Valley University.

"Bitter much? What happened to your peppy optimism and we-can-do-it attitude?"

I wear my positivity like armor. Smile on and words of wisdom on deck, I'm always the first person to look at the bright side to hide the insecurities and fears I don't dare speak.

"It just had a heavy dose of reality. Even the jocks did better than we did," I say as I stare down at my yellow chucks.

When I look up, she gives me a sympathetic half-smile and shrugs. "I don't know about the basketball team, but Mario says the baseball guys get ridden pretty hard about grades."

"I'm sure they get ridden hard, all right."

Vanessa's eyebrows disappear under her long bangs. "That is the weirdest thing you've ever said. Never repeat it."

She's effectively lightened my mood, and I hip check her playfully. "Speaking of riding them hard. Where is Mario? He's usually waiting like a puppy out here."

On cue, Mario comes into view. He's jogging to get to V as quickly as possible, as if it's been days since he's seen her instead of fifty minutes.

"We're going to lunch at University Hall after I stop by the registration office. Come with?"

Not even a full month into the semester and my roommate has already managed to snag a boyfriend. Mario may be a jock, but he seems different. He doesn't have any of the asshole, holier-than-thou narcissism I'd expected. He's pursuing V hard, walking her to and from every class, bringing her flowers, and taking her out on date nights, the works. I'd knock his adoration and classify him as a stage-five clinger if he weren't so handsome and sweet.

Wearing his practice clothes—a cutoff T-shirt and baseball pants—accentuates the whole all-American, tan, blond-hair, blue-eyed, good-guy thing he has going for him. Bonus points that Vanessa is completely smitten. I know this because she's trying way too hard to convince me otherwise. Case in point, inviting me to tag along on their lunch date.

"Can't save you from love today. I'm heading to the library to study."

"That sounds positively boring," she says over her shoulder as she skips off to meet him halfway. They come together, hugging and kissing, completely oblivious to the people shoving around them.

Gross.

Except it isn't. It's actually really sweet.

As skittish as I am about the opposite sex these days thanks to the last guy I trusted, Mario has given me no reason to doubt his intentions. And I refuse to let one asshole taint my view on every other guy for the rest of my life.

Speak of the devil.

My phone vibrates in my pocket, and I fight back the urge to press Ignore.

"Hello?" I answer cheerfully as if the man on the other end isn't the absolute worst.

"Where are you?" He wastes no such effort on niceties.

"I'm on my way," is the only thing I say before I hear the line disconnect.

With a heavy sigh, I head to the library. David paces the front entrance. His dark hair is tousled perfectly and emphasizes the crisp white dress shirt. He stands out among the other students who are dressed more casually. I used to like that about him, how he stood out amongst the crowd. Now, it's just another thing I despise.

"You have it?" he asks before the double doors have even closed behind me.

I bite back every mean and awful thing I've thought about the man in front of me. Polished and handsome on the outside. Horrible and ugly where it matters.

I hand over the folder, keeping my mouth closed.

He opens it, absolutely no regard for its contents. He

can't fathom his actions having consequences, and he's made me all too aware of the ramifications of every single action I've made.

"Jesus, David, you could wait to inspect it until you get back to your room. It's all there. I wrote the answers on a blank piece of paper, so you can fill the worksheet in with your handwriting."

"We aren't in fucking high school, Blair. The librarians aren't sitting around looking for suspicious activity. As long as you keep your mouth shut, no one will ever know."

I grind my back teeth.

He snaps the folder shut and holds it in one hand at his side. "Professor Shoel assigned a five-page paper on a classical music composer. It's due next Monday, but I need it Friday so I can go over it and make sure it sounds like me. The last one you wrote sounded too girly."

Because a *girl* wrote it.

"How much longer are you going to do this to me? I'm failing my own classes, I can't keep up."

Desperation clings to my voice as if I could be anything but desperate.

He sneers, turning his handsome features cold and sinister until the outside matches the inside. "Would you rather I share your nude selfies with the world? Maybe that's what you wanted all along, for me to pass them around and give everyone a little taste."

My stomach twists with shame and regret. "Those pictures were for you, my boyfriend. You know I never meant for anyone else to see them."

"I'm sure you tell that to all the guys, but I'm not buying it." He leans in close, and I hold my breath as if not breathing in the scent of his expensive cologne and mint gum could take back everything. "When I feel like you've learned your lesson, then we're done. You got a problem with that, Blair?"

I hate that I'm in this position. Hate that he put me here. But, mostly, I hate that I don't have the balls to knee him and tell him to go to hell.

"No problem," I mumble.

two

Wes

*J*oel pulls the Tesla into the garage and Z and I pry ourselves out of the tiny sports car. The rest of the team is already here and the splashing and music from out back filters through the house. It's a hundred and eight degrees in Arizona today. August was worse, but we're nearing the first day of fall, and I could literally fry an egg on the hood of the car. Shit isn't normal.

I miss the Midwest humidity. Never thought I'd utter those words.

Sometimes, I'd like to come home to a quiet house instead of the craziness of our non-stop party house, but I get why our place is the hang out.

The White House, which is what it was dubbed because it's white, it's huge, and it was purchased by the university president. Our house is only a few blocks from campus and right across the street from Ray Fieldhouse, making it ideal to walk just about anywhere we need to go—not that we had to thanks to my gimp foot and handicap parking. The only perk of being injured.

The White House is nicer digs than anyone else has. Fuck, this house is nicer than the one I grew up in. The only place I've seen that's nicer than this house is Joel's parents' estate. Estate as in it's too fucking big to just be called a house.

But the pool is really why they're all here. Well, that and the stocked fridge.

I swipe a cold water and head out to sit under the mister. Z grabs a protein drink and follows, taking a seat next to me off to the side and away from the pool hangers.

"Welcome home, roomies," Nathan calls from the pool. He has a cigarette dangling from his mouth and a beer in hand. It's barely noon. On a Monday.

I shake my head at him. I'm not pissed he's drinking and smoking. I'm pissed he's doing it in front of the young guys. He can handle himself. I'm not sure about the freshman.

I turn my attention to Z. "Getting in today?"

He grunts something in response. I've never seen Z get in the pool. We give him shit about it, but I honestly have no idea if he doesn't like getting into the water because it's usually filled with lots of people or because he can't swim. I can't imagine there's anything he can't do.

Quiet. Grunting. Out of the limelight. That pretty much sums up Z off the court. On the court, he's a whole different person. People who have never seen him play assume all kinds of dumb shit about him solely based on his mammoth size, or as he would put it, a big, beautiful black man. The fact that he walks around wearing his headphones oblivious to the world and rarely speaks more than a word or two at a time also doesn't help.

Once people see him play, though, it's like seeing someone in their natural habitat. He's smart, quick, and loud. Dude doesn't shut up on the court.

Shaw tosses one of the ball honeys—Charlene? Charla? Carla?—into the air, and her high-pitch squeal makes me want to cover my ears. There's a whole posse of girls standing in the shallow end, being careful to keep their hair and makeup water free. I wish I were a bigger asshole because I'd really like to go dunk the whole lot of them and watch the chaos that would ensue. Lucky for them, I only think this. Also, I'm not doing a lot of swimming these days with the boot and all, so I just sit back and admire the view. I'm annoyed, but I'm not blind.

So yeah, I'm a grumpy asshole. I haven't always been, but getting injured senior year—the year I was supposed to take the team all the way. Yeah, that would make even the nicest guy go a little douchebag.

The rest of the team mills around, swimming, lounging, drinking, eating all our damn food.

I drain the water bottle and drum the plastic container on my leg.

Bored.

Restless.

Joel appears at my side and flings himself down,

cracking a beer open in the process.

"Rookie is out of control. I can't wait until you're back. Freshman needs to be put in his place."

My eyes go back to the freshman rookie who is front and center in the pool, tossing girls up and lavishing in the attention.

"Three more weeks. Fingers crossed."

"Good because we're screwed if we're depending on Shaw to get us the ball. I know it's supposed to be some big damn deal that he's playing two sports, but shit just makes me nervous. Twice the risk of injury and half the amount of focus."

I nod in agreement. "I'll talk to him and to Mario. I'm sure the baseball team has the same concerns."

"Wanna have a little fun with them?" Joel's attention is focused on the pool and pure mischief coats his expression.

"What did you have in mind?"

"Remember my freshman year when you guys made us crash parties and run plays?"

A chuckle rumbles in my chest. Being a freshman sucked in so many ways. My rookie year, the upper classmen mostly just made us do things like carry their gym bags and act as water boys. Fuck, I'd been so glad to be a sophomore and for a new crop of guys to take the heat. Joel and his class had been an obnoxious batch of freshmen and we'd increased the torture to knock down their huge egos. Come to think of it, Joel's class was a lot like this year's rookies.

"You thinking of taking them out tonight?"

"Yeah, but I think we should elevate – take it to the next level."

Shake my head. "We have practice in the morning, so don't elevate it too much. Coach'll kick our ass if we show up with a bunch of hungover rookies. Exhibition is coming up, and he's chewing Tums like candy."

"Live a little, Reynolds. It's your senior year. We're doing it up right."

"We're? You still got another year."

"Yeah, but it isn't gonna be the same without you and Z. This feels like the last year of something great. Something none of us will ever forget."

Shit. He's right. The season is shaping up to be the best year of our lives, and I'm itching to get out of this damn boot. It's making me cranky.

"Yo, Shaw." My voice booms across to the pool, and he lifts his head slowly, taking his damn time. A chin tilt is the only acknowledgment I get.

"Get me a beer."

Joel cackles. "My man, you don't even drink during the season."

"Rookie doesn't know that."

"No. No. No. Come on, guys. That's sloppy."

Sitting in a plastic chair on the sidelines with my booted foot propped on another, I bounce the ball back and forth under my knee. Back and forth, back and forth. I can't tell if it's making my nerves better or worse. I don't need to be here. It's torture, but there's nowhere else I'd rather be. This is my team. I may be injured, but they're still my responsibility.

"Fifty free throws and two miles on the treadmill and call it a day. We have a big week coming up. Talent only goes so far. Focus. Repetition. Heart.

Already having about a gazillion shots in for the day, I head to the weight room. I can't remember the last time I did leg day, and I've never wanted to squat and dead lift so much in my entire life. I pass Mario and a few of the baseball guys leaving as I enter.

Athletes have our own weight room, but we share it between all the different sports. It's huge—easily big enough for three or four groups to be in here at any one time, but we've all got our own styles. Football guys can't be in here without grunting and talking smack. The swimmers spend more time gossiping like old ladies than lifting. The basketball team likes the music turned up so loud there isn't much of an option to chat.

"Reynolds. Still gimping around, huh? When's the cast come off?"

Mario's guys keep going with a nod in my direction.

"Three weeks. Can't freaking wait."

"Thank the fuck. Those chicken legs of yours are getting damn near embarrassing."

I take his jabs in jest. Mario and I have been leaving our blood, sweat, and tears in this room for four years, and we both know I have fucking great legs.

"Give me a few weeks, and I'll be squatting your pansy ass under the table."

"We'll see." He wipes his forehead with a towel and tosses it on his shoulder. "We're having a party at the house next Thursday. Be cool if you guys stopped by, haven't hung out in a while."

"Yeah, I'll let the guys know. Speaking of the guys,

how's Shaw doing? Team's worried about him splitting his time. I am, too, if I'm honest. We're gonna need him to sub in some this year. Need him to be ready."

"I hear ya. I don't like it, either, but he's the best damn relief pitcher we've had in years. I'll keep an eye on him as best as I can while he's with us."

"Ditto."

Fucking freshman has two babysitters and almost fifty teammates between the two sports, and he's still shaping up to be the biggest pain in the ass I've seen in my four years.

three

Blair

Three days out of the week I work at the small campus café in University Hall. In addition to the café, University Hall houses the university bookstore, a mini convenient store, and a sub shop. Untying my blue apron, I lean on the counter completely exhausted after the lunch rush.

Coffee and a pastry totally counts as lunch in college making it our busiest hour. College kids - we're nothing if not lazy creatures of convenience.

"Hey, Katrina." I let out a sigh as my replacement arrives, signaling the end of my shift.

"Rough day?"

"The worst," I admit. She places a hand to her forehead and then swipes a strand of hair out of her eyes. Katrina is the same age as me but has a total mother-hen vibe. Maybe because she *is* a mother. She brought Christian in with her once. He is adorable, but he's also the best birth control ever. Katrina has her hands full between classes, working, and raising a little man by herself. Puts my own crap in perspective.

"It's nothing I just failed my first statistics test."

"Oh, that sucks. I'm sorry."

"Thanks."

She looks up to the ceiling. "What's the quote you're always writing about failure?"

"We learn from failure not success." I roll my eyes. "I know. I know. But I don't have any clue how I'm going to get an A when I'm already struggling a month into the class. The first month is supposed to be easy."

"You get what you work for not what you wish for." She recites another one of the quotes I often write on the to-go cups.

"It feels more like a suck it up, buttercup kind of day."

She pulls a cup from the counter and fills it with our house brew before handing it to me. "For the road."

I shake my head but grab a sharpie and write the quote on my to-go coffee.

"Another night of disappointed faces when they realize the quote girl isn't here."

That makes me smile. I love that I've been able to add a little bit of positivity. We've all got our struggles and I want to be someone that builds up other people.

The quotes were my idea. A random scribbling when I would notice someone looked like they were having a bad day or seemed stressed. Eventually they became something people looked forward to and I started writing them on every cup. It really isn't so hard to tell who needs tough love or an inspirational pick me up based on their demeanor or tone when they order. The quotes on the sides of the cups have become a part of the café, and it's a legacy I'm proud of.

I trek back to the sorority house with determination and resolve. I won't just ace statistics, I'll destroy it.

Suck it up, buttercup.

Two days later as I'm preparing for class, my inspired mood is appropriately deflated. Another late night of studying and homework leaves me pessimistic and petulant. I hate who I'm becoming. I've worked too hard and have come too far to crumble under pressure.

I decide to dose myself in positivity. Maybe if I feel good about how I look, some of those good vibes will soak into my attitude. I pull on my favorite yellow sundress and matching chucks. With a nod at my reflection, I'm off.

The large auditorium is made up of a semi-circle of three sections that face the podium, which stands front and center. Since Vanessa dropped the class and left me alone in my misery, I opt to sit in the back on the far right.

At exactly one minute before class begins, the eye candy arrives. Kudos for getting my head out of my ass to notice the trio of jocks. Vanessa would be proud. Honestly, what has my life become that I'm so overwhelmed with schoolwork that it took so long for me to appreciate hot guys without Vanessa to point them out?

When Professor O'Sean takes his position behind the lectern, I sit straighter in my seat and attempt to give him the kind of attention I usually reserve for the first week of class, jotting down nearly every word that exits his mouth and tallying the number of times he pushes his glasses up with his middle finger. Is he trying to flip us off or is it just a happy coincidence?

I'm able to focus on independent and dependent events for six minutes and fifteen seconds before I find my gaze wandering across the top of the lecture hall. My eyes go directly to the jocks. One in particular. Foot propped up on the seat in front of him, baseball hat pulled low. His teammates are next to him looking bored out of their skulls, but at least their eyes are open.

Honestly, how did this guy get an A? His tutors must be amazing.

When class is dismissed, I hurry out and then pace the sidewalk.

I can do this.

I *have* to do this.

I turn and face the massive fountain that sits in the center of the quad and take three deep breaths. When I turn back to Stanley Hall, it's just in time to see the three basketball players finally emerge. Statistics is the first class I've had with any of our college's nationally ranked team. They seem to stick together, though, always travelling in groups.

"Hi, excuse me." I smile brightly and step directly into their path.

They exchange a confused look but slow down

instead of trampling over me like a bug, which they could very much do.

All five feet and three inches of me stands taller. I make eye contact with each of them, trying to look friendly and not at all intimidated, which I'm not . . . nope, not at all, and then lock my gaze with the sleeper's. He's the shortest of the three, but the intensity of his navy blue eyes makes it hard for me to find my voice.

"I'm Blair, we have statistics class together." I wave toward the building behind them in case they don't even know what class they just came from. Apparently, I am still bitter about the grade.

"Wes," he says as he shrugs his backpack up higher on one shoulder. "This is Joel and Z."

"Nice to meet you." I look to each of the guys and then back to Wes again, silently communicating he is the one I want to speak to. They don't get the memo. "Wes, can I talk to you for a minute?"

"We'll meet ya at the car," Joel pipes in, and he and Z leave me alone with Wes. It's only slightly easier to think without all three of them staring at me with rapt interest.

"What's up?"

"I was wondering if you could tell me who does tutoring for the team? I noticed your test grade the other day, not that I was trying to see it or anything. Sorry, that sounds horrible. I just happened to glance down as I was walking by your desk. Honest mistake. Honestly."

Deep breath, Blair.

"Anyway, I didn't do so well, and I really need an A in this class. Does the team have someone specifically, or do you guys use the tutor center?"

His eyebrows pull together, and he shifts his weight to his left side, making me conscious that standing here talking to me is probably causing him pain.

Join the club. This whole interaction is excruciating.

"I'm lost. You want information on the tutor center?"

The hot Arizona sun shines bright and sweat trickles down my back. "Just information on the tutor or tutors you're using . . . for statistics."

"You think I have a tutor?"

"I'm sorry. I wasn't trying to be rude, but it's just you're sleeping through class."

He crosses his arms over his chest in a silent challenge. The neckline of his shirt pulls down, revealing a hint of tan chest underneath. Annoyed is a good look for him.

"You don't have a tutor?" The question is no more than a mumble. Or maybe I just can't hear it because my pulse is pounding in my ears. I open my mouth several times and then promptly close it when I can't find the words to apologize. He smirks as he watches me grapple with the realization that I've made a very wrong, very humiliating assumption.

Uncrossing his arms, he takes one step in the direction his friends went. "Tutor center is on the first floor of the library." He points in the direction of the campus library, making me feel about a foot tall. "I'm sure someone there can help."

As I watch him walk away, admiring his gait that's somehow sexy and confident even with the boot, I wonder—statistically speaking, of course—what are the odds that the guy sleeping at the back of the class could not only pull off an A but also manage to get that grade without help?

I have no idea, probably because I'm failing statistics. My guess, though? Not good.

I arrive back to the scene of the crime, aka statistics class, with a cup of coffee, a new pen to inspire better note taking, and a determination to hide from Wes and company. I slip in five minutes early so I can grab a seat and be wholly enthralled when they show up. I don't fancy myself important enough that they'd seek me out, but my humiliation has big plans of cowering and hiding for the rest of the semester.

As if my body is now connected to my mortification, I feel the exact moment they enter the classroom.

Wes Reynolds, Joel Moreno, and Zeke Sweets are quite a trio. Yep, I looked them up. I'm calling it research, but in reality, I just wanted to have all the information on the guy I'd thoroughly insulted. They sit in the middle section at the very top, giving them a bird's eye view of the entire class. If Wes's eyes were ever open, would have been nearly impossible to be out of his line of sight. I'm not invisible, but it's as far away as I can get.

Zeke pulls his red headphones down and rests them around his neck as he squeezes his large frame into the seat. According to everyone I asked (more research, of course), Zeke is already rumored to be going pro after this season.

Wes wears a glare that would frighten small children . . . or grown ass women because I slink down in my seat as I continue to watch him. I have a hard time looking anywhere else, glare be damned. He's unbelievably gorgeous. Hell, they all are. Even Joel, who hasn't looked up from his phone, is strikingly handsome with his black hair and bronzed skin.

When Wes glances around the class and his blue stare lands on me, I become very interested in my notes from the last class, reading over them with a fervor I should have tried before the last test.

When we're dismissed, I hang back, waiting for the last row to leave before making my way up the stairs, but when the auditorium is nearly cleared out and the three musketeers haven't made any move to leave, I'm left with no other choice but to suck it up and hope they don't notice me.

Joel nudges him as I approach. Nothing gets past that guy. It's as if he's Wes's eyes and ears. As Wes's dark blue eyes land on me, I plaster on a big smile and decide to be the bigger person. "Hello."

Wes stands, awkwardly making his way to the aisle and holding on to the back of the chair for support. A flash of pain crosses his handsome features as he meets me on the stairs.

"Ball Buster Girl."

"I'm sorry about the other day. I just assumed . . ."

"That I was a dumb jock who couldn't possibly get a passing grade without the help of a tutor or tutorsss?" He emphasizes the plural version with a hiss as he trails me out of the auditorium. As we come to the door, he steps close and pushes the handle, swinging it open and holding it with one large hand. A gentleman. Interesting.

"To be fair you haven't made much of an effort to look like someone who is trying to get a good grade."

We stop on the sidewalk, and I'm aware of Joel and Zeke hanging back and giving us space. Wes adjusts his hat, lifting it so I get a glimpse of the dirty blonde hair matted down like he'd slept in the damn hat. Right, he had . . . just now.

"I could ace that class even if I never showed up."

"That's an awfully bold statement for the first month of class."

He shrugs. "Any luck finding a tutor?"

"Not yet, but I'm sure I'll have no problem finding someone who passed statistics with their eyes open."

His lips part, and his straight, white teeth peek out. "Good luck with that."

I shove my ear buds in and put on my favorite podcast and head toward the library. By the time I get to the tutor center located on the first floor of the campus library (already knew this without the help of Wes, thank you very much), I've turned my humiliation into focused anger.

Okay, so I jumped to conclusions too quickly, but if he can get an A with his eyes closed, surely, I can manage with a whole lot of determination and a tiny bit of help.

I'm still bristling at the way his indigo eyes laughed at me. He could have politely set me straight instead of acting as if I'd personally attacked his intelligence. Okay, maybe I had, but I mean, how was I supposed to know that the guy sleeping at the back of the class somehow magically aced the first test without help, which I'm still not entirely convinced he did.

A text from Gabby momentarily pulls me from my foul mood.

Gabs: Still coming down next Wednesday?

Me: Of course I am! It's your twenty-first so we're going out!

She doesn't text back, which tells me she isn't exactly on board with my plan to celebrate her twenty-first but knows me well enough to know I'm not going to take no for an answer.

I tuck my phone away as I walk to the tutor center's front desk.

"Hey, Blair, what are you doing here?" Molly, a sophomore sorority sister, asks from behind the sign in area.

"I have a question for you." I lean against the counter and pull out my ear buds.

"Shoot." Molly places both elbows onto the counter.

"What can you tell me about tutors for the athletic teams on campus?"

She scrunches her nose and tilts her head to the side. "Are you interested in being a tutor?"

"No, no. Nothing like that. I just wondered if you could tell me who tutors the athletes. Do they have their own private tutors, or do they come here for help?"

"I'm not aware of any tutoring services specific to the teams on campus. I suppose they could have personal tutors, but I've never heard of it. Why?"

"So, they come here?"

"We don't get a lot of athletes in here despite the assumption they need it. I mean, no more than any other group."

Great, I really am a profiling bitch.

Molly rattles on, "There's a few guys from the football team that come in regularly. Baseball team, softball team, wrestlers . . . yeah, I guess as far as I know the ones that need help come here."

"What about the men's basketball team? Do any of them come in for tutoring?"

She brings her thumb to her mouth and bites on the pad of it while she considers my question carefully. "Not that I can think of."

Damn.

"Do you guys have anyone for statistics?"

She grimaces. "Must be rough if you need help."

I nod. "D on the first test."

"Ouch," she says as she flips through papers hanging on a clipboard. "We have Sally and Tom in today, they both tutor math. I think they mostly do algebra and calculus, but I could put you in the schedule and you could meet with one of them and give it a try. Interested?"

"Sure. Why not? Got anything now? I'm done with classes for the day, and I don't want to come back to campus this afternoon if I can help it."

"Looks like Tom is free after his current session. You can hang over there." She nods to a section of chairs and couches pushed to one side of the room. "He should be done in ten minutes or so."

I stop short of the waiting area, spying the men's basketball schedule on the wall with a picture of the team decked out in their uniforms. The guys stand stoic and unsmiling, and my eyes drift first to Wes. He stands in the back row, wearing jersey twelve. His legs are hidden by the guy standing in front of him, which makes it impossible for me to see if he's wearing the boot. My research didn't pull up any information on his injury, so I don't know if it's recent, what he did, or even if he'll be out for the season. I'm suddenly very curious about Wes Reynolds.

In truth, I've paid very little attention to any of the jocks since arriving at Valley. Freshman year, I'd barely looked at anyone who wasn't in a fraternity. Greek life became a home away from home, and there was something exciting about finding a guy who had the same sort of passion for his fraternity brothers as I had for my sisters. And, of course, fraternity guys love nothing more than they love freshman pledges.

By the end of sophomore year, the guys at socials and parties started to blend together and Vanessa and I'd stopped choosing our weekend activities based on frat parties. We plan on moving out of the sorority into an off-campus apartment next year. I'll always treasure my years at the sorority, but I'm ready to have my own space.

David had been the quintessential frat guy, and I'd fallen for his charm and good looks before I'd realized what a monster he is beneath the shiny facade. Too little too late. It isn't as if I think all frat guys are douchebags based on one bad experience, but it's like getting food poisoning at a restaurant. Even if it was the cook's fault, your brain associates the restaurant itself with a horrible experience and you aren't likely to go back anytime soon.

When Tom finally waves me over, I'm so hopeful I could burst. But my optimism only lasts a few minutes. I'm not an idiot. Far from it. I get the basic principles of business statistics. I've read the book and memorized definitions. It's the real-world application that is just out of reach. Math word problems were the devil in sixth grade, and they haven't gotten any easier no matter how much I study.

Molly catches me on my way out. "Any luck?"

"No." I exhale a deep breath. "There has to be someone on campus who tutors statistics."

"Did anyone at the house have O'Sean last year?"

"I asked around. Nothing."

"I'll see if anyone here knows anything," she offers. "Someone has to have something on him. Old quizzes or tests. I've heard he's old-school and still does everything on paper."

Of course. Why hadn't it occurred to me sooner? Wes must have gotten his hands on tests from someone who'd taken statistics last year. O'Sean seems exactly like the type of professor to re-use the same material every year. That has to be the answer. Wes isn't sleeping through class and magically learning by osmosis. He already has the answers.

four

Wes

"Rise and shine," Joel says as he nudges me. I'm not asleep. I wish I were. My eyes are closed, hat pulled down, but there's no sleep to be had.

"She's coming back for more." The tone in his voice is almost inspired.

I don't have to look up to know who he's talking about, but I do anyway. She's the most entertaining thing about this class. Open my eyes and lift the hat, turn it backward so my view isn't the least bit blocked.

Today she's wearing little pink shorts that show off tan legs, yellow tennis shoes that don't match but somehow work, and a bracelet with a little charm around her left ankle. It's too small to make out, but I stare anyway. Her brown hair is pulled up in a high ponytail, and she has a megawatt smile plastered on her face. A big bow on top of her head is all she'd need to look like head cheerleader of my high school fantasies.

"Wes, hey, can I talk to you for a second?"

"What's up?"

I'm hella impressed by the balls on this chick. She's put her foot in her mouth, not once, but twice, and damn near insulted the entire student athlete population, but she keeps coming back. She has determination and grit. I admire that about her.

I also am not in the least bit offended by her assumption that I'm a dumb jock. I'd be lying if I said I wasn't surprised she came right out and asked who my tutor was, but I know exactly what it looks like. I've fed into the stereotype for years, doing nothing to make it seem otherwise. Well, nothing but get straight A's.

"I have sort of a favor."

"What's up?" I stand to walk with her out of the class.

"The tutor center was a bust. I know you said . . ." She looks like she's choosing her words carefully. "Do you have old study notes or tests from previous semesters?"

"Still convinced I'm not capable of passing on my own, huh?"

"I'm sorry, really, no offense. I just want in on whatever study materials you're using. I can't afford to fail another test. What's your secret?"

The secret? I'm fucking smart. Photographic memory smart and statistics is my whole world, but I can't resist messing with her.

"You know, saying no offense doesn't make whatever you're saying less offensive. It just makes you feel better about saying something offensive."

Joel snickers behind me. I just can't resist fucking with her. She's making it too easy.

"Sorry. I'm really so sorry. What about the other guys on the team? Anyone have any awesome math tutors who aren't available to us non-jock students? I can pay."

"Couldn't say for sure, but I don't think so. Most the guys hold their own academically." I lean in catching a whiff of her hair. It smells good—like sugar cookies or candy canes or something sugary sweet that I want to sink my teeth into. "Shocking, I know."

Her shoulders slump in defeat, and I can tell she's finally accepted that I have no answers for her. At this point, I almost wish I knew of someone to send her to. I don't exactly travel in circles that clue me in on secret study sessions and underground tutor societies.

"Thanks anyway." She gives a little wave with the hand clutched around the strap of her backpack.

Joel catches up to me, and we watch as she crosses the campus toward the library. "Dude. That chick . . ."

"I know," I say, and we continue to stare after her completely awe stricken.

"Quit gawking after the poor girl and let's go. I'm hungry." Z's voice pulls at me just as Blair disappears from sight.

When I turn, Z's grinning like he heard the entire exchange, despite the fact he has his headphones on. Sometimes I wonder if he even has music playing or if he just uses them as a deterrent. I don't have the heart to break it to him that he's intimidating as fuck and probably doesn't need another reason for people not to engage.

Back at the house we sit around the television

watching ESPN and devouring the chicken pasta shit that Joel's mom dropped off earlier. She has taken it upon herself to keep us fed and our pantry stocked. Several times a week we come home to find casseroles in our fridge, index cards with cooking instructions taped to the top of the tin foil.

"Why do girls insist on using eight emojis for every text?" Joel asks without looking up from his phone. His fingers tap at top speed on the damn thing.

"I dunno," Nathan says from the floor. He's alternating sets of push-ups and sit-ups. That's Nathan for you. One minute, he's cramming nicotine and alcohol in his system, and the next, he's doing bonus workouts. I guess it evens itself out. "It's up there with using text slang when it isn't any shorter. Using the number two in place of the word to saves what? Like a half second?"

"I deduct two IQ points for every text acronym or abbreviation," I say around a mouthful of pasta.

"This is why you haven't gotten laid in six months," Joel quips, still not looking up.

"Fuck you. It hasn't been that long."

Close.

I've been busy.

Busy sulking. First a soul crushing loss to end last season and then an injury that's kept me sidelined.

And I'm real tired of girls throwing themselves at me for the thrill of sleeping with a jock. Or in some sort of misplaced show of support to heal my fragile ego. Pity fuck? No thanks.

I know, I know. I got uptown problems.

"What happened to Sarah?" Nathan says as he stands

and starts to jog in place.

"It was Tara, and last time I saw her, she was giving a big Valley welcome to a freshman soccer player."

Joel looks up. "God bless her dedication. She's single-handedly welcomed nearly every jock to campus in her short time here."

"Yeah, she's a real Mother Teresa." Z rolls his eyes. He's adamant about not messing around with girls in college so he can focus on ball and his quest to the NBA, so he thinks we're all petty assholes.

He isn't wrong.

An hour later, I'm in hell. Practice is shit. Shaw has talent, but he's all over the fucking place, trying to prove his worth by taking risky shots and hogging the ball. My nerves are shot. I can't do a damn thing but wait for this boot to come off.

"Reynolds, my office," Coach calls to the sideline when he's done giving orders for the guys to work on shooting drills.

I take my time, already knowing what he's going to say.

He's sitting behind his desk, and though I've seen him in his office before, it always strikes me how weird he looks perched upright like he's working a nine-to-five desk job. Some men just weren't meant for that kind of life, and coach falls squarely in that category. "Come on in, son. Have a seat."

I take the old chair in front of his desk. Thing looks like it's been here since the university opened in the fifties.

"How's the foot? Cast comes off in two weeks?"

"Yes, sir. I'm anxious to get back on the floor."

"And we're anxious to have you back, but the trainers say you may not be back fully for another two to four weeks after the boot comes off. We have the exhibition in two weeks and then our first game the week after. I know it isn't what you want, but have you considered a medical red shirt?"

I grind my back teeth to keep from speaking exactly what I'm thinking. Even knowing this was what he was going to say, it still pisses me off. Hell no, I don't want to redshirt my senior year. Sure, I take the redshirt and I'm still eligible to play an extra year. We get five years to play four seasons, but next year Z will be gone. I'll be done with my degree. It's an option. But it isn't one I'm willing to take.

"I'll be ready. Whatever it takes."

He nods. "Once you step out onto that floor, it gets a hell of a lot harder to take it back. You're sure about this? You can take some time and talk to your folks about it."

Right, like they give two shits about my ball career.

"Positive."

I can tell he's torn. He wants me to play and wants me to take the year to heal properly. I get it. I do. It's risky, but I'm prepared to do whatever it takes to be ready to go and to lead my team to a national championship. We were so close last year. Top four in the nation is good. Most people would be happy with that.

I'm not most people, and I want that national title.

five

Blair

Three more statistics classes pass in the same fashion. I sit, feverishly taking notes, as Wes sits in the back sleeping. Today I've given up the pretense of stellar note taking. My scribbles don't even make sense to me as I write them. It's more about keeping my hands busy and my attention trained forward.

I'm doodling hearts and flowers along the margin of my notepad when Professor O'Sean's monotone stops. The lack of noise is deafening.

"Mr. Reynolds," Professor O'Sean's voice booms off the walls of the room, and every person in the room, including me, duck and pray for invisibility to avoid being the next victim of public shaming in the form of being called on in class.

I keep my head low and peek up to the top row just

in time to see Joel elbow Wes. Slowly, he lifts the hat and sits straighter.

"Mr. Reynolds, can you tell the class the probability of the example on the screen?"

I wince for him. Despite my glee that he's been caught sleeping, no one deserves to be grilled in front of the entire class.

"The probability is three-eights. It's a binomial distribution with a sample space size two to the third equaling eight. Would you like me to list the events?"

My mouth gapes. Wes wears an arrogant smile and boyish charm that makes the guys in class laugh and the girls swoon. Professor O'Sean has a begrudging look as he shakes his head to indicate the answer is sufficient. I'm inclined to be on his side. How dare Wes sleep through class and still know the answer? Here I am, taking notes and hanging on every word, and I still have no idea if I could have provided more to the answer than the scribblings I'd written down in my notes.

Glance at my neatly printed letters. The collection of all possible outcomes of an experiment is called a sample space. Yeah, that isn't helpful. All I've done is copy the definitions.

Without responding to Wes, Professor O'Sean moves on. At least I wasn't the only one who assumed the guy sleeping at the back of the class had no idea what was going on.

I dare another peek at the back row, stilling when I find Wes's gaze on me. He smirks as if mocking me instead of the teacher. My cheeks warm, and I turn quickly and keep my eyes forward for the rest of the class.

"There'll be another short test in two weeks that will cover the material in chapter three. The midterm is only one month away, and it makes up thirty-five percent of your overall grade. These tests are a taste of what will be on the midterm, so I suggest you prepare for them accordingly. Have a good weekend."

Good weekend? He's just ruined any possibility of my doing anything but studying from now until the test. I trudge up the stairs with a pit in my stomach, and a foreboding feeling that I'll be lucky to eke out a C in this class. So much for my stellar GPA and so much for getting into the highly competitive MBA program.

At the top of the stairs, I look up to see that Joel and Zeke wear worried expressions. Ones that I'm sure match my own.

Zeke scrubs a hand over his massive jaw. "Man, I don't think I can learn this shit by then."

Joel nudges him. "Sure you can. Wes could teach this stuff to children."

"Isn't that what I've been doing?" the man himself states dryly.

As I approach, he stands and meets me on the stairs.

"Blair." He says my name like a challenge.

"So, you're what some sort of statistics genius?"

"Your words."

"And in your words?"

"I already told you in my words, I could pass this class even if I never showed up." He shrugs as if it's no big damn deal.

I hold back an actual growl. "That's infuriating."

He grins wide. "And impressive?"

"Maybe, but more infuriating than impressive." I

point toward his teammates. "And those two, *you're* tutoring them?"

"What? No, nothing like that."

Something tells me that's exactly what's happening. He looks almost embarrassed by the prospect. I don't know why it hadn't occurred to me before. I don't need to find a tutor; I've already found the best man for the job. I just have to convince him to help me.

The excitement of my idea must be written all over my face.

"Oh, no. No. I'm not a tutor."

"I know, but you obviously know your stuff."

"I'm sorry. I don't know the first thing about being a tutor, and even if I did, I don't have time. Between practice and homework . . ." He offers another shrug. "There's a reason I sleep in this class."

Nodding, I swallow the lump of disappointment in my throat.

I have no idea how I'm going to convince the statistics God to help me. I don't have anything to offer him. And my schedule is as insane as his until I get David off my back.

Between classes and practice, I don't doubt Wes is strapped for free time. And then there are the parties and the ladies. I'm no fool. I know how girls throw themselves at jocks. Vanessa's told me what it's like. She's ready to throw down every time a girl so much as looks at Mario. And they do a lot more than look.

So far, they seem to have gotten the memo V isn't one to mess with because I guarantee the first time one lays a finger on him—innocent or not—she'll be walking around campus with a black eye or half her hair pulled out.

I digress . . . how do you get a man to do something he doesn't want to do for someone who insulted his intelligence and has absolutely nothing to offer him?

I mull over this question on the two-hour drive to Succulent Hill as I sing along to an old high school playlist. When I pull up to Gabby's house, I haven't managed to come up with any solutions, but I'm in better spirits anyway.

Gabby's mom, who had taken a job that allowed her to work from home after the accident, greets me at the door before I can ring the doorbell.

"Come in, honey. Gabby is upstairs." She rolls her eyes and shakes her head, smiling as if it were totally normal for her twenty-one-year-old daughter to be hiding away.

"Knock, knock," I call as I enter Gabby's room. Unsurprisingly, I find my best friend behind her laptop with eyes squinted behind thick glasses. My life has changed so much since the accident, I moved to Valley and did all the things we'd promised—pledge a sorority and major in business. I even force myself to go to Pilates occasionally.

I got my miracle that day. Whether it was thanks to God or the power of positive thinking, I'll never know for sure, but that day changed me forever.

Gabby's memory returned, but the fun-loving and determined girl I grew up with was lost during the crash. She stayed in Suck Hill, refusing to move away and basically hiding out in her parents' house. Deep down, her ambition hasn't changed. I know this because I almost always find her in front of her computer, studying or doing homework for her many online classes. She's a Valley U student, too, but taking classes online isn't the same as being on campus.

"Come in," she calls without looking up, and then as if just registering my voice, her eyes find mine and a big smile spreads across her face. "Blair."

I make the two-hour trip to Succulent Hill at least once a month to see Gabby and have dinner with my parents. Today, though, is just about Gabs.

"Happy birthday!" I squeeze her tightly and then step back to examine her outfit of yoga pants and tank. She looks fabulous, but she isn't exactly ready for dinner at our favorite local restaurant and pub. "You aren't ready."

She bites on her lip. "I thought maybe we could just hang out here."

"Uh-uh. You cannot celebrate your twenty-first birthday at home."

"But going out is so"—she sighs and then plops back down onto the bed—"soul crushing. I don't want to deal with the pity smiles or stares."

I try to see her as a stranger might. She has two long scars on the left side of her face that cross in an X. I think it makes her look badass, but I can't say I haven't noticed the looks she gets when we're in public.

"I promise to verbally attack anyone who dares to look at you the wrong way." She doesn't look convinced. "Come on, please?"

After a few more minutes of pleading, and twenty more minutes for her to change, Gabby and I head to dinner.

"How are classes going?" she asks as we're seated

into a high-top table near the bar. She fidgets and keeps her gaze turned down, basically ducking out of anyone's line of vision.

"Mostly good. Statistics is a bit of a nightmare."

"You'll manage. You always do." Her voice is proud, almost motherly.

"I actually made quite an ass of myself trying to get a tutor," I admit. I like to fill her in on bits and pieces of college, but I almost always underplay the good and leave out the truly terrible—such as David blackmailing me. Somehow, it makes me feel less guilty about being the one pursuing our dream and hopeful that she might join me someday.

When I've finished telling her how I wrongly assumed Wes was a dumb jock, she is hysterical with laughter.

"It isn't funny," I say but join in laughing anyway. "I was a total ass, and now, I need to convince him to tutor me."

"You're going to have to grovel," she says decidedly. "Try food. Men love with their stomachs."

"I think that ship has sailed. I'll go with helpful acquaintanceship."

As she drinks her first legal adult beverage, I fill her in on Vanessa, who is always a favorite topic. Vanessa's life is way more entertaining than mine, and though, they've only met once, I think Gabby likes to hear our college escapades. And I'd never deny her that.

I've tried on more than one occasion to get Gabs to Valley, but she maintains she's perfectly content at home. I think she's hiding scared, but can I blame her? I'd like to think I'd be able to get out of bed each day and ignore the questioning looks, but I don't know if I'm that brave either. Still, I sometimes wish I could trade places with her. It's her dreams I'm living every day, and I can't help but think she deserves it so much more.

"Oh, hey, I made you a new bracelet to match mine." She lifts her arm and points to an orange bracelet. It's one of about twenty on her arm, but it matches the one she's slid to me across the table. "Another year of friendship."

I tie the bracelet around my wrist and then run a hand over my matching bracelets as I smile. "You know, Valley has a really great arts program, including jewelry and fashion design. You—"

"Not this again."

"Yes, this *again*. Gabby, you should be with me at Valley."

Before I can pitch her my best argument on all the reasons she should be at university, two guys approach our table.

They aren't bad-looking and are dressed as if they just came from work, but they look at least thirty-five. "Can we buy you ladies a drink?"

"Sure. Actually, it's Gabby's twenty-first birthday."

Gabby shifts, letting her hair fall over her face, and stares hard at the table top.

"Oh yeah? Happy birthday. Birthday shots are on us. What's your poison?"

It's silent for two long seconds before she looks up and meets his gaze. She flips her hair back, deliberately drawing attention to the scars. Both men drop their eyes.

"Fire ball," she says and finishes the drink in front of her in a long gulp.

"Coming right up." The men recover from their surprise and scurry off, presumably to get our drinks.

"*That* is why I can't go to Valley. I'd rather hide away in my parents' house than spend all day, every day, watching people react to my face."

"Ignore them. Those guys are idiots."

"It isn't just them," she insists. "Last week, a kid in the dentist waiting room cried when I sat beside him. He *cried*, Blair."

"Your scars are not that bad." I cringe at the way it sounds, but honestly, I don't see her the way she must see herself. She's still stunning. The scars didn't change her obvious beauty – only her confidence. "And anyway, college is different. I promise. No one cares. There's a guy in two of my classes who never wears shoes. He has these dirty, calloused feet, and he just owns it, and no one says a thing."

"Not to his face, just over drinks with friends."

The guys return, cutting our conversation short, and set four shots onto the table.

"What are we drinking to?" The guy closest to me asks.

I grab two shots, hand one to Gabby and lift the other in the air. "To Gabby. Happy twenty-first birthday to the most amazing chick I know. Love you, Gabs."

"Love you too," she says with a smile before we clink glasses and throw back the fiery cinnamon liquid.

Shortly after we've thanked them for the drinks, the guys seem to get the memo that we aren't interested and return to the bar. Gabby and I sit and chat about anything and everything. With each glass we finish, Gabby acts more like the confident and happy girl of the pre-accident days.

"So, Vanessa is still dating the baseball guy, any prospects there for you?"

"I don't know," I admit. "I haven't met any of his teammates."

"Vanessa is dating a hot jock, and you haven't scoped out his friends? What's wrong with you?"

"I've been studying." I point a finger at myself. "Failing statistics a month into the semester."

"Lame. You need to get back out there." I resist the urge to throw the advice back at her. It's too good of a night to ruin.

But Gabby isn't done doling out the advice. "Seriously. You haven't dated anyone since David. What's up with that?"

"Nothing is up with that. I've just been busy."

She gives me a no nonsense look that has always caused me to cave under her peer pressure.

"All right fine. I'll scope out the hot baseball guys."

Satisfied, she smiles. "And report back."

Six

Blair

I haven't seen much of Vanessa since she dropped statistics. She's taken to staying at Mario's most nights, and during the day, our class schedules keeps us out of sync. It goes without saying that when I find her rummaging through our closet singing along to K-pop the next night after work, I'm caught completely by surprise.

"What are you doing here? I thought you were staying at Mario's again tonight?" I ask as I set my backpack down at my desk. Four hours of working at the café has left me with sore feet and a kink in my neck. Not to mention, splattered with the sticky sweet syrups I can't seem to wash off my hands and always manage to smear in my hair.

And worst of all, my quotes went completely

unappreciated tonight. I usually get at least one smile or thanks. So much for putting good out into the universe and getting it back.

"I am, *but* the guys are having an after-hours party and *you're* coming with me."

I attempt a smile that I'm sure looks more like a grimace. "Tonight? Shoot, you know I'd love to hang out, but I'm exhausted and have a class at eight tomorrow."

"Who signs up for eight a.m. classes past sophomore year?" She shakes her head. "And that was your excuse the last two weeks. You're coming."

"It was the only time advanced econ was available."

Vanessa pulls out a red tube top and shakes the hanger at me.

"No, not that one. Last time I wore it, I kept pulling it up all night afraid I was going to flash the entire bar."

"Would have made the night more interesting and maybe you wouldn't have ended up back here alone."

"How do you know I ended up alone that night?"

She raises two perfectly arched brows.

"Fine, I came home alone." It isn't that I'm a prude, but picking up a guy at a bar or party seems so freshman year. Is it too much to hope that a nice guy might notice me in the daylight, completely sober?

"Ever since that asshole David, you've been hiding away all this awesomeness." She waves a hand in front of me and waggles her eyebrows.

"I have a lot on my plate this semester." Vanessa doesn't know that my workload is double what it should be because David is blackmailing me into doing his work. I've considered telling her everything a million and one times, but I know Vanessa's reaction would be to march right over to his frat and kick him in the balls. It's exactly what I want to do every time I think about it, but I won't risk pissing him off and having him expose me in front of the entire college . . . or worse, wind up on one of those revenge porn sites.

I move past her, and I know I've already given in when I find myself scanning the clothes on my side of our tiny walk-in closet.

When we leave thirty minutes later, I've managed to shower and make myself presentable. I let Vanessa talk me into a short black dress that leaves none of my curves to the imagination, but I refused the high heels in favor of my chucks.

Vanessa has practically been living at the baseball house, and when we walk in, she's greeted enthusiastically. The two-story house is small, old, and borderline condemnable, but the upper classmen baseball players don't seem to care as they mill around.

The bars haven't closed yet, so the party is still small, mostly baseball players and their girlfriends and the many single girls vying for the guys' attention. A keg sits in the dining room, and an array of liquor bottles clutter the kitchen counters. Mario already has Vanessa's drink and is walking it over to her when we cross the living room.

"Hey, babe." He hands her the cup and drops a kiss to her temple. He puts an arm around Vanessa and addresses me. "What can I get you to drink?"

I don't even have to think about it. The smell of anything fruity or sweet makes my stomach roll after serving mochas and caramel macchiatos. "Vodka tonic.

I don't suppose there's any lime in there?"

He shakes his head apologetically. "No tonic, either. How about Sprite?"

I nod my approval. I bet if Vanessa wanted tonic and limes he'd not only make sure there were limes but also he'd plant a tree out back.

"He is in love with you," I say when he disappears back into the kitchen.

A panicked look crosses Vanessa's face. "Don't be ridiculous. We've been dating for three weeks."

No one dates the first few months of a new school year. It's all the excitement of new students and different situations. Guys especially, but it isn't just them who reserve the first few months of the semester for hookups and having fun. I'd probably think he was in love with her regardless of the time of year by the way he caters to her every whim, but the fact that it isn't even October yet makes me certain.

Before I can detail out all the reasons why I believe it to be true, Mario is back with my drink.

"Thanks, Mario."

We stand, chatting and drinking, until the house begins to fill. Vanessa and Mario and two other couples claim spots on the couch, sitting on laps and watching the Phillies play the Diamondbacks. Neither being around happy couples or watching baseball are on my top one hundred ways to spend a Thursday night, so I venture downstairs where a makeshift DJ booth has been constructed from a card table and a sheet of plywood. The rest of the dingy unfinished basement has been cleared, and I find a few girls from my sorority holding red cups, shaking their butts, and singing way too loudly. The universal sorority girl version of dancing.

But I don't care that I can't dance for shit or that this basement smells of mold and cheap beer. For the first time all semester, I let it all go. All the worry about grades, David, Gabby . . . it's all pushed aside as I give in to the rhythm of the pop mix booming from two large speakers. This is what college is supposed to be—exhilarating situations without real-world stipulations. After we graduate, we won't be able to go out on a random Thursday night and let the night lead us wherever we want. We'll have jobs and careers to obsess over. Bills and responsibilities. With David on my ass, I've had a taste of what it might be like to have a prick boss breathing down my throat, and I'm not eager to enter that world yet.

"I need air," I yell over the music after the fifth song. Physical exertion has warmed my body and my soul. I move out of the circle, and the remaining girls close the space as I make my way up the stairs. I'm still moving to the beat of the music as I spot some of the basketball players, including Zeke and Joel. They stick out in this cramped stairwell, hunkering their tall frames down so they don't bang their heads on the ceiling.

Joel notices me first, and we pause on the stairwell, holding up traffic on both sides.

"Hey it's stat girl."

I chuckle at the nickname. It'll be flunked stat girl pretty soon if I don't pass this next test.

"What are you doing here?" I ask, genuinely surprised. I assumed the athletes didn't mix much outside of their own houses, and I can't remember ever bumping into any of the basketball team before. I'd like to think I wasn't so frat boy crazy that I wouldn't have noticed.

"Same thing you're doing here," he quips, and we both start to move on as the people behind us get impatient.

I look over the other guys and give them a brief nod. They're staring at me intently, and it's way too much attention for my poor underappreciated lady parts.

Mario and Vanessa are gone from their cozy spot in the living room, so I slip out the front door. The baseball house is sandwiched between two other houses, presumably for other sports teams. All the jocks live nearby, giving them close access to the training facilities across the street.

I follow the wrap-around porch to the side, hugging myself and enjoying the cool air whipping through my hair. September days in Arizona are still disgustingly hot, but the nights are the best. The sky is clear, and there is just a touch of heat in the air.

I inadvertently stumble upon a couple making out on the back side of the house, catching dark figures embraced so closely makes it hard to make out two distinct forms, but I see enough to know I should turn around and walk away. Reminders are everywhere I look that happy coupledom can exist in college. Or maybe it's just happy one-night stands. Honestly, I'm almost desperate enough to consider either as a step up from my current situation.

I quietly return to the front of the house, giving myself a silent pep talk to go in and have fun. Enjoy my carefree college years and ignore the stack of homework

I need to finish. If only for one night.

"No way. *You're* at a dumb jock party?" Wes somehow manages to skip up the steps onto the porch.

Placing my hands on my hips, I give him a playful smile filled with attitude. "I never said all jocks were dumb."

"Just me."

Mario and Vanessa emerge from the shadows, looking rumpled and surprised to see people outside. That shock is quickly wiped away when Vanessa realizes it's just me and Mario calls out, "Wes, man, you made it."

They meet in the middle, slapping hands and doing that one-arm hug thing guys are so fond of.

"You two know each other?" Vanessa asks, stealing my thoughts.

The guys exchange a look that clearly says they think we are the idiots for not knowing they are friends.

"Wes is the only guy at Valley who spends more time at the fieldhouse than I do."

"Yeah, I'm gonna beat your deadlift weight just as soon as I get this thing off my foot," Wes says, nodding his head down to his booted leg.

"In the meantime, what do you say we get you a drink?"

The four of us make our way through the living room. Slowly. I hadn't thought of Wes as a big man on campus, but clearly, I missed the memo. Wes Reynolds – big damn deal.

As if my humiliation hadn't been bad enough before.

Guys yell out to him, slap his back, or ask about the foot. And the girls? If desperation has a smell, I am inhaling it now, and it reeks of flavored vodka and self-tanner. Hanging back, I glance around the room, paying particular attention to the way girls move so they'll be in his line of vision. Even the ones who aren't brave enough to come forward seem to be biding their time until he looks their way.

I grab Vanessa and pull her into the kitchen.

She careens her neck backward as if she can't bear to look away. "Did he get better looking since I dropped statistics, or have I been with one man for too long?"

I roll my eyes. "He puts me on edge. He has this arrogant charm that makes me want to kiss him and punch him at the same time. And I really need him to pass statistics, so I cannot make an ass of myself . . . again."

"Isn't it great? All that muscle and confidence and who would have guessed—brains!" Vanessa fills two cups with vodka and a splash of Sprite Zero and hands me one. "God bless smart jocks."

I play hide and seek with Wes for the rest of the night. To be fair, he has no idea we are playing any such game, but every time he comes into view, I duck out of the room. My theory is that if I don't talk to him, then I can't put my foot into my mouth. I still haven't figured out how I am going to convince him to tutor me, but I have a hunch that getting drunk and begging isn't the way.

Well after two in the morning, I drag myself outside and call the sober driver to take me home.

"You know, it seems you were practically invisible tonight." His voice sends goose bumps racing over my skin.

"Yeah, weird, I didn't see you either. Guess we just kept missing each other."

"You waiting for a ride?" He places both hands into his pockets, which forces me to really look at him. Dark jeans, a gray T-shirt that fits tight across his chest and arms, and tennis shoes . . . well, one tennis shoe.

The look suits him. I can't picture him in a dress shirt or loafers, my usual preference, but he works this look.

"Yeah, one of the girls should be here in a few minutes."

"One of the girls? Roommates?"

"Sort of. Sorority sisters. The sophomores take turns being sober drivers during the week."

"Smart idea."

"You guys don't have some sort of similar set up?"

"Nah. We can usually walk."

"Must be nice to be a guy sometimes and not have to worry about walking home alone in the dark."

He glances down at his body, pulls his hands from his pockets and runs one from his chest to his abs, which is where he lets it rest before pulling up the hem of his shirt just enough to tease me with the hard lines and a promise of a six pack. "I totally understand. I swear that every time I walk home, old ladies are honking and yelling out the window for me to take my shirt off or get in the car."

My mouth waters as I openly check him out. He's joking, but I have zero doubt that what he says is true.

He lets his shirt fall back into place. "Why don't you make the freshman do the sober driving?"

I shake my head and force my eyes back up to his face. "Excuse me?"

"Well, it makes more sense that you'd put that sort of crap job on the newest girls—sort of a rite of passage. I thought it was freshman who got hazed."

"Our freshman girls get the red carpet laid out for them. You don't gain loyalty and sisterhood by hazing."

"No?"

"People are more loyal when they respect and trust you. Respect and trust come from treating people well. A positive first year makes loyal sisters."

"Yeah, but if you put them through hell right away, then you know who will really be there when times get tough."

I consider this. "Fair point, I guess, but we aren't marching to war. Sisterhood is supposed to be fun."

"F-U-N," he says dryly.

The sober driver pulls up to the curb, and we say goodbye. As I walk away, I bite back the temptation to turn and ask him to reconsider being my tutor. I need to figure out what it is he wants or needs, and then I need to strike a deal.

seven

Blair

I stop by the café before statistics Monday morning and then navigate to class carefully with a drink carrier full of coffees and a bag filled with muffins in my backpack. I'm running late thanks to the long line, but it works to my advantage when I spot Wes and crew already in their seats at the back of the auditorium.

"Good morning," I chirp.

"Stat girl," Joel calls out, giving me an easy smile.

Zeke nods, and Wes adjusts his hat just enough to reveal his eyes.

"Coffee?"

Joel and Zeke lunge for the drink carrier. Several girls sitting nearby flash me dirty looks, obviously thinking I've resorted to caffeine bribery to win them over, which is only partly true. They don't even look mad. They look more jealous that they didn't think of it first.

I pull my own drink free and then nudge the last coffee toward Wes. "Coffee?"

He eyes me warily but takes the drink.

"I have muffins too," I say conspiratorially as I take the seat in front of Wes and pull the brown paper bag from my backpack before handing it to an eager Joel. He and Zeke make quick work of the pastries. They don't offer any to Wes, and he doesn't even glance in their direction. He's laser focused on me.

"What are you up to, Blair?" he asks just as Professor O'Sean starts in on the lecture.

Shooting a playful smile, I swivel in my seat.

Halfway through the class, I turn my head slightly to get a glimpse of Wes, certain he'll be sleeping again, but I am surprised to find him staring at me. Our eyes lock, and I offer a small wave. He lifts a brow as if he's still trying to figure out my angle, but I just smile sweetly and return my focus back to the front.

When the class is over, I take my time packing my things.

Wes waits until the class has filed out and steps down a stair so he's very much in my way. "What's your play? Coffee and muffins just because?" He narrows his eyes.

"I work at the café on campus." I don't meet his gaze.

"You worked before class?"

Looking up hesitantly, I admit, "Well, no, but it was on my way."

Wes shakes his head. "Thanks for the coffee. I actually managed to stay awake for once."

He gives me a salute with his cup before he shuffles away.

"Wait," I call. Before his steely blue eyes have a chance to regard me in that arrogant, calculating way, the words spill from my lips. "One score makes happy *one* player. An assist makes two happy."

"Uhhh, what?"

"The quote on your coffee." I can feel my face warm and know I'm beet red. This is humiliating. Did I really use coffee and a cheesy basketball quote to win him over?

He lifts his fingers and turns the cup until he can read the words I scribbled.

I hang my head. Might as well go all in at this point. Too late to pretend this never happened. "I was wondering if you wanted to get together sometime this weekend to study? I can work around your schedule."

"Aww man, you mean I drank bribery coffee?" He looks down at the cup in his hand and curls his lip, eyes still smiling.

"Not bribery," I protest. "Friendship coffee. Come on, I need help. Just one time. Let me join you guys the next time you study, and I'll never bother you again."

It'll be easier to ask for more help once I've shown him what a quick learner I am.

Joel nudges him as he tips his head back finishing his coffee. When he's drunk every drop, he speaks, "You know Z and I are going to need to talk it out a bit more, let her join. Plus, girl used a Tony Kukoc quote. Mad props for that. Wait are you the café quote girl?"

I bite my lip and nod.

Wes shoots him a look to zip it, to which Joel just shrugs. Zeke just watches silently, but there's the slightest upturn to his lips.

"Fine. Be at the house at four this afternoon."

"Yes!" A victory smile breaks out on my face, and I don't even care if I look as ecstatic as I feel.

I hold on to those good feelings until I meet David at the library. He's disheveled, clothes wrinkled, hair mussed like he's been running his fingers through it. I hold back questions about how he's doing because, frankly, I don't care if he's having a rotten day.

"We had a pop quiz in computer programming," he says as I take the seat across from him.

It's the only class he didn't shove off on me because most of the work is done in class. You'd think he'd be able to manage one freaking class on his own, but apparently, he can't. I pass over the folder filled with the latest assignments he gave me without saying a word.

"I convinced Professor Reilly to let me do some extra credit to make up for the grade."

"Un-fucking-believable," I mutter as he hands me the paper with directions for the additional work. "I don't know shit about programming, David."

His lip twitches on one side, and he takes out a heavy textbook and plops it down between us. "Thought you'd say that."

I'm still staring at it baffled when he stands. "Need it by Tuesday next week."

Awesome. Add programming to my list of classes this semester, why the hell not?

I read the directions five times. Yep, five. I give up and shove it in my bag. I'll deal with it this weekend.

My shift at the café ends at three thirty, so I reek of coffee and whipped cream as I walk up the sidewalk toward a house I can't believe belongs to anyone I know.

It's only a block from the baseball house so I guess it's fitting – most the jocks live near the fieldhouse. But this isn't like any other off campus house I've seen. It's huge, and the lawn is manicured with shrubbery and flowers. It's obviously landscaped professionally and often.

I check the address three times. It's only when I hear the faint sound of a basketball bouncing from inside that I believe I'm in the right spot.

Wes's instructions were not to knock, so I disregard all manners and push open the door and hold my breath, preparing for anything.

Standing in the entryway of the massive place, I gawk. The room I share with Vanessa would fit inside the foyer.

Zeke comes down the stairs, sans shirt, a pair of long shorts slung low on his hips. I try not to stare but I figure it would be a crime not to admire all that muscle. A series of tattoos trail from his left shoulder all the way down to his fingers. He nods to me and attempts a small smile. His gesture makes me take a deep breath and relax.

"Hey, Zeke," I pause. "You know where I can find Wes?"

"He's in the gym upstairs."

"The gym . . ." My voice trails off as he continues past me walking toward an open room with a large television mounted on the wall. Unsurprisingly, it's tuned to ESPN and a couple of guys are lounged back in big armchairs that look like theater seating.

"You aren't coming?" I call after him. Joel mentioned they'd need help too.

He shakes his head and keeps going without saying any more.

Oh-kay. I walk up the stairs, the sound of basketballs leading me to the court. It's a half-sized version of the one at Ray Fieldhouse and even has the roadrunner mascot painted on the sideline.

Three guys are positioned around the hoop, a ball cart full of basketballs between them, but Joel and Wes huddle together on one side. A shirtless Joel stands with his hands on his hips, watching Wes carefully. Wes has a basketball in one hand and uses his other to emphasize whatever he's saying.

I walk slowly toward them as I take in Wes's focused and determined face and the way he so effortlessly holds the ball, dribbling it occasionally or palming it with one large hand, fingers splayed out to cover what seems like half the ball. It doesn't look like he is even aware he is doing it. The ball is an extension of his hand.

Joel nods slowly, as if a light bulb is being switched on in that pretty head of black hair. He holds both hands out, asking for the ball as he cuts to the top of the three-point line. Wes passes, a crisp fast move that has the ball in Joel's hands before I can be thoroughly impressed with the way he moves. The ball arches to the net and in. The guys move toward each other happy smiles on both their faces as they exchange some words I can't quite hear.

"Hey." I hang back a few feet, giving them room for

their bro moment.

Joel and Wes turn to me in unison.

"Stat girl," Joel says with a smirk. "You're just in time. We're just finishing our study session. He's all yours."

Joel has the sort of charisma and good looks that convince girls to do dumb things like make out with their friends or follow him to his room.

Or send nude photos.

I shake away the negativity and give his sweaty forehead and chest a once over. It doesn't look like much studying has taken place, but I'm not about to argue that point.

Joel lifts his head to Wes in acknowledgment. "Thanks, man." He bounces the ball to Wes and tips his head to me. "Catch you later."

"It's just the two of us?" My voice is a screech, but I'm too nervous to care. "I thought Zeke and Joel were joining us."

"They had some stuff they needed to do this afternoon, so we studied early. They're good, so that just leaves you."

We stare at each other for a moment. Well, I stare. He is probably trying to figure out what is wrong with me while simultaneously devising a plan to get the crazy, gawking girl away from him. He has to be used to that by now, though, right?

"You ready?" Wes finally asks.

"Sure. Yep. Great," I manage with more confidence than I feel.

"We can study downstairs in the television room, but I think some of the guys are down there hanging out, or we could go to my room."

"Your room," I blurt too quickly and then fumble to cover my slip. Great, now I sound like I just want to get him alone. "I mean, the quiet would be good."

"Cool." He motions for me to go before him, and I backtrack out of the gym and into the hallway.

"This way."

I let him take over, and I follow him past open bedrooms while I openly admire the living arrangements these guys have. I've counted three bedrooms already. Each one is large and set up almost in a dorm format with the same bed frame, desk, and large flat screen mounted on light yellow walls. And the bedding and décor isn't bachelor style mismatch stuff picked up from Target. It's all in team colors, and the roadrunner mascot makes an appearance in much of it.

"This is me."

His room looks exactly like the others, but I still scan it from floor to ceiling, looking for clues that make it different. Make it solely his.

"This is your room?" I turn and grin. "What no balcony or bathroom?" I say sarcastically.

"Joel has the master since his dad paid for the house."

My attention snaps to Wes, and the wheels turn as I piece together what I've read about the team and his last name clicks. It should have since it's plastered all over campus. "Joel Moreno. He's a Moreno, like, Moreno Hall and—"

"The president of Valley University? Yup."

Wes grabs the statistics book and a pair of glasses from his desk before taking a seat on his bed.

"Chair's yours if you want it, or you can sit up here. Big bed." He slides his glasses on and then flips open the book, and I swear it's like someone turns on a wind machine. The black rimmed glasses take him from hot jock to hot *smart* jock, and I know this must be what it's like for guys watching a supermodel eat a double cheeseburger. It seems all wrong, and yet, it is sooo right.

"You have specific things you want to go over? Questions? I'm not a tutor, so I don't really know the right way to do this."

I take a seat on the edge of the bed. My heart rate spikes just being this close to him. "Joel and Zeke seem confident enough so whatever you taught them in the past few hours seem to contradict your modesty."

He scrubs a hand over his jaw. "Yeah, all right. How about we start with measuring variation in data sets?"

For the next thirty minutes, Wes basically recites the book as I ask questions and pour over the notes I've taken in class. He never looks at the book before he answers. He flips through it a few times when I mention something in reference to a chapter number, but he seems to be an encyclopedia.

His effectiveness, though . . . I mean, I have read the book on my own, but I'm not even remotely close to understanding a fraction of what he does.

Zeke walks in and then freezes. "Sorry, didn't realize you two were still studying. Practice in ten."

Wes takes off the glasses and sits back on the bed, resting his large frame against the wall. He clears his throat like all the talking has made him lose his voice. I suppose lecturing to a person for an hour could do that.

The Assist

I gather my notes and shove everything into my back pack as I try to lift the fog that has settled over my brain. This is worse than the confused and drugged feeling I have when I leave Professor O'Sean's class. I'm more confused than ever. Between the glasses and his general hotness, I barely registered a word he said.

When someone likes the way a person's voice sounds, they often say they could listen to them read the phone book. Yeah, that's basically what just happened. He read me the stat book and his smooth voice and handsome face mesmerized me, but I learned absolutely nothing.

I stand and shift toward the door. "Thank you for the, umm . . . help. See you guys on Monday."

Wes follows me to the door with a scowl on his face. "Sure. No problem. Hope you got what you needed. I'm sorry to cut out, we have late practice tonight."

"Practice on Friday nights, huh?"

"Every day. We have an exhibition game coming up."

I nod and shift one foot farther as I consider asking if I can come back for more help just to see him put the glasses back on. It wouldn't help my grade, but it'd certainly brighten the day. "Thank you again."

I spend the rest of Friday night finishing David's music appreciation paper and Saturday alternating between trying to figure out this stupid computer programming assignment, trying to study for statistics, and figuring out what I'm going to do when I fail the midterm and have to drop the class with an incomplete. I'm taking four classes this semester. That isn't counting the four classes David is enrolled in but passing along to me. I'm drowning in assigned reading, research, and assignments.

As the quiet sorority house starts to buzz with excitement of girls getting ready for a Saturday night out, I finally give up any pretense of absorbing any more information.

With no other plans for the night, I find myself back at the baseball house. I shoot Gabby a text to let her know I'm back and scoping out the hot jocks. She replies with about ten smiley faces. I'm standing with Vanessa, Mario, and a freshman named Clark, who hasn't left my side since I walked through the door unattached. He's funny, charming, and cute, but I have one eye aimed on the door as he trails on about his first months in the Arizona heat. And if my pulse accelerates at the sight of Joel and Zeke entering the party . . . well, I'll blame that on the alcohol and not the blip of hope that another player might not be far behind.

"I didn't realize the baseball team was tight with the basketball team," I say to Mario and Clark, trying for nonchalance. "Aren't you guys supposed to have some sort of rivalry or something over gym time and national titles?"

Clark pipes in. "Basketball team is cool. It's the soccer guys we don't like."

Mario gives Clark a glare. "We don't have beef with any of the jocks."

A steady stream of guys I now recognize as basketball players follow in behind Joel and Z. It looks like the whole team is here . . . sans one. Maybe Wes is busy memorizing more of the statistics book. How does someone get that sort of knowledge? I consider myself bright, but he has some sort of effortless genius. Or it appears effortless anyway.

I wave to Joel and Zeke as they look out over the crowd but resist the urge to go hang out with them and ask where Wes is. Maybe he's just late like last time. I don't know why I'm hoping for the latter, but as I let Clark attempt to dazzle me with more conversation, my nerves start to fray a bit more each time the front door opens.

"Listen to me go on and on, tell me about you, Claire."

His inability to even remember my name annoys me and snaps me out of my trance. "You know what? I think I'm gonna go home and study. I'm failing statistics, and I'm stressing and . . . well, I won't bore you."

I turn without waiting for his reply and curse the heels that are pinching my feet with every step. I knew I should have stuck with my guns and worn my chucks, which make much better getaway shoes.

"Wait, can I get your number?" I hear him call but hurry my pace and don't stop until I'm a block away and it's clear Clark has given up the chase. I laugh to myself. Did I really think a guy who couldn't even remember my name was going to follow me to get my number?

I keep walking, waiting to call a sober driver, telling myself it's because it's still early and it is a nice night to walk a bit, but when I arrive at the front of Wes's house, I stop and look up at it for signs that he's inside. The faint sound of a basketball being dribbled catches my attention, and I smile, imagining Wes inside hard at practice. Maybe it isn't even him, he has another roommate I haven't met, and Wes did mention that all the guys on the team hung out here. Still, I want to imagine it's him practicing and that's what kept him from a night out with his friends.

I take another step down the sidewalk and pull out my phone to dial the sober driver when I realize the sound I'm hearing is outside. It's the echo of a basketball hitting pavement and not the gym floor inside. Curious, I ignore every single girl horror story thing I've learned about trespassing and being out alone at night and I walk toward the noise. The parking garage for the house curves around the back, and in the far corner, they have a basketball hoop set up. The rusted backboard and chain look out of place with the immaculate house. It's funny to me that anyone would be out here playing when they have such a nice court inside.

In the darkness, I can't make out his face, but the movements are all him. Even without the cast, I think I would be able to pick him out of a silhouette lineup of athletes.

I cross the lot, taking advantage of the view. He's tossed his shirt on the ground and wears a pair of athletic pants that zip at the ankles but are open on the right leg around his cast. The late summer night has cooled, but sweat beads up and shines in the light the streetlights cast around him.

"Hey, Reynolds. Didn't anyone tell you it's Saturday night?"

He stops under the hoop, but he doesn't stop dribbling as he stands to his full height. "Best time to be out here. Got the whole court to myself."

"And no spectators to appreciate the view."

"If you build it, they will come . . ."

"How's that?"

He palms the ball and extends his arm toward me. "You're here."

"I'm not much of a spectator." I close the distance between us and take the ball from him. I turn the ball over in my hands and then dribble it twice, hyper aware that he is watching me. I stop a couple of feet in front of the hoop and shoot the ball.

"Yes!" I call out when the ball rattles around the rim and goes through the net.

"Nice shot." He catches the ball and passes it back to me. I shoot it again, but the basketball gods are fickle, and it bounces off the rim.

"Try again."

He passes it back to me, and I take my time lining up and concentrating at the free throw line. The ball sails up, and I hold my breath until it swishes through the net. Gabby and I played one whole year of junior varsity basketball before we determined we were not cut out for competitive sports.

"Two out of three. You have a spot for me on the team?"

"Sixty-six percent would have you riding the pine."

"What about you? You gonna be ready to play this season?"

He looks down to the cast and grimaces. "Comes off next week, but I won't know what sort of shape I'll be in until then."

"What'd you do? If you don't mind my asking."

"I don't mind," he says and dribbles the ball slowly. "Stress fracture. I hurt it in practice about a month back. Just came down on it wrong and that was it."

"I broke my arm once. Missy Thomas pushed me off my bike. My cast was pink, though."

He looks down at his black cast and then pushes his bottom lip out in a pout. "They didn't give me that option."

"Too bad."

He tosses the ball to me almost as if he's forgotten I'm me and not one of his teammates.

"So, really, why are you out here on a Saturday night and not out with the guys? I saw Joel and Z and a bunch more of your teammates at the baseball house. Were you busy memorizing more textbooks?"

He arches a brow.

"I took a guess. The way you know statistics, I assumed you spent your spare time memorizing it."

He chuckles. "Photographic memory. Plus, statistics is my life."

"How do you mean?"

"Well, say I get fouled taking a shot and get two free throws. Each shot has two outcomes: make or miss. So, there are four possible outcomes. I could miss both shots. Miss the first shot and make the second. Make the first and miss the second."

"Or make both."

He grins. "Exactly."

I stare at him as he moves around the court, and I process what he just told me. "Oh my God. This is how you've been tutoring Joel and Z."

He shrugs. "Not tutoring, just explaining it in terms they understand. They're smart dudes, but ball is our life. So, by giving them examples about shit that doesn't mean anything to them is a lost cause."

"Wes, that's genius. Can you show me more? Explain it like you've been doing for Joel and Z?"

Scrubbing his hand over his jaw, he studies me carefully. "I don't know how much sense I'm going to make talking ball stuff with a chick in a dress and heels."

"Don't let the outfit fool you. I can keep up."

"That so?"

"Yep. I'm not some prissy sorority girl."

He gives me a once over that sends a shiver through me.

"Okay, well, I am, but it isn't *all* I am. I've played basketball before."

"Yeah, how long ago was that?"

"It was a while ago," I admit. "Come on, please?"

"The sorority girl wants the dumb jock to tutor her? It's pretty funny, really."

"Sorry I assumed you were a dumb jock."

"You're only sorry because you need my help."

"I'll play you for it."

"Play me for what exactly?" He cocks his head to the side.

"More of your tutoring services."

"You think *you* can beat *me*??" He raises a brow as he spins the ball around in his hand. He's showing off, but I'm very much enjoying it.

"Not one-on-one." I hold my hands out, and he bounces it to me. I moved to the side of the basket, dribble once and pull up and shoot. As the ball goes through the net, I turn to him. "We'll play PIG."

One side of his mouth tugs into a half smile, but he retrieves the ball and dribbles it to where I stand. I hold my spot, so he moves behind me, the warmth from his body swallowing me up. He leans down so that his lips are a hair's breath away from my neck. "I'm seventy-five percent from the left wing. You sure this is your play?"

I turn my head to meet the arrogant glint in his eye and nod. "I'm not intimidated."

That's a lie, but I'm not about to show any more weakness in front of this guy.

Without taking his eyes from mine, he raises the ball over my head and shoots. The sound of the ball swishing through the net is the only indication it went in. That, and the swagger and cocky athleticism that ooze from him as he retrieves the ball.

And so it goes. I take shot after shot, taking my time and concentrating like I haven't since the SATs, and then he makes the shot while watching me. It's infuriating. And seriously hot.

When I miss, he takes over, picking spots all over the court and moving back a foot each time. Miraculously, I manage to capitalize twice, and we're tied, both having P-I.

"Only one more letter."

"Don't count your chickens before they're hatched." Lining up at the free throw line, I turn away from the basket and hold the ball with two hands. I hear him snicker, but I keep focused on the shot. Trying not to overthink it, I toss it up and over my head and then crane my neck around to watch as it rattles through the net.

"You got trick shots," he says, sounding more impressed than anything.

"Trick shots? Does it somehow count less this way?"

He chuckles and shakes his head. "Fair enough."

He lines up in my spot, peeking over his shoulder once before facing away from the basket and tossing the ball up into the air. The ball hits the front of the rim and bounces back to him.

"Yes! I did it! I beat the conference assist leader."

"Seems you do know my stats."

Heat floods my cheeks. "I might have looked you up. I won! I won!"

"You got lucky. I demand a re-match."

"Nope. I won fair and square." I walk off, grabbing my purse and phone from where I left them.

"You're leaving?"

"I know when it's time to walk away. Tomorrow at two work?"

I don't look back, but I can feel him smiling after me. "See ya then, baller."

Wes

"All right, the probability of success remains constant for all trials. In other words, the probability of me making a shot is always fifty percent no matter how many times I shoot."

The words fall out of my mouth without thinking, which is good because all I can concentrate on is how fucking adorable she looks as she lines up at the free-throw line in her short shorts and Valley T-shirt. Eyes focused on the hoop, she dribbles three times and then pauses with the ball up to her face before shooting. Fucking adorable.

And I'm not the only one who is taken with Blair. The whole team is here, hanging on Sunday afternoon, and she won them all over the minute she waltzed in with paper bags. It looks like she wiped out their entire pastry counter, but she waved off any notion that it was a big deal as she'd tossed the bags onto the counter with no need or want for thanks or acknowledgment. The gesture gained her both.

It isn't just the food, though. Only two type of girls come over to hang at the house. Type one is the ball honeys who have only one objective—landing a basketball player. Those girls are tossed around and become frequents lounging in the house at all hours willing and ready to be used for the bragging rights that she landed a ball player. I stay far, far, like outer space far away from those girls. The second type is girlfriends and those are far and few between. Zeke's made it very clear he isn't dating until he's signed an NBA contract. Nathan parties too much for any girl to take him seriously, and Joel refuses second dates like he's afraid it binds him contractually to marriage and kids.

But Blair isn't either of those things. She isn't settled down with any of the guys, and she most definitely isn't a ball honey. Right now, though, she looks like a cross between the two—hotter than both but taking the best of each. Being all domestic and feeding and taking care of us but looking too hot to be in a relationship. No sane dude would let his girlfriend wear what she has on right now in a house full of other guys.

Joel and Z shoot around us. Joel pipes up when he thinks of something to add. He's smarter than people give him credit for. He just doesn't like to make a big show of it. Z stays quiet like he always does, but he's listening. He's always listening.

"Sounds like you have it down," I say reluctantly. As much as I didn't want to tutor her, I'm clinging to our time together. What I feel borders on disappointment that it's over so soon. "How about a rematch?"

"PIG again? You sure you want me to embarrass you in front of the guys?"

My teammates have trickled in from around the house and the pool and mill about, but they don't intrude, just linger on the sidelines watching.

"Nah, one on one. First to three points. I'm at a distinct disadvantage here with the boot and all."

"You're like a foot taller than I am," she squeaks and waves her hand, gesturing from my feet to head.

"I'll even give up my good hand." I put my right hand behind my back and walk the ball to her. She looks up at me with a cocky grin that is sexy as hell. I can see the hesitation as clearly as I can see her determination.

Pulling her bottom lip behind her front teeth she looks like she is in deep concentration as she tries to figure out her next move. I hold the ball out to her, and she reaches for it. I'm faster and move it out of her grasp as I shake my head. "If I win, I want no mention of last night's loss to anyone. I have a reputation to uphold."

Her brown eyes sparkle. I push away the thought that I just referred to a girl's eyes as sparkling as she speaks. "Buying my silence?"

I nod.

"What do I get if *I* win?"

"I'll keep tutoring you."

I'm not even sure I've been all that helpful. She's a sharp chick, she'd have figured it out on her own. I wonder if she can see through my weak attempt to see her again.

"Give me the ball, hotshot."

Ball in hand, she telegraphs her every move, giving me a distinct advantage even with only one good leg. She has no poker face and when she fakes left while looking right, I'm already prepared for her to make a move. What I'm not prepared for is Joel standing in my damn way.

"What the hell, man?" I ask as I nearly trip over him while Blair dribbles undefended to the basket and tosses up an easy shot just under the basket.

"Sorry," Joel gets out between chuckles, clearly amused at my expense.

Nathan calls out the score from the sidelines. "You're rusty, Reynolds. Weak defense."

Blair saunters back to me, swinging her little ass side to side as she dribbles like she's just walked on to the team. She dribbles the ball right up to me. Her hair is pulled up into another high ponytail, and it flips from side to side. "One to zip."

"You got lucky."

I take the ball and palm it in my left hand, dribble side to side, front to back. She tracks the ball with a focus that makes me want to keep showboating. Thank you, Pistol Pete. I spent an entire summer doing ball handling drills until not having the ball in my hands felt like the loss of a limb.

The guys around the gym have stopped any pretense of minding their own damn business and all eyes are glued on us.

"Show off," and "Steal it, Blair." ring out in steady succession. It's clear who they are routing for, and it aint me.

Traitors.

I make my move to the basket, spinning around her as best I can with the boot weighing down my right foot. Z steps forward just as I'm preparing to pull up and puts his big body between me and the basket. No way am I getting around him with a bad leg. Even with two good ones, he would still be a wall that is hard to break through. I get the shot off, but he's thrown me enough that it rattles around and bounces out without going through the net. Z rebounds and tosses it to Blair.

"What the hell?" I stop and glare at my center just as Blair whizzes by me again and makes another short shot.

"This is sabotage," I mutter as I watch Z and Blair high-five.

To be clear, I want her to win . . . but I don't want to get my ass handed to me.

My teammates are very squarely on her side. She brings the ball back to me with a smile so sweet I want to kiss it off her . . . and then beat her. Girl or not, I have my pride, and the more she taunts me, the harder it is to let her win.

While she stands there waiting for my reaction or for me to make a move to the basket, I decide not to risk it and shoot the ball from where I stand at the top of the three-point line. The surprise on her face turns to a frustrated, and maybe impressed, frown as the ball swishes through the net.

The gym erupts with boos. I turn to the guys sitting around the sidelines and nod toward them. Wise guys, the whole lot of them. I meet Shaw's gaze. No surprise that he's the loudest heckler. "You keep at it, and you won't see the ball all year, Rookie."

He pipes down, but the rest of the guys continue to

let me know how much they want her to hand me my ass.

"Aww, come on, don't be a poor sport," Joel says as he shoots a wink to Blair and beckons her over to him.

My "friends" huddle around her, leaning down so they can . . . fuck, I dunno, come up with a game plan?

"What the fuck? I'm only using one hand and I have a boot on my foot."

Silence. They ignore me and keep whispering until finally Blair nods frantically and smiles. She takes her spot at the three-point line and then holds her hands out for the ball. I'm nervous and maybe a little pissed that I'm going to lose like a chump. There's a big difference between letting someone barely eke out a victory over you and whatever the hell is going on right now.

I'd be lying if I didn't admit I'm also a little turned on watching her strut around all dark hair and long legs in a tight little petite package. It's all very confusing.

"You ready for your whole team to watch you lose to a girl?" she taunts as she dribbles twice and then dares to crossover to her left hand right in front of me. She's goading me, trying to get me to make a move, and my hands tingle to oblige.

"Your win is going to be tainted in lies."

"A win is a win."

She steps closer, putting her right hip into me and keeping the ball on her left side. She's surprisingly good with her weak hand. The long strands of her ponytail tickle my arm and chest as I put pressure on her side. The air between us shifts and maybe that was her plan all along because she doesn't seem nearly as affected as I am. I wrap my left hand around her tiny waist, nudging her backward. I hadn't planned on getting this handsy or aggressive, but she's making it hard to remember this is a friendly game. A friendly game that I wanted her to fucking win.

"You smell good," she says on a breathy whisper so quiet I'm sure no one else can hear.

The statement catches me off guard, but I manage to get out a weak thanks.

"I guess you aren't used to your opponents noticing things like that."

"If they did, they definitely wouldn't say it."

"They're probably too busy trying to keep up with you to notice. You're a really good ball handler. Some of the things you can do with the ball in your hands is just insane. Where'd you learn to do all that?"

"I, uh, well . . ." I clear my throat while I try to figure out how to respond to that, but it's too fucking late. She pulls a spin move that wouldn't fool a preschooler toward my bad foot and is off. I turn just in time to see her pull up and make another damn shot just under the basket. No block, no assist—all her. I lost to a fucking girl. A hot girl, but a girl none the less.

Z and Joel laugh their asses off, and the rest of the guys rush toward Blair. They have her up in the air on their shoulders before I can even hobble over and rebound the ball.

"You played me," I yell to her over the noise. I doubt she can even hear me over the guys, but I don't miss the triumphant smile plastered on her face and surprisingly I think my smile is almost as big . . . just not victorious.

nine

Blair

After my victory, the guys take over the court for their own game, leaving me, and much to his obvious dismay, Wes, on the sidelines.

"Come on, we can finish studying in my room where my teammates can't get in the damn way."

If I were a better person, I'd let him off the hook tutoring me since I clearly had help beating him. But now that he started teaching me like one of the guys and shown me what a good tutor he is, I'm not about to pass up the opportunity.

Also, he's hot. I mean I'm not shallow enough to only entertain the idea of hanging around hot guys, but when they're hot and fun to be around *and* they can help me get a better grade? Yeah, I'm grabbing the opportunity any way I can.

In his room, I pull out the Chewy Sprees tucked away in the side pocket of my backpack and reward myself with two. One for learning something and one for beating him.

He doesn't bother grabbing the statistics book this time as he sits on his bed and winces as he props his foot up on a pillow.

"You all right?"

"Yeah, just gets sore if I don't elevate it every few hours. You want to cover covariance next?"

"Sure."

"All right, let's do the definitions first and then we'll go into scenarios."

He fires off terms and I reply, parroting back the information I've read and memorized from the text.

At each nod from him, indicating I have the right answer, I pop another candy into my mouth.

He raises a brow. "I can't remember the last time I saw someone eating Sprees."

"Want one?"

"Dear God, no." He looks absolutely horrified at the idea.

"Come on. Have one. Live a little." I wave a red candy in front of him, and he grimaces, pulling his lips into a tight line.

His refusal only eggs me on, and I lean on my knees to get closer and press it into his lips as he tries to keep me from getting the candy into his mouth. I swear you'd think it was poison the way he fights.

"Come on. One piece."

His lips part slightly, and I drop the candy in and sit back. I watch his face carefully. The grimace turns to intrigue and then pleasure.

"That's good," he says finally. "Give me another."

I hand him the pack and he tosses a handful of colorful candies into his mouth.

"Hey, that's all I have left." I swipe my precious Sprees back and frown at the two remaining. "Now how am I going to study?"

He shakes his head. "I could rub behind your ears and tell you good job."

"Just ask me the next question," I grumble and hold my candy tightly.

He gives me a scenario, and I fumble to remember anything we've just covered.

"You know the parts, just put them together."

"Ugh, I suck at this part. The essay questions kill me." I close my eyes and focus. Negativity isn't going to get me anywhere. "Stay positive. I can do this. I've already come a long way. I know more today than I did a week ago. I just need to keep putting in the effort. *I can do this.*"

"Uhh . . ." He cocks a brow, and I realize I've been muttering aloud.

"Sorry, you weren't meant to hear that last part."

"What the hell was that?"

I'm sure I turn a hideous shade of red as he stares at me like I've officially lost it. "A pep talk. When I'm feeling down about something, I try to flip it, phrase it to better represent my achievements instead of focusing on the things I can't control. Positive thinking attracts miracles."

"You're weird," he says but winks and goes back to drilling me.

We continue long after the Sprees are gone, and my eyes start to glaze over. "I need a break," I finally admit when I can't take it any longer. "All the definitions are jumbling in my mind."

"You want to stop for the night or . . ."

"I just need a short break. You ate all my rewards, and I'm losing focus." The loss of focus might be in part due to the way he's sprawled out on the bed, making me picture all sorts of scenarios that involve fewer clothes.

He snickers. "I'm afraid we don't have any candy in the house."

"Of course, you don't." He probably fills his sculpted body with carefully proportioned meals meant to fuel the long hours of practice and training. Not pure sugar.

A knock at the door snaps my attention toward it. Joel's face appears, hand covering his eyes. "Everyone decent in here?"

"We're studying, asshole."

Joel stands to his full height and lets his hand drop. "I know. Just messing with ya. It's six."

"Again, we're studying."

"Take a break then." Joel turns, and I'm looking between them, trying to figure out what is so important about six o'clock. "Movie starts in five. Nathan said to tell you he wants extra butter on the popcorn this time."

Wes looks sheepish as he explains, "It's movie night."

"Yeah, I got that." I chuckle. Standing, I begin to gather my things. "I can finish studying at home. I've taken enough of your time today."

"Nah, stay. We can go over it again after the movie." He must read my hesitation. "It's cool. It's just the roommates. We kick everyone else out for movie night." He pauses. "You don't talk during movies, do you? Nathan demands silence."

"And buttered popcorn, apparently."

"You in?"

I drop my bag. All that awaits me at home is reminders of David and the shitstorm he's made of my life. "Why not?"

Wes takes me by the movie room while informing me he's on snack duty for the night. "Popcorn? Soda? Beer?"

"Soda'd be great."

"Save me a seat. I'll be back in five."

Joel arrives as I'm trying to decide where to sit. "Yo, Blair, you met Nathan?"

I shake my head and stretch out my arm to take the elusive fourth roommate's hand. "Good to meet you."

"Nice work on the court today. I thought our boy was gonna lose his shit." Nathan's hair is longer, hanging about chin length, and he tucks a strand behind his ear as he speaks.

Joel plops down in a one of three seats in the front row and Nathan hovers next to him. There's one seat left in the front and four in the back. I take a step to the back row and then hesitate.

"Your boy usually sits in the back by himself. Lucky him. I'm thinking this was his plan all along—leaving room for pretty girls to sit beside him."

My face flushes at Joel's playful flirting. Z and Wes enter the room, and I sigh a breath of relief. Wes, for all his arrogance, has a presence that puts me at ease. I'm starting to trust him.

Wes cradles three huge bowls of popcorn. He hands one to Nathan, places one on the empty seat that is presumably Zeke's, and then tucks the other at his side. Z has five sodas stacked up in his large hands and tosses them to the guys and then walks one back to me with a shy smile. The whole thing is so casual and homey that, when we settle into our seats, I grin at the whole charade. Who would have guessed this is how they spend a Sunday night?

I learn the pick rotates each week, and tonight it's Zeke's choice. Nothing could have surprised me more than him picking a Tom Cruise romantic comedy, *Knight and Day*.

"Seriously?"

Joel tosses popcorn in Zeke's direction. "Z's working his way through all of Tom Cruise's movies and taking us along for the ride."

"I've never seen this one," I admit.

I recline the seat and curl up. I'm sitting next to Wes Reynolds watching a movie. No big deal, just a Sunday night Netflix and . . . well, there's no chill, but a girl can pretend.

ten

Wes

I sleep through movie night ninety percent of the time,
but there's a zero percent chance of that tonight.

Cameron Diaz should have my eyes glued to the
screen, but she pales in comparison to the intrigue I
have for the girl beside me. I don't know what Blair's
story is. All I've been able to determine so far is that
she's a sorority girl, driven, and sexy as hell. So, basically,
nothing that every other dude at campus couldn't have
figured out with a cell phone and social media account.

Blair yawns and stretches her hands over her head.
The movement lifts the hem of her shirt and exposes
the creamy, flat skin of her stomach.

I need to get laid before our next study session or I'm
likely to embarrass myself with a boner that has nothing
to do with my love of probability.

As Tom and Cameron fill the screen, Blair is riveted. It gives me a chance to study her better. Her dark brown hair is pulled up in a ponytail that falls past her shoulders. I like when she wears her hair this way giving me an unblocked view of her small features and delicate neck. The tank she wears shows off her rack, which is the perfect size for her body. They aren't so big she looks like she'll fall over but plenty for me to palm in my large, skilled hands, which is as likely to happen as Tom Cruise somehow *not* ending up with Cameron Diaz at the end of this movie.

I don't have to ask her to know she isn't up for a one-night stand. She has complicated and relationship written all over her. And I don't have time for that. I don't even have time for the study sessions I now owe her.

I shift in my seat and slam the back of my head into the chair to get my thoughts off sex, catching Blair's attention in the process.

"You okay?" she whispers.

"Yeah, just wondering when Tom's going to start kicking ass." It's the first thing I can think of, but she buys it.

"Shh." Nathan's shushing is louder than our talking, but I don't point that out. Guy is serious about movie night, and I'd be lying if I said I hadn't grown to love our weekly ritual.

"Want some popcorn?" I lean over the arm of the chair to whisper the question.

She nods, and instead of handing her the popcorn, I lift the armrest and scoot closer so I can place the bowl between us. Nathan shoots a dirty look over his shoulder at the noise from our shuffling, and I kick his chair. "Calm your tits, man."

The rest of the movie is spent in silence. When Cameron and Tom cross the border into Mexico and the end credits roll, Joel jumps up to turn the lights on and the television off. We have early practice on Monday mornings so we don't usually waste any time hitting the sack after movie night.

"How many left on the list?" Blair asks Z.

He grins. "Everything he's done since. I'm watching in order."

Joel groans. "The early years were the worst."

"I enjoyed *A Few Good Men* and *Risky Business*," Nathan says.

"And *Interview with a Vampire*," Blair adds. "*Jerry Maguire.*"

"Girl knows her Tom Cruise." Z looks positively impressed.

"You wanna cover probability theory one more time?" I'm gonna be tired as hell for six a.m. practice if she says yes but I'm thinking it might be worth it to spend a little more time getting to know her.

"Actually, I'm exhausted, and my brain is mush. I feel good about what we covered today, though. I think I have it."

We head up the stairs with the guys, and Blair says good night to them all like they're tight now. In my room, she grabs her things, and I lead her back down and outside. She unlocks her car and places her backpack in the passenger seat. "Thank you for helping me. You really don't have to keep—"

I cut her off before she says something stupid like I

don't have to keep tutoring her. Of course, I do. It's the only way I'm going to figure her out, and that's become as important as my need to see her succeed. "I have weight training in the afternoon tomorrow, but I could meet you at the library say around seven?"

She looks relieved at my offer. "That'd be great. What's your major anyway?"

I think about giving her my quip about the Final Four being my major. That's all most people really want to hear about anyway. But the fact that Blair sees beyond my stats makes me want to be honest. "Officially, it's business, but basketball is the only thing I've ever seen for my future." I could leave it at that, but I don't. I keep going. "I'll deal with the real world when the season is over, find some bullshit job if I have to. What about you? What are you going to be when you're all grown up?"

"Oh, man, I don't know." Her eyes light up, and I feel like I'm seeing my first real glimpse of Blair. "I have one more year and then hopefully my MBA. My end goal is to be an influencer, an entrepreneur, a badass female boss. I want to inspire people and work beside others with the same sort of passion."

She stops rambling and ducks her head as if she's just realized how much she's said. "Anyway, something business related, which is why I need an A in statistics. O'Sean is the program coordinator for the accelerated MBA track, so I need him to like me."

I nod. She's given it a lot of thought, and I haven't allowed myself to think about anything beyond March.

"Thank you for your help. I really appreciate it, and you're a good teacher. Maybe you should consider that when you start your bullshit job search."

She slides into the car seat, and I close her in. She rolls the window down and tilts her head to look up at me, a playful smile sitting on her lips. "And, for the record, you really do smell nice."

eleven

Blair

"Sorry. Training ran late," Wes apologizes as he takes a seat across from me in the library.

I wave him off. It's only two minutes past, but I'd been so buried under the newest assignments David shoved off on me I hadn't even noticed.

"No worries. I was just finishing some homework."

He grabs the programming book in front of me and flips through it, holding my place with a finger. "You're taking a computer science class? I thought you were business?"

Shit.

I take the book back and shove it into my backpack. "Most businesses run on computer science."

I think I heard David say that once, so there's a slight

chance it's true.

"So, I worked through the practice questions in chapter six. I think I showed my work right, but can you take a look?"

He nods as he rummages through his bag, unzipping every pocket and dumping the contents onto the table—two mechanical pencils, a notebook, a folder, and a bottle of Icy Hot. The bag is clearly empty, but he keeps riffling through the pockets.

"You forget something?"

"I, uh, was hoping I had a granola bar or a forgotten pack of trail mix. I didn't have time to eat."

Extra points for skipping food to hurry to meet me. The tally is somewhere in the millions at this point.

I check the time and close my laptop. "University Hall is open for another thirty minutes."

His eyes light up at the prospect of food. "You don't mind?"

"Nah, I need to stock up on Chewy Sprees anyway. *Someone* ate all mine."

He sweeps everything back into his backpack as I do the same, albeit much more carefully.

The sun is setting as we walk, disappearing behind the mountains and taking the daylight with it. The colors that paint the sky with its descent take my breath away. I used to hate sunsets. Hate the signal of another day ending without accomplishing everything I wanted. I preferred the sunrise and the prospect of a new day filled with possibilities.

It was David who made me fall in love with them. He'd told me that sunsets were meant to be shared. That, unlike sunrise, which was about individual reflection, they were a gathering and celebration of a day spent with people you cared about. I'm sure it was a line he heard somewhere, or worse, made up on the spot to win me over, but even if everything else about my time with him had been a lie, the idea of sharing sunsets stuck.

"You lost?" Wes interrupts my thoughts and motions toward the University Hall, which I nearly passed.

I point toward the horizon. "I was just admiring the sunset. Arizona has the best sunsets."

"Better than wherever you're from?"

"Well, no. I'm from here."

He laughs. "So, your data point is one?"

"I don't need to go anywhere else to know *that* is the best sunset."

He looks up as if he's really seeing it for the first time. "It's pretty good. I'll give you that. Better than any I saw in Kansas."

"Kansas, huh?"

He nods. "Yep."

"Ruby slippers, Dorothy, tornados, the Wicked Witch, and Todo . . . that is literally everything I know about Kansas."

He chuckles. "Not a lot else we're known for, I guess. *The Wizard of Oz* and the Jayhawks."

"The what hawks?"

"University of Kansas Jayhawks. One of the best college basketball teams in the nation." He looks at me like his explanation should jog my memory. I'm not about to tell him I know next to nothing about college basketball, let alone which teams are the best.

"Why'd you decide to come to Valley instead of being

a Jayhawk?"

"According to my father, I did it purely to piss him off."

"Did you?"

He smiles sheepishly. "No, not entirely, but it was an added bonus."

"So why Valley?"

He holds open the door for me as we enter University Hall and runs the other hand over his chin. "Got Z to thank for that. I played against him my senior year of high school in an AAU championship. Coach Daniels recruited Z hard, everyone did. When he signed with Valley, he put in a good word for me. Never even talked to the guy off the court. Anyway, I owe him. It's been incredible playing alongside him. Players like Z don't come around very often. He has the kind of talent that people will still be talking about in twenty years."

"I heard he's going pro next year."

"Yeah, definitely. He should be a first-round pick, but it depends on how the season goes. If I can get us to the final four, he has a shot at a top five spot. Joel could go, too, if he doesn't screw it up with the partying and women. He has another year yet, though."

"What about you?"

"Nah, doubtful. I could maybe get drafted in a late round, probably spend some time on their minor league teams, but I'm just focused on the next five months."

"I'm surprised," I answer honestly. "I can tell how much you love it, and you're obviously talented enough to play with guys who are going pro, why wouldn't you want to go for it or at least try? You might be surprised, and worst-case scenario is that you don't make it and you can fall back on your business degree."

He grins, which is not at all the reaction I am expecting. "You have spunk. I like that. I just need to focus on getting the team to that national championship. Z and I have been working toward it for four years, and it's so close I can taste it."

We go our separate ways to get supplies for our study session and then settle into a table where I sip coffee and Wes devours a sandwich and chips. He quizzes me on binomial distribution between bites, and I find I mostly know the answers. I'm picking it up faster now, whether because it's clicking or because Wes is that good, I don't know. I'm leaning toward the latter.

I'm able to concentrate more too. It isn't that his looks don't affect me anymore, he's still mind jumbling hot, but as I learn more about him I realize the outside isn't even the sexiest thing about him. He's intelligent and polite and just . . . nice.

When they dim lights at University Hall signaling closing time, I'm reluctant to leave but I know Wes has other things to do. Guilt for tricking him into helping me gnaws at my conscious. I should probably let him off the hook now and tell him I can finish preparing for midterms on my own.

"Same time tomorrow?" He asks as he scrolls through his phone and then taps out a message.

"Uh, yeah, sure. I work at the café until four, but I'm free after that."

"Shoot," he says and stops on the sidewalk.

"What's wrong?"

"Joel has a late class tomorrow night."

I stare at him trying to figure out how Joel's schedule

impacts his.

"He's my ride," he finally says as he stares down at his phone. "I can't drive yet with the boot."

"Oh, right. I'm sorry. I completely forgot. I could come to the house again if that's easier?"

"Yeah, that'd be great."

"How are you planning to get home tonight?"

He shrugs. "Joel's coming to pick me up."

I laugh, something about Joel playing chauffeur makes me adore their friendship even more. On cue, Wes points to a black sports car pulling into the parking lot behind the library with no regard for the speed limit. Joel pulls up to the curb and grins up at us through the open window. "I feel the need . . ."

Wes shakes his head, but I don't miss the big smile on his face as he finishes the quote. "The need for speed."

He looks over sheepishly. "*Top Gun.*"

"I should have guessed."

"You need a ride, stat girl?"

"Nah, it's a short walk." I point in the direction of the sorority house.

Both men look at me stubborn and hard. "You are not walking across campus at night by yourself."

Valley isn't exactly a hub of violent crime, but I can see any retort I could make would be in vain. They aren't letting me walk.

Wes holds the door open for me, and I slide in to the back of the car that still smells new and expensive. It fits Joel, who I haven't gotten a good read on yet. He's flirty and playful and seems to be so different from Wes and Z, but they're close. I can tell their friendship goes beyond ball.

"What kind of car is this?" I ask as I run my hands over the soft leather. A large screen rests in the middle of the dashboard and Joel taps it to set the music for the drive.

"Tesla 3." Joel turns to me, mischief in his eyes. "Ever gone zero to sixty in three seconds?" The way he says it sounds positively dirty.

I shake my head slowly, afraid what my answer means.

Joel's eyebrows raise, and he smiles wickedly. Before I can brace myself, he speeds off so fast I forget to breathe. Holy shit. Wes careens his neck back to check my expression, and the wolfish smile he gives me only speeds up my already racing pulse. Zero to sixty. Yep, I'm falling just that fast.

twelve

Wes

I barely get the threadbare Valley basketball T-shirt pulled over my head before I hear Blair walk up the stairs toward my room. Her footsteps are tentative and soft, a definite distinction from the heavy ones of any of my roommates.

She knocks on the doorframe as she peers in. "Hey."

"Hey." I take in her tan legs and the tiny white shorts that cover places I want to see and taste.

I squeeze my eyes shut to try to erase the thoughts. I recite the presidents backward in my head and then open my eyes to find Blair bent over in front of me to get something out of her bag. An innocent act, but the way her T-shirt gapes open and gives me a view of her rack? Not so much.

She stands straight all business and pep. "I spent

some time going over the first two tests to try to determine what this one might look like."

We settle onto my bed, sitting so close her hair brushes against my shoulder. "I think I'm good with the short answer questions, but the essay killed me last time. What do you think he might ask us to do for this one?"

I take her last test and read the essay question and her answer. Then re-read twice because my head is not in it.

"I think he'll have us compute probability of events."

We take turns coming up with scenarios and then computing the probability. She chews on the end of her pencil in thought, and I'm mesmerized by the way her lips part and her teeth rest gently on the rubber end. This woman is going to kill me a slow, achingly painful death.

"Every single example you used was basketball related," she says looking back over our scenarios that she's carefully written in her notebook.

I shrug. "It's what I know."

She raises both eyebrows as if she's daring me to think beyond ball. I clear my throat. Only two things currently occupy space in my brain. Ball and . . .

"The probability of you letting me kiss you." My throat feels like gravel as I continue. "Possible outcomes include allowing and not allowing. Each outcome has a probability of point five."

Her eyes widen, and she shifts uncomfortably. Her voice is quiet and throaty. "No."

The sting of rejection hurts. I thought I'd seen interest in the way she looked at me. And not just my brain and what I could do to help her or my status as a jock for some sort of ego boost. Interest in *me*. I flip open the textbook, hiding my disappointment and giving my fingers something to do. "It was just—"

She rests her hand on top of mine. The G-rated touch sends X-rated thoughts. "That example doesn't work because not allow isn't an outcome."

Her words register, and my fractured ego repairs itself and then alley oops a beautiful lob that ends with my mouth capturing hers. Slam dunk.

Fuck, I don't even care that the thoughts going through my head are screwed-up ball references. I can usually compartmentalize the aspects of my life that don't revolve around my jersey, but this girl's lips against mine feels like the sweetest victory.

Our tongues tangle, and she grows bolder, running her hand up to my chest before fisting my shirt as if she's afraid I might run away before she's ready.

Baby doll, I'm not going anywhere as long as you're touching me. I keep the thought to myself but do my best to show her that truth by placing a hand at her hip and deepening the kiss. I smile into her mouth when I taste the lingering sweetness of Sprees and something that is uniquely Blair. Damn, I had been curious about kissing her and assumed it'd be nice, but now that I've kissed her, I don't wanna stop.

The door swings open, "Hey, man, I invited some girls—"

Joel stops short when he catches Blair scrambling away from me and placing the back of her hand to her lips.

"My bad. Looks like you already have plans for the night." His grin makes the stiffy in my pants deflate. Fucking Joel.

"Ever consider knocking?"

"Ever consider locking the door?" He throws back.

Blair scoots off the bed. "He's all yours. I have to finish a paper tonight anyway."

Joel backs out of the room, leaving me alone with this girl who has my head spinning. I half-hoped kissing her would cure my interest, prove that she was just like any girl, but it didn't. I want to do it again.

"Sorry about Joel."

"It's fine." She waves me off. "I really should get going."

I shove my hands deep into my pockets. "Okay."

I walk her downstairs and past the noise of the party forming out back.

She stops just outside the door and peers back at me. "So, I'll see you in class tomorrow?"

"Actually, no. I'm getting the boot off late tomorrow morning. Professor O'Sean is letting me come in during his early office hours to take the test."

"There goes my idea of cheating off you."

I chuckle and run a hand through my hair. "After that stunt you pulled on the court Sunday, I wouldn't put it past you, but you don't need it. You're ready."

"I hope so. I need to pass this class. No, I need an A in this class."

"I'll get you your A."

And I know I will. I've taken on her grade the same way I've taken on Zeke's first round pick. I don't know what it means or even why, but I can see the possible outcomes, and I know the probability of walking away is the least likely of them all.

thirteen

Blair

When I arrive at class the next morning, I take the seat in front of Joel and Zeke and wordlessly hand them the muffins and coffees I grabbed from the café. They both turn the cups straight to the quotes and smile.

Professor O'Sean walks up the stairs to begin passing out the tests, so I offer them a nervous smile and wait, tapping my pencil against the desk and praying that I've retained some of the knowledge that came out of Wes's beautiful mouth. Thoughts of his mouth lead to dissecting the kiss that still burns my lips, which is pretty much all I've been doing since it happened.

The first person stands and takes their completed test to the front with five minutes remaining. O'Sean's tests are no joke—long and arduous. A minute later the room becomes a hub of energy as the whole class finishes or maybe just gives up. I wait for the last possible minute, going over each question, re-thinking my answer, and ultimately changing nothing. I know this stuff.

Joel and Z wait for me just outside the classroom.

"Longest test ever," Joel mutters.

I nod as Zeke elbows Joel and points behind me.

"I'll be damned. He's back!" I hear Joel and Z share their excitement with some sort of hand clapping, but as soon as I look over my shoulder, it all becomes background noise. Wes is walking toward us. The off balanced gait I've grown accustomed to in such a short time is replaced with a strong, sleek elegance.

"Hey, how'd it go?" he asks, a genuine smile filled with trepidation like he's afraid I've failed and his tutoring didn't help.

I'm very aware that his eyes rest solely on me. "Good. I think."

He wraps his arms around me, taking me completely by surprise. "Knew you could do it," he mumbles and then just when I'm about to swoon from the feel of his hard body wrapped around mine, he ruffles my hair like a big brother might do to his annoying little sister.

He pulls back quickly and steps toward the guys.

"You're back?" Joel asks looking down at his foot. "Please tell me you're back."

Wes's face lights up as he does a little dance side to side. "I'm back, baby."

Z grabs Wes in a bear hug and then pulls back. "With me." He lifts his hand up to his head. "Without me." He drops the hand to his waist. "With me," Z repeats and smiles as he lifts his hand back up.

Wes chuckles. "Definitely with you."

The three of them grin and chuckle as they share their Tom Cruise movie quote moment, but I can't peel my eyes off Wes.

Oh no.

I'm totally falling for him. First, I let him kiss me, and now I'm getting all mushy inside watching him have a bro moment. Making out with a jock is one thing, falling for one? That spells disaster, and I can't stomach any more relationship disasters.

"Let's grab lunch at The Hideout to celebrate all the things. Another statistics test done and the boot is off! It's a damn good day," Joel interrupts my thoughts and just like that I find myself back in the small sports car with enough testosterone to power it Flintstone-style.

The Hideout is the most popular restaurant and bar near campus. The décor is sports themed and judging by the warm welcome they receive as we slide into a booth, I'd say the employees are fans.

Wes and I sit across from Joel and Zeke, who are deep in debate mode over whether Coach should start Nathan or some rookie who neither Joel or Zeke seems to like. Wes angles his body toward me and nudges me under the table with a knee.

"Tell me honestly, did you use basketball references in your essay?"

"Nope," I say proudly.

"No? All my good basketball examples went to waste?" His eyes light up. "Wait, did you use my kissing example? Please say yes!"

I flush, and my eyes fall to his lips, remembering the way they felt against mine. "I took your examples and flipped them to football terms instead. Professor

O'Sean prefers football."

"He does?" Wes tilts his head to gauge my seriousness.

I nod. "He used the Cardinals as an example twice last week during the lecture."

"Well, I'll be damned. Maybe I shouldn't have slept through class."

He winks, and my heart does a little pitter patter.

"How's the foot feel?" I ask as the waiter brings our food.

"I'm cleared for practice today."

"Wow, just like that, huh?"

He nods. "Exhibition game is on Friday, so I don't have a lot of time to get my guys ready."

"Your guys?"

"I'm the point—the leader on the floor. Z and I have been playing together since freshman year, Joel and Nathan a year later, but we have younger guys who aren't meshing as well as I'd like yet. Takes a lot of time together."

"I'm impressed."

He waggles his eyebrows. "Oh yeah?"

Joel and Zeke get quiet as they start piling food into their mouths. I eye the food in front of Z. Two sandwiches, chips, and a milkshake. I don't comment. He has to be close to two-hundred and fifty pounds, so it's probably a drop in the bucket.

"I can't wait for practice." Joel chews, and his body practically bounces with excitement. "Coach letting you play the exhibition?"

"He'll let me play." By the tone in his voice, I venture that Wes is used to getting his way on the court. And probably off it.

"What about you? Are you coming to the exhibition?" Joel asks, stealing a chip from my plate.

I swat playfully at his hand. "What exactly is an exhibition?"

The table goes silent. Even their chewing stops.

"Wait a minute. Have you ever been to a Valley basketball game?"

I bite my bottom lip and try my best to look sweet and innocent. "No."

"Never?" Wes drops his sandwich and stares at me.

"Well, I watched last year's tournament on television."

He shakes his head. "The exhibition game is like a scrimmage or practice game where we split into two teams and play each other."

"When is it again?"

"Friday night at seven," Wes answers.

Joel steals another chip, and I pretend not to notice. "And there's a party at the house after."

"Cool. I'll see if I can round up some of the girls."

"You're a sorority girl?" It's more of a reminder than a question. "Yeah, bring some friends."

I pull my plate back as he reaches for another chip. "My friends are too good for you."

Turns out a lot of the girls from the house already made plans to see the exhibition game.

"I had no idea people came to these," I whisper to

Vanessa.

"They didn't until they started making it to the Final Four."

The cheerleaders and Ray Roadrunner, our lovable mascot, dance in the center of the floor to Magenta Riddim, but I'm too nervous to follow any of it with any real focus.

"You're gonna have to stop bouncing your leg like that you're shaking the whole row."

"I'm sorry. I'm just so nervous."

"Why are you nervous?" Vanessa asks with a smirk.

"I don't know."

"You like him."

I shoot her a look as the crowd around us erupts. Turning my attention to the floor, I watch as the team runs onto the court. I spot Wes right away even in their matching warm ups and shoes.

But it's Joel who steals the show by joining in with the cheerleaders and doing the ridiculous dance perfectly in step with them. If Wes is cocky, Joel is an attention whore. He eats up the female screams and shouts as he shows off his dance moves.

Vanessa and I stand and cheer with the rest of the student section.

"I can see why you like him. The man is seriously fine. He really knows how to rock the whole hot athlete thing."

"That he does." I motion with my head toward Mario, who is standing on the other side of Vanessa and talking to one of his buddies from the baseball team. "So, does Mario. He's hot and nice—the total package."

She checks to see if he heard our conversation and

then hushes me. "Don't say that shit where he can hear you."

"You're spending every night with him, I think he knows you're into him. Give it up, V. You aren't playing this cool."

She scoffs but smiles. Turning my attention back to the team, more specifically to Wes, I'm completely transfixed by the way he moves—quick, confident. He oozes athleticism, and—crap, I'm totally into a ball player. No, not just a ball player. *The* ball player. Do they even date?

Obviously, they kiss girls in their bedrooms.

After a short warm up, the guys split up into two teams: white and blue. Wes and Zeke don the home team jerseys while Joel and Nathan are on the blue team.

I'm lost in all of it, in all of him. Sure, I've seen plenty of games between high school and the NBA games my brother made me watch when we were kids. I mostly know the rules and the lingo, but I've never been so invested. I wring my hands every time he shoots the ball. I scream like a total fan girl every time he makes a shot, but I'm keenly aware of how badass he is leading his team. They trust him. They look to him. They follow him.

Z's also surprising. The quiet guy I've come to know is a total trash talker on the court. I can't hear him, but his mouth moves constantly while the ball is in play. On defense, he mumbles what I assume is razzing commentary to his opponent. And on offense, he calls out for the ball, pumps up his team with pep talks and attaboys.

Joel's personality is exactly the same on the court.

He's arrogant, but he backs it up by leading his team in points and looking good doing it. The cheerleaders yelling just a little louder for him doesn't go unnoticed, and I have a sneaking suspicion he's earned their favoritism with a lot of sexual favors.

I don't have a read on Nathan yet, but his game face is as intense as his desire for silence during movie night. His longer hair is pulled back in a nubby ponytail. If I'd passed him on campus, I never would have pictured him a jock. He has a grunge style that I thought died with Kurt Cobain.

The game ends with Wes and Z's team on top. Joel and Nathan look pissed but still accept fist bumps from Z as they walk off the court.

Part of me wants to hang around and wait for Wes, but I have no idea how long he'll be or what his routine is like. I don't even have his number. And if I did, I wouldn't know what to say. I mean I guess we're friends, but it isn't the friend in me who's anxious to see him again. The girl he kissed last night, on the other hand, is ready to stalk him into a dark corner and demand a repeat performance to verify it was as mind-numbingly good as I remember.

"You ready?" Vanessa asks as the people around us start to clear out. "Mario says everyone is going straight to The White House."

"Sure." I watch Wes until he disappears completely into the tunnel that leads to the locker room. "Let's go."

fourteen

Wes

"Nice job out there," Z says as he removes his headphones from his locker and places them around his neck.

"You too. You keep playing like that, and you'll be a top-round pick for sure."

He grunts, but I don't miss the smile. I take his future as seriously as he does. It's my job to get the ball to him, so if I fail, then he fails. That isn't gonna happen.

"See ya back at the house," I call after him. When the rest of the guys go, I unwrap my foot and hobble to the shower. Pain throbs as I wash quickly, leaning on the wall to take some of the weight off it. I'm supposed to be easing into it, but I only have one mode—all out.

"How's the foot, Reynolds?" Coach asks as I step out of the shower with a towel around my waist.

"Sore, but good. It felt strong out there."

He nods and eyes me carefully. When he seems convinced I'm telling the truth he nods again. "All right. Take it easy tonight. I know you guys are celebrating, but make sure you ice it before bed and check in with the trainers first thing tomorrow before practice. Need you strong out there."

"Yes, sir."

"And, Reynolds? Spend some time with Shaw. He has potential."

Just the mention of the rookie irritates me. "He's a hot head."

"So were you." He pushes open the door and taps the doorjamb twice with a fist. "Nice work out there tonight. Good to have you back on the floor."

When the door closes behind him, I slink down on the bench and flex my foot to try to loosen it up a bit.

I'm back.

The party is loud, and people are everywhere when I get back to the house. I push through to my room and throw my bag onto my bed. I'm not really in the mood to party, but I am hoping a certain brunette will show up. I spotted her at the game, which might have had something to do with my refusal to ask coach to pull me even after my foot started throbbing.

"Fifteen points, three assists, and either two or three steals. I lost track trying to keep count of all of it." The object of my thoughts stands in the doorway of my room. "And I can't believe Zeke."

"He's pretty incredible."

"I meant the talking. The guy never shuts up out there. Who knew?"

I laugh. "Yeah, he saves it all for the court."

She steps into the room and holds out a beer. "Drink?"

I shake my head. "I don't drink during the season."

"I don't think Joel got that memo. He's halfway through a bottle of Jack downstairs."

She moves to sit on my bed, and I take a seat at my desk.

"Your foot hurts." A crease forms between her brows, and she speaks with certainty.

"A little sore."

"You should probably have it elevated." She moves into action, looking around the room before zoning in on a chair propped up on the other wall. She pulls it across the room and then motions for me to put my leg up. "You have any ice in here? Or is it heat that you need?"

"Shit. I should have grabbed an ice pack from downstairs."

She bites her lip and looks as if she is considering leaving to go get it. She's gone into full-blown mama bear mode. It's hot, but I don't want her to leave.

"Hand me that beer."

She obliges, and I place the cold can against the side of my foot just above the top of my shoe. I should really take it off and ice it properly, but I don't want to give her any reason to rush off. "Guess I did need that drink after all."

She shifts as if she doesn't know what to do—or worse, as if she might leave.

"Sit, please. You're making me nervous pacing around."

She does, and we study each other with the bass from downstairs vibrating the floor below us. "Did you enjoy your first game?"

"I did."

I'm not convinced. "You don't sound very sure."

"I was a nervous wreck. I don't know how you do it. Every shot, every pass . . . I'll have an ulcer by the end of the season."

I like that she's already planning on going to more games. Like that I popped her ball cherry. Hell, I even like that having her there made me work that much harder.

I swing my foot down off the chair and stand. "Move over."

Before she can protest, I sit on the bed next to her and scoot until my back rests against the wall. My feet still hang off the edge, though. A detail that doesn't go unnoticed.

Blair moves so she's facing the headboard and I angle myself to face her and move my legs onto the bed. Without a word she places her still mostly cold beer against my foot.

Her phone pings, and she sits forward to retrieve it from her back pocket giving me an eyeful of cleavage. A gentleman would pretend not to notice, but there's no part of her covered flesh I haven't already imagined in vivid detail.

"It's Vanessa. She and Mario are leaving."

"Already? Party just started."

"I think they're far more interested in being alone than a party with half the university."

She pulls the beer away from my foot and lets her legs hang off the edge of the bed. "I should go. I rode over with them."

"I doubt they want a third wheel for what they have in mind. Stay. I'll get you a ride home later."

"You sure I'm not keeping you from your adoring fans?"

"Got my number-one fan right here."

She cocks a brow. "I'm your number-one fan? I'm not sure what that says about you, considering I've only been to one game."

"I guarantee you're the only one here who tracked my stats tonight. It was three steals, by the way." I wink, and she blushes. Truth be told, it's fucking hot that she watched me close enough and cared enough to keep a tally.

"So, I surmise there's no boyfriend. If there were, he'd have tracked you down and kicked my ass by now."

"Was that a question?"

"Yeah." I laugh out the word. "Is there a guy?"

The tiniest shake of her head is my answer. "And you aren't dating anyone and on top of the list for every girl downstairs. I'm actually surprised I'm the only one who thought to come upstairs."

"Smart girl." I worry a little about the talk she might have heard. I haven't dated anyone since freshman year when I realized I didn't have the time or energy for that while playing college ball, but I'm not ignorant to the rumors and talk that have me sleeping with or paired up with a different girl every week. Not true, by the way. Girls are too exhausting to go through them like Joel does.

She rolls her eyes. "I just wanted to check on you. I saw you favoring the leg as you went up the stairs."

"I'll be all right. Feels better already. So, why no boyfriend? I haven't heard any chatter, but I'm not blind."

"You have the weirdest way of asking a question that feels like it isn't really a question."

I cross my arms behind my head and wait for her to answer.

"I've dated a little, but nothing serious."

I'm content to keep her to myself in my room. Hell, I didn't even want to party before she showed up, but Blair isn't an easy nut to crack. Maybe the atmosphere downstairs and another drink or two will loosen her up. And I don't mean that in a crass way. I'm more interested in learning something about her than getting in her pants. At least for tonight.

"You ever seen a six-six guy do a keg stand?" I ask as I stand and hold out my hand to her.

She puts her delicate hand in mine. "No."

"Let's go find Joel then. It should be just about showtime."

I wrap an arm around her shoulders and make sure to lean some weight on her so she feels like she's helping me. Part of me does it to claim her, selfish man that I am. Mostly, though, I just want an excuse to touch her.

Joel is exactly where I expected him to be—the center of fucking attention on the back patio. Girls hang off either side, and he's telling one of the five stories he tells every damn time he gets drunk. He stops mid-sentence when he spots Blair and me.

"Reynolds!" He calls out my name and lifts the bottle in his hand. "About time that you two lovebirds decided to show your faces."

I grin but feel Blair shrink a little in my arms. Fucking Joel. "Don't be jealous that I got the hottest girl on my arm."

It's a dick thing to say, considering the two on his, but I'll trade their annoyance to make Blair feel less unsure. I nudge us through to an outdoor patio set. "Shaw, wanna give me and Blair your seats?"

He growls at me and doesn't budge.

"Come on man, I need to get off my foot."

He nods to the girls next to him, and they leave slowly, taking their damn time as he glares at me.

"They always do what you say?" Blair asks when we are seated.

"I wish. The freshman are the worst. Takes half the season to get their egos in check."

"Who keeps yours in check?"

"Ball busters like you."

I pull her closer so she's all but on my lap. She doesn't resist, and my dick starts making plans. A girl stumbles past us, covering her mouth like she is about to puke, and Blair and I watch in combined horror and fascination as she moves like lightning into the house.

"Not exactly how I pictured our first date."

"This is a date?" Her voice borders on panic.

"Kinda feels like one. We're hanging out together, and I plan to try to kiss you at the end of the night."

"No," she states adamantly and turns to face me.

"You don't fall into a date. A date is planned . . . intentional."

"That right?"

"Yes." She leans back into me. "Now, ask me on a real date."

I chuckle. "Ball buster."

She shrugs, telling me she isn't budging on the subject. Not that I mind, exactly, but I haven't been on a real date since . . . well, I can't remember, but it probably involved high school and a dark movie theater where I could try to cop a feel.

"Go out with me."

It's her turn to laugh. "Was that a question or a command?"

"Blair Olson, will you go out with me?"

She shrugs again. "Yeah, I guess so."

This girl. "But, uh, even though this isn't a real date, I'm still kissing you later."

"Promise?" She turns her head to face me, bringing our lips inches apart.

I stare at her mouth as she moistens her lips like she's waiting for me to make a move. Instead of answering with words, I capture her face with both hands and pull her to me. What I'd planned to be a quick kiss—a taste of the promise I made—turns serious fast. There's nothing quick or innocent when it comes to my response to this girl. She hums into my mouth, and I deepen the kiss, not giving any fucks about making out in the middle of a party.

My dick aches as she molds her body to mine and wraps her arms around my neck. We're as close as we can get without lying down on the floor and going at it.

I weigh that scenario out in my head before breaking the kiss. "Think we should probably go back upstairs if you want to continue this."

Pleas say yes. Please say yes. Yep, I'm cool as a cucumber on the outside but straight up begging on the inside. Her eyes dart from my mouth to the party, taking in what we've done and where we are. She looks more stunned than embarrassed, but then she pulls away and runs shaky fingertips across her lips.

"I should go."

Well, hell.

"But pick me up tomorrow night for our date?"

fifteen

Blair

"He's here." I read the text saying as much and smooth my dress down. I do a final turn side to side to see myself in the mirror from every angle.

Vanessa lies on her bed, watching me obsess. "Want me to go downstairs and ask him what his intentions are?"

I laugh, easing some of the nerves that have taken over my shaky hands. "As entertaining as that would be, maybe we should wait until at least the second date to scare him off."

Or until I get laid. I know it's probably a terrible idea to sleep with the guy who holds my statistics grade in his hands, but a girl can only be expected to have so much restraint.

"Better to know now before you waste a perfectly

good Saturday night."

Most people I know don't even go on real dates, let alone on a Saturday night. Weekend nights are pre-filled with frat parties and nights out at the bar. The rare occasions I've been asked out on a real date, it's always been something mid-week. A Monday night coffee date, a Tuesday dinner, sometimes even a Thursday out together at The Hideout. Fridays and Saturdays are reserved. I'm willing to risk missing a party to go on a date with Wes. One almost certainly ends with me coming back alone, but the other . . . has possibilities.

The sorority house is a two-story home with bedrooms on both floors and a basement with a kitchen and dining room, laundry room, and our chapter room where we hold meetings. Vanessa follows me down the stairs from our second story room and into the first-floor entry way/living room. Men aren't allowed beyond the entryway unattended, so essentially it serves as our "suitor waiting area." It doesn't see a lot of suitors for all the previously mentioned reasons.

Hostess duty is a real thing in the house, a chore shared between all of us, and it seems Molly has jumped at the opportunity to play hostess. She hasn't only let Wes in, she's proceeded to fawn all over him. I hold back a giggle as I watch him lean back away from her as she tries to snake a hand up his arm. An arm that leads to those hands I admire so much. He looks up as I appreciate my first glimpse of him in date attire—a black T-shirt, dark denim jeans, and tennis shoes—a different pair from what I've seen him wear before, and I'm suddenly curious how many pairs of sneakers this guy owns.

I stop at the bottom of the stairs and Vanessa pushes ahead of me. She waltzes up to Wes and eyes him carefully.

"You gonna give me the talk, maybe show me your gun collection before you let me take our girl out?"

"Nah, I don't think it's necessary to tell you I'll either personally kick your ass or pay someone to do it for me if you hurt *my* girl. I'm sure it's also not necessary to tell you that a badass chick like Blair deserves a gentleman. Where are the flowers? Chocolate covered strawberries?"

I groan, and Wes looks embarrassed. V, however, keeps going.

"I expect that, for the rest of the evening, you bring you're A game. I'm talking door-opening, attentive, no-looking-at-other women, hold-her-hand, chivalrous shit."

"Okay." I step in front of Vanessa and take Wes's arm. "I think we have it from here.

Wes chuckles and lets me lead him to the door. I give V a small wave over my shoulder. Her intentions are good. She knows enough about the shit David pulled to understand why going out with someone new is both nerve-wracking and exciting. We've almost made it outside when Wes stops abruptly and turns. V still stands in the doorway watching us.

"Don't worry about our girl. I'm well aware of just how badass she is."

Wes leads me to a small black SUV and opens the door for me. I flush, assuming he's following V's orders. "Don't let Vanessa get in your head. She's—"

But my protest is cut short. He winks and leans in.

"Would have opened the door for you either way. It gives me more time to check you out. You look amazing."

"Thank you. You too."

Wes drives us to a small bistro on the outskirts of town. It's well out of the three-block radius that most university students venture out of, and I wonder if it's a coincidence or if he's purposely taken me somewhere we won't be seen.

"I've never been here," I say as he helps me out of the car. A blue awning welcomes us, and inside, I'm surprised to find the décor a mix of local sports memorabilia and amateur artwork. Canvases are hung artfully around the small space with the artists' names boldly displayed on gold plaques underneath. Jerseys ranging from tee-ball size to high school are lined up on one wall like a walk through a lifetime of an athlete. It's a bizarre design, but it feels welcoming none the less.

"Hey, Wes Reynolds." A man with a mess of unruly gray hair that makes him look like a mad scientist appears from behind the counter. His smile falls, and he pauses. "Did you get the days mixed up? Game is next week."

"Nah, came here to eat." Wes places a hand at my back. Those long fingers splay out across my lower back. The heat of the contact makes me feel secure and possessed all the way down to my toes. "Cal, this is Blair. Blair, this old man is Cal."

"She's with you?" Cal gives Wes a shocked look and then tosses a wink in my direction. "Honey, he didn't kidnap you, did he? You're free to go. I have a bat under the counter here and I'd love an excuse to take some practice swings."

Wes snorts and lifts his foot. "The boot is off, old man. You can't catch me now."

Cal's expression softens, and he rounds the counter, zeroed in on Wes's leg. "You're really back? Coach letting you practice and everything?"

Wes nods. "Yep, all the way back. Even let me play the exhibition game last night."

"Well, all be damned. Don't tell Mason or he'll be pissed we missed it." He looks to me apologetically. "Sorry for the language. My boy loves to watch Wes play. Thought we were gonna have an angry teenager on our hands this season, and trust me, that would have been good for no one."

"Those your son's jerseys?" I ask, pointing to the multi-colored, multi-numbered shirts.

"Sure are. Mason's a baseball player, but he loves watching basketball."

"Kid's gotta wicked curve ball," Wes adds.

Cal beams with pride. "Your table is open." He nods toward the small seating area.

As Wes leads me to *his* table, I ask the obvious questions. "You have a table? What is this place?"

Wes throws his arm over the back of the booth, looking as comfortable as if this really is his table. "Cal's wife owns a cleaning service and does some work for Joel's family."

He looks up sheepishly.

"Which means she cleans The White House." I connect the dots.

He nods. "She started bringing by food, got us hooked on the grilled cheese and homemade pies. Z and

I started coming here to get our fix. So, yeah, I have a table."

He winks, and I'm a total goner. Instead of trying to impress me by taking me to a restaurant where we would have maybe shared a bottle of wine and asked about the daily specials, he brought me to a hole-in-the-wall bistro that requires him to drive off campus and where he has his own table. This feels so much more real.

Cal brings us menus and a pitcher of iced tea, which Wes pours for both of us before almost draining his own glass.

"Best damn iced tea this side of Kansas."

I must be staring at him with a perplexed expression because he looks around and then asks, "What? Got something on my face?"

"No. I'm just trying to figure you out. What's the game he mentioned?"

"Mason has a home game next week."

"And you're going?"

"Wouldn't miss it."

"So, you help your teammates study, you tutor failing students in your spare time—"

"That one was not my choice, if I remember correctly," he points out.

"You attend high school baseball games and support local businesses . . . you're like a decent guy under that arrogant, egotistical exterior."

He holds a finger up to his lips. "Shh, not so loud."

"No, honestly. It's hot."

His mouth pulls into a big smile. "Well, if you put it that way."

"What's your family like back in Kansas?"

He visibly stiffens, but the smile only falls for a second before it's back. "If I tell you we had Sunday dinners every week and I call my mom every day is that going to get me extra points?"

As if he needs them.

"Depends on if it's true."

A tall kid with shaggy hair desperately in need of a haircut brings our food to the table. Wes stands to shake his hand. "Mason, how's it going? How's the arm?"

Mason bobs his head and cradles his arm protectively. "Good. I'm starting next week."

"I'll be there."

Mason's face shows his excitement, but he gives a one shoulder shrug like he's too cool for school.

"Mason, this is my friend Blair."

I offer a wave. "Nice to meet you. Good luck next week."

Mason does some sort of blush, nod, wave before he disappears into the back.

"Good kid," Wes says as we dig into our food. "Parents too. They're at every game, home and away. I know it can't be easy working the hours they do, but they make it work."

"Do your parents make it to many games? Must be hard being so far away."

He doesn't look up as he answers. "They'll be there if we make it to the Final Four."

All right, that seems to be a touchy subject. I let him lead the conversation after that, which includes him asking me the most random questions about myself.

How the coffee shop quotes came about, my favorite songs and books and television shows. I can barely get in a question back as he fires them off one after the other. It's surface-level stuff, but one thing I learn for sure about Wes Reynolds is that, despite the lack of information he gives me about himself, he's damn good at making me feel special and wanted.

Wes

I drive back to campus after dinner, but I'm not ready to end the night, so I park at the house and then usher her across the street to Ray Fieldhouse. Going inside would only lead to me kissing her, and trust me, I want that, but I promised this girl a date.

"Tell me something about yourself that has nothing to do with basketball."

I gape. Something that doesn't pertain to basketball. What does that leave? And when was the last time anyone asked about me without mentioning basketball? It became part of my identity somewhere along the way and separating it from me leaves . . . someone I don't recognize.

"What were you like in high school? What are your parents like? What's your favorite color? What do you want to do after college?"

"That's quiet an interrogation. I'll give you one. My favorite color is orange. I like the new addition to your bracelets, by the way." I pull at the orange string tied around her wrist. One of about twenty on her arm. All of them are different colors, and some are faded and frayed, but the orange one looks new.

"Thank you."

"What's up with the bracelets? Do they stand for something?"

"A friend makes them for me. For us. Friendship bracelets. It's sort of our thing. I started making them for us in middle school, and we've worn them ever since."

"Girl friend or guy friend?" I ask, feeling insanely jealous at the prospect of her having that sort of attachment to some other guy. It's ridiculous because whatever we're doing is casual. That's all I have time for right now, no matter how cool of a chick Blair is or how much I wish I had more time to really get to know her and date her like she deserves.

Vanessa was right about one thing—Blair deserves all of it, all the romance, and I'm not that guy. Maybe after the season, but nothing can get in the way of getting back to the Final Four.

"Her name is Gabby. Wait, how did this get turned around? You're supposed to be telling me about you."

"I'd rather talk about you."

"A question for a question then. Where in Kansas did you grow up?"

"Just outside of Kansas City. You?"

"I'm from Succulent Hill, it's a couple of hours south of here. You have any siblings?"

I shake my head.

"I have an older brother. He lives in Phoenix and is married with two adorable kids."

"What's your greatest fear?"

She balks, thrown by the deep question. I can almost see the answer on the tip of her tongue, but she holds back. "I don't know."

"You don't strike me as someone who isn't self-aware. What scares you?"

"Failing." Her voice comes out quiet, barely a whisper. "And letting people down."

Silence falls between us. I get that fear because it's tied so closely to my own. What if I can't get the team whipped into shape? What if Z is looked over for a big NBA deal because his team lets him down? Yeah, I get the fear of failure. Guilt washes over me for being such an ass about helping her with statistics. It obviously is as important to her as basketball is to me.

"Come on, let me show you something."

The gym is empty and dark. I love it this way. I love it packed full of people on game day, too, but no athlete gets that without a lot of days and nights with only the echo of the ball bouncing off the wooden floor.

I lead her up the stairs to the very top and we sit on the blue plastic seats so we can take in the darkened gym.

She's quiet and pensive, as if maybe she's trying to figure out why we're here. Or maybe she is counting down the seconds before she can make a run for it. Bringing a girl to a deserted gym probably is not on the top one hundred best first dates.

"This is my greatest fear." I lift my arms on either side.

"Bad seats?" she jokes.

"Being a spectator and watching the game from up

here, smart ass. It's my final year, and I'm not ready for ball not to be the center of my life."

It's terrifying, actually. No, terrifying doesn't seem like a strong enough word. Anxiety wracks my body when I think of being one of those guys watching from the sidelines, talking about the good ole days. As a kid, it felt so far away, but every day, I get closer to it all going away, and I don't know what that looks like. Don't even want to think about it yet. One final season. This is it. This is my moment to soak it all in. I can deal with the rest later.

"Have you thought at all about what you'll do next year?"

I shrug. "Not really. I know I should be thinking about it, making a plan, but I just can't. I need to focus on the season and the season alone, and when it's over, I'll figure out what's next. Speaking of, I don't know any way to say this that doesn't make me sound like a conceited prick, so I'm just going to say it."

She raises both eyebrows but nods for me to continue. "Dating isn't really an option for me right now. Vanessa is right, you deserve more than anything I can give you."

"So, this is our first and last date?" Her voice is filled with humor. Not what I expected.

"I like hanging out with you. I'd like to see more of you, but I can't make any promises beyond that."

"Vanessa means well, but what she wants for me and what I want aren't the same thing. I've dated guys who promised me the world and didn't make good on it. I appreciate your honesty, and I get it." She grabs my hand and interlaces our fingers. I've avoided touching her too much tonight, because I'm finding that, with Blair, each touch only makes me want her more. "You have an incredible gift. I don't know if I've ever loved anything as much as you love basketball, and I can't pretend to understand your fear, but I know the things I'm most scared of tend to be the things that push me the most. No risk, no reward. So that's how I'm choosing to look at whatever this is between us."

"You're smarter than you look."

"That's the nicest thing you've ever said to me."

I shake my head. I don't know what I'm doing on a real date, acting like a gentleman and talking about fears and life goals, but the time I spend with Blair feels so much more substantial than even the best of fucks I've had with other girls. "No. *This* is the nicest thing I've ever said to you. I think you might end up being the best thing that ever happened to me."

She blushes, and I wonder if I've put my foot into my mouth or scored points. I stand and offer her my hand. "Come on."

With her small hand cupped in mine, we walk back to the basketball house. It turns out this dating thing isn't so bad. I've almost even forgotten about sex while I've learned more about what makes Blair tick. Nah, that isn't true, but I did enjoy myself more fully clothed than I ever imagined I would.

Joel bounds down the stairs dressed to go out when he spots us. "Hey, it's Bless."

We share a confused look.

"Blair and Wes. Bless. You know, it's like your couple name."

Blair giggles. "I guess it could be worse, our couple

name could be Weir."

Joel slaps me on the back as he passes us on his way to the door.

"Don't get into any trouble," I warn. "We have practice in the morning."

"Yes, Dad," he calls and then, as if just remembering, he calls out, "Oh, hey, Blair, how'd your test turn out?"

She looks shell shocked, and I shoot Joel a glare.

"Don't worry, I'm sure you did great. Z and I both passed."

He leaves, and Blair turns to me. "Grades are up? Up where? How do you know?"

"O'Sean posts them on the student portal before he hands them back."

I lead her to my room and hand her my iPad so she can log in and check her grade.

Tension hangs heavy in the room while she pulls up her grade and then sighs. "I got an A," she says like she almost doesn't believe it. "Oh my God, I really got an A!"

I smile and say a silent thank you to the math gods. Then nix that because I did this. Props to myself. "Congratulations."

She hands the tablet back to me and eyes me warily. "You weren't going to tell me grades were up, were you?"

"I was planning on mentioning it about the time I dropped you off."

She punches my arm playfully.

"I had faith in you . . . well, and in my excellent tutoring."

I toss the iPad onto my bed and wrap my arms

around her waist, drawing her against me.

"You were okay, I guess," she says, her voice husky and tight as it travels straight to my balls.

"Admit it." I lean down and let my lips linger just over hers. "Admit I'm a good tutor."

Instead of answering, she closes the space between us and brings her mouth to mine. I consider pulling back and making her say it for all of a second before her soft tongue brushes against mine, I'm lost and exactly where I should be all at once.

She threads her arms up and laces them behind my neck, forcing her up on her tiptoes and putting her flush against me. Not daring to break away from her, I mumble, "I'm taking your non-answer as confirmation."

She chuckles into my mouth in response and then pulls back, breathless and flushed and sexy as hell. "If I admit you're a good tutor, will you wear those sexy glasses again?"

"You think my glasses are sexy?" She drops onto the bed, and I grab my reading glasses from my desk. If I'd known that tidbit sooner, then I'd have been playing it to my advantage already. "You mean, these glasses?"

Her eyes light up and her tongue darts out to wet her lips. She gives the faintest nod before sitting up on her knees and reaching for me. "You're like the best of both worlds—hot jock meets hot nerd."

"All I just heard was you calling me hot."

She rolls her eyes. "Don't act like you don't know it."

"Oh, *I* know it." I brace myself over her and look into her brown eyes, which dance with amusement. "I'm just happy to hear you agree. Makes my next play a little less risky."

I kiss her and tumble us back onto the bed. My glasses are getting in the way. I've never made out with a girl while wearing them before, but then again, I've never had one react like this to my need to see clearly. Most girls are far more interested in the jock side than the nerd side. Or maybe I just never let anyone see anything but the jock. Until Blair, I wasn't exactly winning girls over with my *brain*.

Eager limbs and mouths tangle together. Neither of us wastes any time giving into the electrical pull between us. I run a palm up and down the leg she's draped over me, ankle to thigh and back. Blair hums as her breasts rub against my pecs, hard nipples poking through the material of her little black dress.

An angel and a devil sit on either side of my shoulder, or more accurately a little Vanessa and a little me. Vanessa's warning about Blair deserving a gentleman isn't lost. Sure, I've cleared my conscience by letting her know I can't commit to anything serious, but she isn't the kind of girl you sleep with and never call again.

Our kisses are frantic, and her hips rock into me, beckoning me to do something with the raging hard-on pressing into her. Trailing my fingers back up her leg, I let them slide under her skirt and to the lacy material of her underwear. No wait, it's a thong. Christ, this girl. I cup her ass and growl. *Mine*. Serious or not, I'm *serious* about this ass.

When my fingers slide under the scrap of material covering her pussy, she falls back onto the bed, arching her whole body into my palm. Her eyes flutter open and lock onto me. "Oh God, I think I might come just watching you. The way you're looking at me right now and with those glasses."

She sighs, emphasizing how close she is, and my chest shakes with a silent laugh as I move one finger inside her. "Just watch me then."

She does exactly that as her body trembles under my touch. I'm mesmerized by this girl. Her heart hammers in her chest, and she whimpers and pants, squeezing around my fingers and moaning loudly as she finds her release.

Her eyes close behind dark lashes, and she whispers my name on a sigh.

"That was the hottest thing I've ever seen," I say, hearing the wonder in my own words. Damn.

"Ditto," she mumbles without opening her eyes.

Music starts to play from another room, and the bass vibrates the wall. "I think Z might be trying to drown out your sex sounds."

Her eyes pop open, and she pushes up onto one elbow. "Oh my God, he can hear us?"

I shrug. "Well, I can sure as shit hear his music, so it goes to reason . . ."

"You could have warned me or, I don't know, gagged me."

A gag? As hot as that sounds, no way I'd want to miss out on hearing the way she responds to my touch. "I'll remember that for next time. Speaking of, when can I see you again?"

She buries a smile into the crook of my neck. "Will you wear the glasses again?"

Hell, I'd forgotten I was wearing them. "Any time you want."

sixteen

Wes

"Shaw take Reynold's spot."

My foot is killing me, but I still resent the substitution. I take a seat on the sidelines next to coach.

"How's your foot?" he asks, keeping his eyes glued forward watching the guys run through our plays against a full court defense. Our season opener is Sunday, and the team isn't where I want it to be. Coach's face tells me he feels the same.

"It's fine," I grit out.

"Doesn't look fine out there. You're favoring it. Stay off it, ice it, check in with the trainers." He finally looks at me, taking his eyes from the action on the court. Concern, or maybe just disappointment, etches his features. "We need you ready."

"Yes, sir."

Coach blows the whistle, and the guys stop as he starts barking at them about lazy defense.

Hanging my head, I welcome the pain in my foot. It reminds me that I have one season left. This is it. I don't have delusions about playing in the NBA. Maybe I could make it as a late pick, but it just hasn't ever felt like the right path for me. There are better, faster, and stronger point guards out there. My mental game is what's kept me competing at this level. That, and a whole damn lot of dedication. Guys that make it beyond college, though? They have it all—mental, dedication, and raw talent. Guys like Z.

The man himself takes a seat next to me and wipes a towel across his shaved head. I know he's here as a silent comfort, but I can't bring myself to feel anything but anger and self-pity.

"This fucking sucks." I sound like a bratty teenager, but Z only nods with a grim acceptance of what I'm saying.

"Did you see that behind the back pass Shaw tried to pull off? Crazy kid is gonna cost us games out there trying to be the next Jason Williams."

I hear the question in his statement. "Fuck. I'll work with him. He has talent. He's just trying to force too much too fast."

Z tosses the towel and stands. "The guys are going to Theta house tonight. You in?"

"Nah. Blair and I are going to watch Mason play. He's starting pitcher tonight."

The big center grins, which is a rare sight on his serious face. "Another date with Blair. She sleeping over this time? Do I need to make myself scarce to avoid your headboard banging against our shared wall? I could stay in Joel's room."

"I think the theater room couch is a more sanitary spot than Joel's room."

We both laugh and cringe at the same time because Joel getting the master on the other end of the house was probably the best for all the roommates. No one wants to be within hearing distance of his room. The guy's room is a revolving door.

"You're a lucky man." The words hang between us and the irony isn't lost on me that we both seem to be coveting the other's life. I never imagined Z wanting anything other than ball. "Blair is great. I'll find somewhere else to stay tonight so you don't have to worry about me listening in. Enjoy the night with your girl. Hers is probably a much better shoulder to cry on right now than mine, anyway."

"I don't know, big guy, I think I might feel much safer in your big beefy arms." I bat my eyelashes at him and the tension lifts.

"You're the best point man I've ever played with."

He walks off, and I'm glad he doesn't try to tell me everything will be okay or some other cheesy cliché. The game is a few days away, and I'm having serious doubts that my foot can hold up through forty minutes of play.

When I get to the house, Blair is already there. She's on the sofa, bare feet pulled up and crossed, she's the picture of comfort. I could get used to coming home and finding her here. I love that she feels at ease with my friends, it's just another way she positions herself above the rest.

Joel stands in the middle of the living room, turning

with his arms held out to his sides like he's a princess twirling in her fancy new dress. Except this Latino princess holds a basketball in one outstretched hand.

"What the hell is going on in here? A fashion show?"

He tosses the ball at my head, which I catch because I've got reflexes like a cat.

"Blair is helping me pick a shirt for tonight."

Ball in hand, I take a seat next to Blair and pull her closer before delving any further into whatever messed-up, dress-up game is going on.

"Why the obsession over attire tonight?"

It isn't that Joel doesn't always dress nice, but he's never asked me, or anyone else I know, if we approved of his outfit. Dudes don't do that. He'll be asking if his butt looks big next.

"He struck out getting a number this afternoon and is now all bent out of shape." Nathan's voice is filled with humor and judging by the death glare Joel shoots him, I know it's true.

That makes me smile. "Aww, you poor, poor schmuck."

"That isn't what this is about. It was one girl. One girl." He flashes his index finger, but he sounds so desperate and whiny we burst into laughter.

"Fuck you all," he says but smiles. He runs his hands down the shirt and rolls the sleeves up on either side. "So, this one is good?"

Blair nods. "You look hot. Black is a good color for you. It gives you the whole dark and mysterious thing with your skin tone and dark hair."

"Easy, now." I pull her fully onto my lap.

Joel winks at her. "*Muchas gracias, linda.*"

"Yeah, definitely do that." She bounces with excitement. I don't think she knew he spoke Spanish, and she's obviously a fan. As is the rest of the female population when he busts it out.

"Do what?"

"Talk in Spanish. Not all the time . . . but drop it in casually. Accents are sexy."

"All right, all right." I squeeze her waist. "I think your work here is done."

She kisses me on the cheek as she stands. "Actually, I just stopped by to see if I could rain check on dinner. I need to finish a paper before Mason's game."

This girl's dedication to schoolwork is insane. "Sure. I'll text you before I head over."

She winks and gives a little wave, and I watch her fine ass until the door closes behind her.

"Soo . . ." Joel's tone reeks of a loaded statement on deck. "You and Blair . . . things getting serious?"

"What? No, it's just . . ." I don't know how to finish that statement.

"If you're having sex, then it's getting serious. You wouldn't be mixing business with pleasure unless it's serious."

"I'm not mixing—you know what? I'm not even gonna go there."

"Wait, wait, wait. You haven't slept with her?"

"Is that really so ludicrous? I've only known her a few weeks." Fine it's bonkers that I've spent so much time with her and we still haven't had sex, but I don't want to admit that it's a big deal.

"Uh-huh. Uh-huh." He scratches his chin and wears a shit-eating grin. "So, does that mean tonight is the night?"

"We're going to a high school baseball game, not looking to do jail time for indecent exposure."

"Don't bullshit me. Tonight's the night." Joel practically sings the words as he dances around.

Nathan draws a heart with both index fingers. "She completes you."

"Fuck off, both of you."

"I gotta shower." Nathan stands and hustles toward the staircase.

"Hurry up. I'm leaving in fifteen, and I need to make a stop for condoms," Joel yells after him and then looks to me. "You good? Need me to put some in your nightstand?"

My answer is to lob the ball at his head.

"Okay, fine. I'll lay off. You probably need to go take care of business anyway. Since she bailed on dinner, you have time to rub one out before and after your shower."

I groan. "For the love of all that is holy."

"What? Please tell me you aren't planning to show up to the game without clearing your head?" His shocked expression makes his eyes go ridiculously wide, mouth gaped open. "Dude, you go in there without taking care of business, and you're gonna embarrass yourself and the whole male population."

I shake my head and let it hang down between my knees. Is this how a panic attack starts? I seriously need new friends—the kind who don't interfere in my damn business.

seventeen

Blair

"So how does it work? Do you remember everything you've ever heard or read?"

Wes shakes his head, eyes focused on the pitching mound where Mason warms up. "No, not everything. Some things I remember more easily than others, same as everyone else."

"You just recited all the US and French presidents in order. That isn't the *same as everyone else*," I mock his blasé tone.

"The way I remember things is different. I see it in more detail. I can recite the presidents because I spent a year in fourth grade staring at a timeline banner the teacher posted above the white board. My memory allows me to remember it more clearly than other people, that's all."

"So annoying and hot at the same time," I mumble under my breath.

"What was that?" He takes his eyes off the field and leans in. "Did you say I was hot again?"

"Your brain is hot. The rest of you"—I let my gaze rake over him and I purse my lips—"is okay, I guess."

"What if I told you I can recall in vivid detail every outfit you've ever worn."

I narrow my gaze. No way that's possible. Do guys even notice clothes beyond the amount of skin they show?

He takes my silence as a challenge.

"It's true. The day you called me a dumb jock you were wearing a yellow dress. Your hair was down, and you looked fine as fuck pacing the sidewalk and practically stomping your feet to pry information out of me."

I cover my face. "That's so embarrassing."

"Wanna know what else I've committed to my amazingly hot memory?"

By the way he says it, I have a few guesses that make my heart lurch. "What?"

He leans in until our sides touch from shoulder to knee. He looks at my mouth and brings the pad of his thumb to the corner. "The sounds you make when I touch you. When I kiss you here, you make this adorable little hum."

The noise sings from my throat on command.

"And when I touch you here . . ." Long fingers wrap around my thigh and move up until his palm stretches from hip to the bundle of nerves, which is throbbing at the prospect of what his magnificent mouth and hands can do.

"Wes." His name comes out sounding more like a plea than a warning.

He grins and moves his hand back to a more appropriate spot on my knee. Damn appropriateness. "You say my name in the sexiest way."

We're still staring, holding each other hostage with that promise of an end to the sexual tension banging between us, when the umpire calls out, "Let's play ball."

We watch Mason pitch six innings before he's pulled to rest his arm. Six excruciatingly long innings, where I spend more time tracking touches and glances than the strikes thrown from the pitching mound. I meet Maria, Mason's mom, and we make our apologies to her and Cal as we duck out before the end of the game.

"Can I convince you to stay tonight? We have early practice tomorrow before we leave for our game up state. I won't be back until Sunday night."

Convince me? Is this guy serious?

"Okay." I one word it to avoid the squeal that threatens to embarrass me.

"Can we swing by the sorority house on the way? I need to at least grab a toothbrush and a change of clothes."

"All right, but I'm coming inside with you. I want to see your room." He turns the car in that direction, and his excitement about our impending sleepover makes my insides tingle.

"You know you aren't technically allowed in my room," I say as I walked us to the side entrance, which is the closest one to my room and hopefully the easiest to sneak him in. "So, be quiet and try to blend in." I wave a hand in front of him and then giggle because there is no way he is going to blend in.

Thankfully, the house is empty since it's a weekend, and I shut the door, closing us into the safety of my room. I busy myself grabbing the essentials for a sleepover while Wes roams around my room taking it all in. He looks absolutely ridiculous in my and Vanessa's ultra girly room with the low ceilings and purple walls.

"Who's this?" He lifts a frame, my and Gabby's faces pressed together as we smile into the camera. It was taken right after the accident, and the fresh scars on her face would make me hate the picture if it weren't for the big smile on her lips. It was the first genuine one I remember seeing after the accident.

The pity in his voice makes me irrationally defensive, and I take the frame from him and place it back onto my desk. "My best friend Gabby."

He looks guilty at my reaction. "The one who makes the bracelets?"

I nod. "She was in a car accident senior year. That is how she got the scars."

"I'm sorry."

I can hear the sincerity in his voice. "Thank you. She's actually why I want to rule the world. It was her dream for us to be lady bosses."

"She here at Valley?"

"Sort of. She takes online classes and lives back in our hometown."

He places a kiss on my forehead and takes the bag I dropped onto the floor. "Ready?"

"Yep."

"Bless is out," he says and winks.

There are those tingles again. I secretly love that he uses our ridiculous couple name. Bless is out. Bless ready to get it on.

eighteen

Blair

The White House is empty when we return. Wes tells me we have the place to ourselves for the night, and we settle into the theater room, legs and bodies intertwined. The television is on, but I have no idea what we're watching. I'm lost to him. His kisses, his hands, his words.

"Why'd you start playing basketball?" I ask as his calloused palms caress my calves and move up, higher and higher but never quite reach the apex of my desire before moving back down. My hands have taken on a mind of their own, tracing the lines of his stomach and arms. If he doesn't tear off my clothes soon, I'm going to combust. I can feel how much he wants me—it's pressing against my stomach, but he makes no move to take off my clothes. I thought sleep over was code for sex.

"Girls, obviously."

I swat at him. "Seriously."

"I don't know. I can't really remember a time I didn't play. My parents worked a lot, so they overcompensated by putting me in every extra-curricular activity possible from rock climbing to piano to origami . . . you name it, I tried it."

"Origami?"

He nods, a big proud smile on his face. "Yep, but basketball was the first thing I was really good at. I guess it sounds lame, but basketball was something that got me attention. My dad was always working long hours, coming home about the time I was getting ready for bed at night, and then all of a sudden, he was around more, getting home in time to shoot hoops outside and coming to practices. He was proud of me, and I wanted to keep that feeling. I loved it, don't get me wrong, but I loved it more because of the way people treated me. The attention didn't last, of course, I mean not from my parents, but the way other people praised me filled that void."

"I don't think I was ever that good at anything," I admit with a small laugh. "I was okay at sports, got decent grades, but it must be really incredible to have a true talent for something."

"I have other talents." His fingers trace up and down my sides in slow movements that leave me equal parts wanting more and wanting just this. "These origami fingers can do magical things."

"I may have already noticed how good you are with your hands." My voice is filled with want and desire even to my own ears.

He dips his head, his lips finding my collarbone. "It isn't just my hands that are talented."

I respond with something witty and sexy, I'm sure, but the words don't register above our combined sighs.

His phone vibrates in his pocket, and I'm so keyed up I nearly groan at the hum of pleasure against my hip. "Let me just make sure it isn't one of the guys needing a ride or something."

I pry myself off him reluctantly, and Wes fishes out his phone. "Fucking Joel," he mutters and stands before he adjusts himself—no shame. Wes lets out an audible sigh. "Give me five?"

"Everything okay?"

"Yeah. I just need to take care of something."

Wes leaves me, and I sit, tapping my toes and impatiently waiting for him to return. I do a swipe under my eyes in case any eye makeup has smudged, run my fingers through my hair, check the bra and panty situation to make sure they aren't all twisted. I've been wearing my best lingerie for weeks now just in case.

Minutes pass, and I listen for any indication of what he's up to. What in the world could he possibly be doing?

The answer should be me. He should be doing *me*.

An idea forms, and I hesitate for half a second before bounding up the stairs to Wes's room and grabbing my overnight bag.

There's no sign of Wes. Maybe he went to Joel's room for something? I quickly pull the shirt I'm wearing off and then pull on the Valley jersey. Without a mirror, I can't properly check my reflection, but I have a feeling

Wes is going to enjoy seeing me wear his name and number.

I'm contemplating removing my shorts and just making my intentions ultra-obvious, but he appears in the doorway. He's holding his phone and tapping away like he's sending a text. When he sees me, he stops short, fingers still over the screen. "Holy shit."

"You like?" I turn so show off the back and, yes, my ass because I know it looks fantastic in these shorts.

"Come here."

We meet in the middle, and I give myself over to him. His touch, his kisses, the smell of him . . . I breathe him in. Everything moves slowly, he's taking his time as if there's no rush when I'm so keyed up I might die if things don't move faster. I'm forcing myself to let him take the lead, and it's as if his restraint is something of Gods and not mere mortals like myself.

I whimper when he finally brings two rough palms up under my shirt, but just as his hands graze the bottom of my lacy bra, he pulls back and lets his hands fall to my hips.

The restraint I've been holding on to snaps. "You're either some sort of saint or you just aren't as into me as I'm into you."

He laughs, a deep throaty sound that I feel shake his chest. "I promise you I'm no saint and I'm definitely into you."

"Then what is it? I have my sexiest lingerie on and I'm practically throwing myself at you. Can we please get naked now?"

He groans and pulls at his hair with both hands. "Fucking Joel."

The mention of Joel catches me by surprise. Seems like a weird time to chat about his friend. Maybe their friendship really does know no bounds.

"Did Joel do something? Say something?"

"He just gave me maybe the worst advice ever."

I wait for him to say more, utterly confused.

"This is embarrassing, but I guess I'd rather risk humiliation then have you think I'm not into you. I'm *so* into you—so much so that I took fucking Joel's advice."

"I—"

"Joel lives by the motto that you shouldn't show up on game day without getting your head in the right place." He says it so quick that I'm pretty sure I heard him wrong.

"I'm sorry, what?"

Why the hell are we talking about basketball right now?

"You know . . . clean the pipes, buff the wood, polish the rocket?" He uses both hands to point to his junk. "Joel jerks off before—"

"Ewww, okay. TMI. I do *not* need to know about Joel's pre-game rituals."

"No. Fuck. I'm going to kill him." He takes a deep breath and lets it out. "Joel told me I should jerk off before we had sex. It's been a while, and he was worried about me making an ass of myself." He continues muttering under his breath, but I'm doubled over in laughter.

He finally joins in, and it only eggs me on. I'm laughing so hard tears are streaming down my face while simultaneously wondering if it is the end of romance when you find out the guy you want to have sex with is taking matters into his own hands . . . literally.

"So, just now . . . while I was downstairs?" I motion at his crotch, which sets me off again.

He scrunches his nose like he knows he's said too much. "Fuck, this is humiliating."

I try to rein in my laughter. He's clearly embarrassed. "Guys really do that? You jerk off before having sex for . . . what reason exactly?"

"I know it sounds dumb as fuck now, but Joel was convincing."

"Joel seems like the last person to take relationship advice from."

He runs a hand through his thick hair in frustration. "I really fucking like you, Blair."

"I like you, too, but why does that require . . ." I wave my hand in front of him. There's no way I can bring myself to say it again.

"I panicked. Joel got in my head. I wanted tonight to be perfect. So, yeah, I listened to my douchebag roommate, but don't think for a second that my restraint has anything to do with not wanting you. I fucking want you so much I listened to *Joel.*"

"That's oddly sweet, but I think I'd prefer come in your pants to this jerked off version that has me ready to hump your pillow. I want the perfect, can't-keep-his-hands-off-me, afraid-of-embarrassing-himself-because-he-might-explode-at-any-moment guy I'm falling for. Just you."

"Fuuuuck." He drawls out the word and closes his eyes.

I slide my hands up his chest and link my arms around his neck. "Okay by you?"

He nods and just as I'm feeling fully in control, he has me on the bed and is braced above me. His muscular arms press into the mattress, caging me in as he stares down at me like I'm everything.

He stands and pulls his T-shirt over his head before lying back beside me. Hooking a finger into the V of my shirt, Wes tugs just enough to show a bit more skin. "I really want to see what's underneath, but damn, you look good wearing my jersey."

"The whole point of putting it on was for you to take it off."

He grins and slides his hands to the hem and slowly inches it up as if he wants to delay the surprise underneath. "So beautiful."

As he stares down at me and his navy eyes darken, I fall a little deeper under his spell. He's everything I never knew I wanted or thought to fantasize about. Smart, fun, loyal, and smoking hot. His muscular body moves with elegance and confidence that is as hot as it is commanding.

I'm not nearly as patient as I scramble to get naked and then free him of his jeans and boxer briefs. Maybe I should have aspired to the Joel Moreno life motto, because the sight of Wes's naked body is nearly orgasmic on its own. His penis is the kind of perfection that romance novels are written about.

"Need to study this gorgeous body," he murmurs against my lips. The heat of his gaze rakes over me. True to his words, he looks at me as if he wants to memorize every detail as he trails kisses down my body. He places one at my belly button that sends a tremble down my spine.

"Can you study later . . . or maybe during?"

His smile is slow and cocky. "So impatient."

One long finger trails up my inner thigh and slips inside me, causing my hips to rock into his palm. He fucks me with one finger and then two, circling my clit with his thumb. I open my eyes to find his gaze still hard and studying.

His hands are magic. As my moans fill the silence of his bedroom, his lips find the pulse in my neck, and he sucks hard. My orgasm tears through me at rocket speed, and I call out his name as I shatter.

"Perfection." He dusts kisses down my body, places a kiss on my hip, and then trails back up. "I want to hear you say my name like that again."

He reaches to the nightstand and pulls out a condom, and I watch on greedily as he slips it on. I'll happily say his name any way he wants, as many times as he wants, if he makes me feel like that again.

I stare hard at his beautiful penis as he fists it and guides it to my entrance. I'm mesmerized as our bodies join. He stretches me gloriously, and I let out a sigh of complete contentment.

"You good?"

Good? No. Fan-fucking-tastic.

"Super," I say as I reach up and rub both breasts.

His size and strength and endurance make me realize what I've been missing out on, and I suddenly comprehend the devotion of the jersey chasers.

His eyes stay on me as he pumps in and out at a delicious pace that promises another bone-melting orgasm. I struggle to keep my eyes open, but the way he looks at me, as if somehow this is a big deal even though we've said from the start that this is casual, is as hot as the rest of him. He has promised me nothing but has given me everything.

I push away all thought, letting the sensations overwhelm and pull me under.

"Wes," I say as my lids close with the pressure of my second orgasm.

He slams into me harder grunting out my name as he shudders through his release.

The next morning, I wake to an empty bed. I miss the heat of him immediately. I open my eyes and stretch my limbs, feeling the soreness of last night and bask in it. Wes is gone, which I knew he would be, and the house is quiet. I sit up in his bed and spy my name written on a note on his desk. Pulling the blanket around me, I stand and walk over to it. I pick it up and turn it over, but the note says nothing else. I frown until I spot what's resting behind it—a paper rose folded intricately and perfectly. I lift it and clutch it carefully to my chest. Damn, he really is good with his hands.

nineteen

Wes

We're on a high after winning our first game of the season and end up at The Hideout when we get back to Valley. It's packed, especially for a Sunday night. Blair sits on my lap, and Z and Nathan are across the table from us, arguing over who is getting the next round from the bar.

"I'll get a round. I want to go say hi to Vanessa, anyway."

I let her go, watching as she pushes through to the other side of the bar where Mario and Vanessa sit with a group of baseball guys, including Shaw, who is still on my shit list. Rookie had two turnovers in the six minutes he was on the floor. The same six minutes I sat on the bench and watched in combined frustration and pain.

Nathan's phone rings, and he silences it as he shakes

his head. Z glances over and smirks. "Don't ignore your momma, boy. What the hell is wrong with you?"

"I'll call her later," Nathan insists.

Zeke reaches over and picks up the phone, answering it before Nathan can stop him. "Hello, Mrs. Payne. It's Zeke."

Nathan grumbles and reaches for the phone, but Z moves the phone to the other ear. "Thank you, ma'am, I appreciate it. The team played well today. Yeah, your son is right here. Good to talk to you, Mrs. Payne."

He hands the phone over to an angry-looking Nathan.

Jealousy eats at me. I absently check my own phone. Nothing. I feel a bit like a sullen child who is sitting around and wishing his parents would call or text or in some way acknowledge that he had a game today. I know they're a thousand miles away and it isn't like I expect them to make it to every game, but a *good job* or *I'm proud of you* text once in a while would be nice. I guess a hardship of being the parents of an elite athlete is that it gets old watching your kid win trophies and travelling to games every week because somewhere along the way, my parents totally checked out. They probably assumed they'd told me enough times they were proud that they could just stop.

"I think I'll help Blair."

I see the pity in Z's eyes. Nothing gets past him, and I may not express my disappointment in my parents, but he knows me too well not to pick up on it.

Mario slides off the bar stool as I get near. "Congrats on the game. How's the foot holding up?"

"It's getting there," I tell him. It's my new canned

answer since it's the only thing people want to hear.

I look past him to Vanessa but missing in action is Blair. Did I pass her? Where'd she go?

"Hey, Vanessa." She eyes me warily, clearly still not convinced that I'm not gonna drop kick her friend's heart. Kiddie gloves are on with Blair. All the way on. I'm doing my best not to screw this up. She's a cool chick, and I like spending time with her. "Where'd our girl go?"

"That douche canoe David grabbed her." She points to the corner of the bar where Blair is talking to a guy I don't know but instantly don't like. He's backed her into a dark space and leers over her in a way that sets all my alarm bells off.

"David?"

"Her ex-boyfriend," Vanessa says. Blair and I haven't gotten into the specifics of our past dating life. She mentioned she dated, but she played it off like it was no big deal. By the way Vanessa looks at me, it's clear Blair left some important things out.

I step toward them, trying to keep an air of calm while I'm nothing but a knot of defensiveness as I approach.

"Everything okay?" I ask, leaving a few feet of space between myself and the back of the prick talking to my girl. Yeah, my girl. I'm regretting not laying down a claim.

Blair's demeanor changes when she sees me. Her shoulders sag in relief but then stiffen as if she feels some weirdness about being caught talking to her ex. David turns with a scowl and gives me a once over.

"Mind your own business. We're having a

conversation that doesn't have anything to do with you."

Aww, hell no. I place myself between David and Blair. "My girl looks upset. I'd say that's my business."

His lip curls. "Your girl?" He looks to Blair for verification. I don't bother checking her reaction because I can practically feel anxiety roll off her in waves.

"Wes." I extend a hand, and the bastard glances at my palm and then dismisses it. Dismisses *me*.

"I'll call you tomorrow." With a final patronizing glance, David turns and disappears into the crowd.

I wait until he's completely out of sight before I turn to Blair. "You okay?"

Her hands shake in front of her. "Yes. I'm fine. You didn't need to do that. We were just talking."

I cross my arms and study her. I'm calling bullshit, but I can't decide if she's playing it off because he's an asshole or because she's embarrassed I caught her in a dark corner with another guy. "Friend of yours?"

"We dated last year. He was just asking about classes. I'm sorry if it looked like it was anything."

"No reason to be sorry. You looked upset, and I wanted to make sure everything was good."

"So, that wasn't you peeing all around me?" Her lips pull into a knowing smile, calling me out for referring to her as my girl.

I rub a hand over my jaw. "Might have been a little of that."

"Don't worry." She closes the space between us and throws her arms around my neck. It's her go-to move, and I love the way it presses our bodies together. The contact immediately sends communication down below. Red alert, hot girl is touching you. Yep, I'm fourteen years old again. "I have zero interest in David. He's a total . . ." She waves a hand at my ear like she's grappling for the right word. "Douche canoe."

"You ready to get out of here?" Ex-boyfriends, reminders of parents who don't give a fuck? Yeah, I'm ready to bounce.

She places her hand in mine and tugs. "Bless out."

twenty

Blair

"Blair, what is all this? Your bag weighs a ton."

Vanessa struggles to move my backpack from the small table at the library so she can sit.

I barely look up from my laptop. "I have a paper due in econ, reading for American literature, and about a million other things before my shift at the café this afternoon."

"You stay at Wes's last night?"

"How do you know? Did you go back to the house?" Screw my paper, if Vanessa knows I wasn't at our place, it means she wasn't with Mario.

"Yeah, I just needed a night off from Mario." She says it flippantly, but the perfectly curled hair and extra makeup speaks volumes.

She's overcompensating.

"Oh no, why? I like Mario." I've done my best to keep my opinions about Vanessa's boyfriend to myself because nothing scares her more than approval, but Mario seems great. I've never seen Vanessa happier.

"It's just too much. *He's* too much. I keep waiting for all his scary flaws to appear. I mean, no man can possibly be as perfect as he is. Seeing David last night reminded me that perfect on the outside hides a whole bunch of crazy on the inside."

Great. The aftermath of Hurricane David continues to unveil more damage. "Mario is nothing like David."

"Or maybe Mario is just good at hiding his crazy like David is."

"What's this really about? David and I have been broken up for months, you've dated other guys since my break up."

"I . . ." She pauses and twists the gold ring she wears on her thumb. "I like him," she says quietly.

I hide my glee that she's finally admitted it. "Then, please, for the love of God, don't let David be the reason you don't trust Mario."

"I was worried you were going to fall back under his spell when I saw you two together. What did he have to say at the bar last night?"

I consider telling her the truth, but if she knew just how calculating and horrible David really is, then she might see that as a sign to steer clear of men, and I don't want that for her. David is an asshole, but he doesn't represent every guy. I sure hope not, anyway.

"Not much. Wes walked over, and David took off."

"I saw that! I was so freaking glad when Wes got between you two. I only wish he'd punched him."

I laugh, mostly because I'd wished that too.

"You aren't thinking of getting back with David then? Because you're finally starting to seem like the old you."

I'm starting to feel like the old me as well. "No, I'm absolutely not getting back together with him. What's more important is when you're going to tell Mario how you feel."

She stands, clearly the interrogation has gone beyond her comfort level because we're talking about her feelings, and V doesn't do feelings. "Why would I do that?"

After she leaves, I spend the next three hours in the library and then hustle over to the café to relieve Katrina. She's beyond frazzled and knee-deep in supplies as she restocks everything.

"Everything okay?"

"My sitter just bailed, and I have to pick up Christian at daycare in ten minutes."

"Go. I have this."

She looks around at the mess, hesitating. I know she'd do the same for me in a heartbeat, so I place my hands on my hips and smile. "Seriously, go. It's no big deal."

"I owe you," Katrina says, hopping over the box and untying her apron.

Monday afternoons are slow after the lunch rush, but Monday evenings are not, so I enjoy a bit of down time stocking shelves and singing along to the cheesy nineties' music playing over the university station.

My mood is high until David walks through the door. His demeanor makes it clear he's here to see me and knew he could catch me alone. I hate the way my body responds like it's a fight or flight moment. I desperately want to be emotionally detached enough for his presence not to send me into panic mode.

"What do you want, David? I'm at work."

"Tall house blend." Black like his soul. "And put one of those inspirational quotes on there for me, would you?" He has the audacity to wink.

I remind myself that killing him would only get me thrown in jail while I get his coffee and write "Choose kindness" onto the cup. "Here ya go."

He looks down at the quote and smiles.

"You're banging the basketball team now, huh?"

Arizona has the death penalty.

Arizona has the death penalty.

"My life isn't your business anymore, David."

"Oh, but it is. Especially if it interferes with our arrangement."

"I've done everything you've asked."

"That bullshit paper you wrote on Chopin got me a B. You're distracted, and it's fucking up my GPA."

"I'm distracted because I'm doing two people's homework."

"I need this one on Friday." He slides me a piece of paper with the details. David's been careful to leave no electronic paper trail. Only paper copies that we both know would easily be dismissed if I ever went to anyone and tried to tell them what was going on. "It better be an A paper, Blair. I'd hate to have to embarrass you in front of your new boyfriend."

The thought of Wes knowing about any of this makes the muffin I ate fifteen minutes ago feel like a brick in my stomach. Trapped and angry, I watch him walk out of the café and vow to end this somehow, someway.

twenty-one

Wes

*B*lair and I sit on the floor of the gym while we wait for Z and Joel so we can all study for our next statistics quiz.

"You play over Thanksgiving break?" she asks, clearly surprised by this revelation that we have a tournament the weekend after Turkey Day.

"Yep, it's one of our busiest times. With no school, we get to focus solely on ball. Christmas break is the same."

"So, you don't get to see your family?"

I shake my head but don't meet her eyes as I say, "We get a full week off for Christmas. I'll see them then. I usually go to Joel's house for Thanksgiving. Mama Moreno invites the whole team and anyone else who doesn't have anywhere to go."

She lets out a little huff that's her adorable version of being appalled. "My family is ditching me this year. My brother and sister-in-law invited my parents on a Disney cruise. I think I'm gonna go home to see Gabby, though. Plus, it'll be good to get away for a week." Her tone has bite, and I wonder why she's so anxious to go home to an empty house.

I can't bring myself to feel too sorry for her. Judging by her annoyance, I'd guess this is the first time she hasn't seen her folks during a holiday break. I was probably like that the first time my parents bailed too. Now I'm just indifferent. Well, I'm trying to be. After years of my parents planning vacations that in no way work around my schedule, it's clear they don't care if they see me for Thanksgiving or Christmas.

"Let's do this," Joel calls out as he and Z enter the gym. "I have a date in an hour."

The stuff we're going over tonight doesn't lend itself that well to my usual basketball analogies, but it's good to be on the court with my boys and my girl. When Nathan shows up, clearly bored and looking for something to do, we give up statistics altogether and start running through plays. Blair fills in the place of our power forward, Malone. She's about a foot and a half shorter and a buck fifty lighter, but she's way better to look at.

Damn, it feels good. Nah, feels *right* to be playing around with my roommates and to have Blair here.

"You guys wanna hit The Hideout?" Nathan asks the rest of us as Joel hustles off the court to get ready for his date.

"Negative ghost rider," Z says and shakes his head.

"We could have a pool party," Blair pipes up, looking beyond excited at the possibility. "I've been carrying my swimsuit in my backpack for weeks waiting for an opportunity to get in that pool."

"Pool party it is." Nathan claps his hands together. "I'm gonna invite a few people."

"I'm out." No surprise that Z isn't interested in swimming.

"What about if we set up the projector, put on a movie poolside?"

Z narrows his gaze. "My pick?"

Chuckling, I rack the balls. "Yeah, you can pick."

He hustles off the court, and I reach for Blair so I can wrap my arms around her. "Twenty bucks says we're watching something with Tom Cruise."

She laughs and then we head up to my room to change, and she slips into a hot pink bikini that makes me hard on sight. I don't know how word got out so fast, but when we get down to the pool it's already filled with people. Nathan is in the pool, a cigarette hanging from his lips and a beach ball raised above his head. Z's taken up residence in one of the lounge chairs pulled up in front of the projector and has attracted a circle of girls who are faking interest in *Mission Impossible*.

I lead Blair to the shallow end of the pool, and she wriggles her butt into my crotch and leans against me. We're more spectators than active members of this party, which suits me just fine.

"Last year, where would you have been right now?"

"With V. Before Mario, we were inseparable."

"And what sort of trouble would you two have been getting into on a night like this?"

"We'd have been at one frat party or another." She sighs. "I dated David for most of last year, so we usually went to Sigma."

"Dude seems like an asshat, how'd you two get together?"

"He can be very convincing when he wants something. He showed me what he wanted me to see, and I gobbled it right up. He was sweet and charming at first."

"And then?" My chest tightens with all the shitty things he might've done to my girl. I saw a glimmer of what he was like pissed, and I didn't like it. "He didn't hurt you or anything, right?"

"No, he was never physical. It was little things like he talked shit about everyone, even guys he was tight with. He got mad when I so much as said hello to another guy, and he didn't like me going out with V if he wasn't there, stuff like that. When I'd try to talk to him about it, he made me feel like it was my fault."

"I'm sorry."

She shrugs and turns to face me, wrapping her arms around my waist. "I don't want to waste another second regretting my time with him. I can't take it back, any of it, but I would if I could."

There's more hurt than she's shared, judging by the dark look in her eyes, but far be it for me to push her to relieve her painful past. "Come on, let's dry off and then grab some food. Joel's mom brought by enchiladas and she made me a gallon of sweet iced tea."

"You can't make your own tea?"

"I can; just don't." I pat her ass as she steps out of the pool in front of me.

She grabs her towel and drops onto a lounge chair as she wrings out her hair. Her nipples salute me through her top and when she realizes what I'm staring at, she quickly wraps the towel around her chest. "Perv."

Instead of grabbing my own chair, I pick her up and sit down, placing her between my legs. She leans back against me and then startles when she feels the bulge in my board shorts.

"Your fault," I murmur in her ear and brush a kiss against her shoulder.

Turning, her eyes focus on my crotch as she bites on her bottom lip. She drapes the towel over my lap, and I watch, amused by what she might be planning and a hell of a lot turned on at the endless possibilities.

She slides her hand up the leg of my shorts and curls her fingers around my shaft. I exhale through gritted teeth as my balls draw up tight. It isn't the first time a girl has given me a hand job in public, but it's the first time one did so without the hope of being seen. The way Blair looks at me, it's about me—us. She doesn't want to be caught. She just can't keep her hands to herself, and God, is that hot.

No one is paying us any attention, but I sit upright and pull her closer to better block us just in case. She pumps and squeezes at a pace that already has me teetering on blissful release. She's so beautiful like this. Blair deep in concentration and filled with determination and pep for the task is breathtaking. Her lids are heavy with lust and her breathing labored even though I haven't even touched her. I won't out here. I'm a selfish guy and want her pleasure to remain mine alone.

My hips thrust forward, and a knowing smile pulls at her lips. She hums as if my pleasure were hers, and that little sound is all it takes. Ecstasy jolts through me, and I come with her name on my lips.

Between practice, games, and Blair, the weeks pass in a blur. A blissful blur. Team is playing well and starting to mesh like I knew we could. Even the rookie is annoying me less. Bus rides back from away games are tense when we lose, but tonight, the mood on the bus back from New Mexico State is light. We only get two days off for Thanksgiving break, but it's the most we'll be free from now until the end of the season.

"You're heading home with Blair tomorrow, huh? Does that mean you two have made your relationship official?" Joel tucks his phone into the seat back pocket in a clear sign that he isn't going to let the conversation end with a yes or no answer.

"It isn't like that. She knew I wasn't going to be able to make the trip to Kansas and she felt bad. Her parents aren't even going to be there. They're on some Disney cruise."

As I replay the conversation in my head, I'm sure that part of what I've said is true. She did invite me because she felt guilty I couldn't be with my own family, and she probably felt some sense of obligation to include the guy she's banging.

My reaction is the one that has me worried. I've never been to a girl's house for a holiday. I've been invited, sure. But I always turned them down with some sort of lame excuse such as not wanting to intrude or needing to catch up on schoolwork or claiming I had extra practice. I can usually just throw out the words ball and schedule to get out of anything I don't wanna do.

I've never wanted to go, therefore, I haven't. When Blair asked, I surprised us both by saying yes.

"Mama Moreno is going to be disappointed you aren't coming to our house again."

I smile. "Mama Moreno. How is she? Still doing the barre classes?"

Joel's eyebrows disappear into his hairline. His mom is seriously hot. Not like hot for a woman her age, either. She's just hot. Everyone gives him crap about it, myself included. His reaction is just too much not to screw with him.

"Don't try to change the subject to my mom to get out of talking about Blair. You like her. She's the first girl you've dated in the three years I've known you. You are smitten kitten."

"Sure, of course I like her. She's great."

"But?"

I shrug. "Why does there have to be a but?"

"You tell me."

"There doesn't. I really like her."

"Wooooo." Joel covers his mouth too late, the noise carries, and the guys around us are looking. "Wes likes a girl."

"Pipe down or I'll tell them I'm dating your mom."

I pull out my own phone to busy myself and avoid Joel's questions and am pleased to see a text.

Blair: You were amazing. I watched the game with Vanessa and Mario. Fifteen points, seven assists, one steal. My man is on fire.

Me: You missed my most important stat: four.

Blair: What stat is that?

Me: The number of orgasms I plan to give my girl when I get back.

A text from my mom flashes in my notifications.

Mom: Great game tonight. Your dad and I caught part of it in the airport. We're boarding soon but wanted to tell you Happy Thanksgiving!

Me: Thanks, Mom. Enjoy your trip.

Mom: Love you!

Another text from Blair pops up.

Blair: Ooooh, in that case. I better finish my school stuff. See ya soon!

Me: I love you.

My hands freeze after I press send. Oh shit. "Shit." Joel looks over and cocks a brow. "Problem?" I scrub a hand over my face. "I just told Blair I loved her instead of my mom."

"You're gonna have to explain that."

"I was texting my mom and Blair at the same time. I meant to send it to my mom."

His eyes widen. "What'd Blair say?"

I wake the screen, "Nothing. She went silent."

Joel sucks in air through gritted teeth, grimacing and putting a sound to the panic strumming through my pulse.

"What do I do? Oh my God, what do I do?"

"I dunno. This one is out of my league. I don't tell girls I love them, and if I somehow screwed up and did, they wouldn't believe me anyway."

"Your player status is not helping me right now. What do I do? Do I tell her it was an accident or just hope she doesn't see it? Can you recall text messages like email?

"Well, do you?"

"Do I what?" I stare at the screen. This little device is going to destroy me.

"Do you love her?"

"What kind of question is that?"

"Oh, come on, it isn't that ridiculous of a notion. You're spending all your spare time together."

Oh my God. It's been three minutes with no response. Did she block my number? Is she gonna ghost me? Holy fuck.

"Still no response?"

I slam my head back into the headrest. "Nothing. She's probably busy changing her number."

"Okay, calm down. Tell me this, if she responded right now and said it back, how would that feel?"

The Assist

I consider that for a moment. Her reaction—or non-reaction, as it currently stands—aside, how would it feel to have Blair love me?

"It'd feel good. I guess. Fuck, I dunno. It's too soon. I don't have time for love."

"Love don't give a rat's ass if you have time."

I'm taken aback by that sentiment from Joel. "When did you start waxing poetic on love?"

He shrugs and stands, turning his body so he can place one hand on the headrest of his seat and one on the seat in front of him. "Yo, boys. Our point man needs a little girl advice. Anyone got any experience with texting blunders? Specifically telling your girl that you love her for the first time over text?"

The bus erupts with noise. Some cheers and words of encouragement and some heckling me as if I were on the opposing team.

Coach, who sits two rows in front of us, moves to the aisle and the bus quiets. His suit jacket is unbuttoned and hangs open. He's a commanding man, and not just because he's our coach. We respect him beyond that.

"Sit down, Moreno. You're the last person who should be giving Reynolds advice."

A collective chuckle waves through the bus and Joel sits.

"Good game tonight, guys. We're going to take tomorrow and Friday off." Applause rings out, and Coach lifts a hand. "But I expect you all to be back Saturday ready to practice hard."

The bus comes to a stop at the fieldhouse. "And, Reynolds," Coach says as I stand and move past him in the aisle, "for the love of God, don't text anything else.

Some things are meant to be said and heard. Go tell her in person."

I practically run from the bus to the locker room, where I deposit my gear. I shower quickly, pulling the plain white T-shirt over my head while my skin is still damp.

Z puts a hand on my shoulder before I can sprint off. "The guys and I are heading to the Moreno house tonight. Happy Thanksgiving man."

I know them staying at Joel's tonight instead of The White House is for me, and I would kiss his bald head if I could reach it. "Happy Thanksgiving."

Shaw notices my urgency. "Might want to slow your roll. Too eager, and you'll scare her away. Chicks smell desperation like dogs smell fear."

I don't dignify his remark with a response, but as I walk up to the front of the house, I do make a point to take my time, slow my breathing, and get my shit together.

The house is quiet—almost eerily so. I take the stairs to the second level two at a time, unable to restrain my desire to see her any longer.

The light in my room is on, and Blair sits at my desk, earbuds in and a notebook in front of her with a pen poised in one hand. She stares straight forward in deep concentration.

I cross the room quietly, taking in the number twelve jersey she wears with my name printed across the back and the cut-off jean shorts that are inched up, showing off those legs that I can't get enough of.

She's stunning.

I tug on one of the earbuds, and she startles, letting

out a little squeal and pressing a hand to her heart.

"You scared me." She pulls out the other earbud and uncrosses her legs. "I can usually hear you three coming from a mile away."

Her eyes dart past me like she's expecting to hear or see signs of my roommates.

"They decided to stay at Joel's parents' house tonight so they could sleep in and then roll out of bed in time for Thanksgiving dinner."

"No such luck for us. I promised Gabby we'd stop by to see her in the morning and then stay for lunch with her family. I hope that's okay. She's dying to meet you."

"You mean to grill me?"

What is it with girls always wanting to interrogate the guys who date their friends? I've never once considered inserting myself into one of my buddy's relationships. Hell, if I did, I'd be more likely to tell them to run away than to warn them against hurting my friend. Perhaps that's the root of the problem. My buddies, my teammates, and I are typically stereotyped as the ones breaking hearts.

In the case of Joel and some of the other guys on the team, that's probably true. But I'm not looking to break her anything. I don't have time for games. The life that Joel lives doesn't interest me. He uses women as a distraction from his time off the court, a rush to tide him over until the next game or practice. Not me. Distractions are expensive.

My edge on the court is that I've studied and prepared better and harder off the court. Allowing a woman to have that time is like giving away some of my edge. And she's the first girl I've ever even considered doing that for. A smidge of edge for more of Blair.

"I can't wait to meet her," I say and mean it.

I stare at her, wondering if she's going to say more. If she's going to mention the love-bomb I dropped. She doesn't.

I should be relieved, but the way she's avoiding it makes me realize I *want* to talk about it. I want her to acknowledge that this thing between us is something important.

Petty as it is, I want her to voice that my loving her, real or not, is a big freaking deal. If she weren't in my life, I'd spend the night reflecting on the game and my performance and looking for areas to improve.

But, now, I just want to focus on her.

"So, listen about my text—"

She waves her hands in front of her. "No explanation needed. Your iPad was displaying the text notifications from your mom. I put it together that you meant it for her."

I glance down at the desk where my iPad is docked. Well, that was easy. Way too easy. "Right. Okay then."

I force a smile. Her notebook lays open to where she's been taking notes. With a head nod in its direction, I ask, "What were you working on?"

She hesitates and nips at the bottom of her lip before responding. "It's nothing. I was just listening to a podcast on goal setting."

I'm intrigued. What college girl spends a night before a holiday listening to podcasts and taking notes?

"May I?" I reach for the notebook, eyes on her. I won't tease or taunt her, and I won't look if she doesn't want me to, but I really hope she lets me. It's a rush when she finally nods and my fingers brush against the paper she's scribbled onto. I read through what she's written, keenly aware of her discomfort. Her hands clasp in front of her stomach, and she studies her cuticles with an intensity that they don't warrant.

"This what you're always listening to between classes? Business podcasts?" I'm not sure if she can hear the pride in my voice, but I am proud. She's hella smart, and this makes her more attractive to me in some way like I've discovered her weird matches my own. Numbers and ball are my poison, looks like hers is business.

"Not *all* the time. Sometimes I listen to music."

"It's really cool." I hand her back the notebook. "You really are going to take over the business world."

She shrugs. "I don't know. I listen to them more hoping it'll spark some inspiration on a career path than anything else."

"I thought you were decided on being a boss lady and all that."

"I have, but I don't want to spend my life climbing the ladder at some fortune 500 company. I think I might like the idea of a career as a business woman more than the life of actually being one. I can't figure out where my skills will be best utilized."

"You'll figure it out."

"I guess so. It feels like everyone else already knows exactly what they want, and I don't. And I desperately want to feel that kind of passion for something."

"You want passion, huh?"

I'm rewarded with a smile and playful glint to her eyes. "Doesn't everyone?"

After sliding my hands around her waist and down the curve of her ass until I reach smooth legs, I glide my fingers around the hem of her shorts.

"You look good wearing my jersey." I want to buy her one for every day of the week so she'll walk around with my name and number like a brand. She belongs to me not because I want to own her body and mind— although, I'm a dude with a pulse so of course I want that—but because she wants to belong to me. I can see it in her eyes and in the way she studies me. I don't need her to say she loves me. She's mine, and that's enough. Still, I press her. I want to hear the words come from her mouth.

"Does this mean you're mine? I can brag to all my buddies that I got the hottest girl at school?"

She snorts as if to blow off the compliment, but I don't let her get away with it that easy. I slide my hand up inside the leg of her cutoff shorts until the tips of my finger brush against lace. She stills, and her eyes flutter closed for an instant. My lips find the corner of her mouth and stop before making contact. I can feel her breath, warm and shallow, on my face. "You are hot. Gorgeous, smart, sexy as fuck. Own it, Blair. Thinking you're anything less than that is an insult to me. You think my girl is ugly?"

Her lips part and pull into a smile. "No, your girl is fine."

"Fine as fuck," I mutter and capture her mouth.

twenty-two

Blair

Is being someone's girl the same as being their girlfriend? I'm contemplating the differences as we drive to Succulent Hill. Wes is driving, and I'm sitting in the passenger seat exhausted and satiated. He made good on the sex stats last night and this morning, not resting until my limbs were weak and my mind mush.

I could just ask him, but I'm a little afraid of the answer. I know he *likes* me. Suddenly that doesn't feel like enough. And if being his girl is really his way of calling me his girlfriend, then why is the word so hard for him to say? What we're doing doesn't feel any different from what I've done with other *boyfriends*. Except, it kind of does.

I push back my disappointment, the niggling voice that wishes he would have stormed through the door last night and told me, accident or not, he does love me. Stupid, I know.

If Wes hasn't been clear on labeling what we mean to each other, he has been loud and clear on basketball being number one in his life. His life revolves around the sport, and even with as much time as we spend together, I know that I'm the other woman, so to speak. The mistress when he's away from his true love. And even as I allow myself to think this, I know how dumb it sounds.

Wes is who he is because of his passion. Taking ball away from him would take a piece of him that I love. I admire his dedication, but I can't help but wonder what it would feel like to have that kind of passion directed at me. Is there any room for him to love anything else the way he loves basketball?

Ugh, my mind circles around my insecurities, and I stew, too afraid to voice any of it. Every guy wants a desperate girl begging for love and attention. Yeah right.

I need to just focus on the things I can control, like my career path. I've been searching for my purpose since I arrived at school. I love business, but I haven't found my place in a field that encompasses so much. After throwing myself into the cause with books, podcasts, vlogs, inspirational blogs, the only thing I've become passionate about is my quest for passion.

Wes puts the cruise control on and shifts so he can flex his foot.

"Your foot still bothering you?"

He waves me off with a shake of the head as he rests one hand on my leg. "All good."

I turn toward him to revisit a conversation from last

night. "Gabby won't grill you. She isn't like Vanessa. Actually, no she's a lot like Vanessa—or she used to be. I should warn you, though, she is really sensitive about her scarring."

He nods, and his eyes go thoughtful. After a moment of silence, I stare ahead, watching the familiar sights of my hometown come into view. When he finally speaks, we're pulling up in front of my parents' house.

"We all have scars we're trying to hide. Gabby's are just more obvious. I'm excited to meet her. She's important to you, she's a part of you, and I want to know all of you."

His words are a promise, and I hold on to them as we step out of the car and walk to Gabby's house.

Whatever fears I had about Wes meeting Gabby are short lived. They embrace like old friends, and as we sit in the living room after lunch, college football on the television as background noise, they chat like little old ladies at the hair salon. My face hurts from smiling even as my most embarrassing moments have become the topic of conversation.

"Blair always fails to mention that the reason Missy Thomas pushed her off the bike is because Blair was showing off. She was the first to get rid of her training wheels, and she rode up and down the street, ringing her bell and rubbing it in all our faces."

"I did not. I was just excited and my parents would only let me ride in our cul-de-sac." My attempt to defend myself falls on deaf ears. Wes and Gabby are in stitches, paying no attention to my rebuttal.

Traitor, I mouth to my friend and tug on the end of one of the bracelets on her arm.

"Oh, I almost forgot." Gabby reaches into her pocket and pulls out two matching bracelets of blue and yellow. She hands one to me and the other to Wes. "I made them with twelve strands of thread to represent your number."

"Matching bracelets?" I stare at her a little dumbfounded. It's one thing to wear best friend bracelets but a matching bracelet with my sort of boyfriend who is keeping me firmly in the I-like-you zone is a whole different thing.

Wes wraps the braided thread around his wrist and holds it out, indicating he wants me to tie it. "You embarrassed to match me?"

I roll my eyes and tie it securely before reciprocating and holding mine out to be tied with the others that don my arm. He shakes his head and nods to the other arm. He wants me to wear it on my right arm. It's bare, and a shiver takes my whole body as I pull my left back and extend my right.

He seems to understand the significance of wearing it separately from the others because a playful smirk rests on his lips, but his eyes are dark and serious.

As he ties the knot snugly, my heart squeezes with possibilities and hope. I search for meaning in the gesture as my eyes flit to the many bracelets that adorn my other arm. The colors vary from vibrant to dull, but as a whole, they complement each other to create beauty. Years of friendship are living art that I wear daily as a reminder of years gone by and dreams that are still unfulfilled.

This new bracelet, shiny and colorful without the grime and dirt of the real world to mar it, represents a new dream that I hadn't realized I wanted until I met Wes. A life shared with new hopes and dreams. Like the others, I know it will soon be tested for durability and strength, but I feel certain of one thing as I stare at our matching jewelry. I'll strive to hold on to Wes and our time together with the same passion and intensity that I've strived to hold on to Gabby and the plans we created when we were just kids. Bottom line, if he decides he suddenly doesn't have time for me, I'm going to be crushed. I'm in deep.

As we stand to hug Gabby and say our goodbyes, she wipes tears from both cheeks. Wes hangs back as I embrace my friend.

"What's wrong? Why the tears?"

She shakes her head and pulls back. "Ignore me. I'm just so happy for you. And maybe a little jealous too. You really did it . . . the whole college experience we always talked about. I know I'm not supposed to be ungrateful or sit around wishing things were any different from how they are. I've mostly made my peace with it. I don't want you to think I resent your happiness, no one is more proud of you. I promise. But—"

"Gabs, of course. You're allowed to feel that way. You can still have all those things. You just have to decide you're ready."

We share a sad smile, having spoken truths we usually leave unsaid. She turns to Wes and cocks her head at him. "Take care of her and promise you'll come back. I want to hear more about how amazing she's doing. She underplays it."

His eyes slide to me and back to Gabby. "I bet she

does."

After more hugs and promises to return, Wes and I walk down the street toward my parents' house. At the front door, he cages me in by putting both hands around my hips and pressing my back against the door.

"Thanks for letting me come. Gabby is something."

"She liked you too."

"I get it now. I see the way she drives you."

"She was always the one who wanted to rule the world. I just wanted to be by her side while she did it." The words taste bitter.

"That doesn't make you less worthy."

"Maybe not, but it feels that way."

He's quiet for a beat before he responds. "There are two types of ball players. Those with more talent than heart and those with more heart than talent. You'd think it'd be the ones with the most talent who perform the best, but it isn't."

"This coming from the guy who was sleeping through statistics. Where was your heart?" I tease.

"I've been running stats for myself and my teammates for as long as I can remember. That class is cake because I studied it early on in order to understand basketball."

"And none of that is talent or brains?"

"Sure, of course. Listen, Joe Schmoe off the street who's never touched a ball before isn't likely to be able to beat Lebron, but when you're talking players of a roughly equal talent spectrum, heart wins out. Sure, the most talented guys make some shots, pull off things I couldn't dream of, but they never really become a part of the team. When it comes game time they never mesh, and we're a team out there. We practice seven days of the week, year-round, and it rules our lives. Talent burns out before heart."

I consider his words and how it relates to me. Am I all talent and no heart?

"You have as much heart as you do talent," he says as if reading my thoughts. "You show it in everything you do. I've never met anyone with more heart than you. You're holding on to dreams of your best friend long after most would have abandoned all hope. When you figure out what *you're* passionate about, you'll be unstoppable. It's time to decide what your dreams are. As shitty as it is, Gabby may never be ready to stand by your side running a company, so whatever plans the two of you had back then have to be shifted some. Why are you holding on so hard when she's making it clear she just wants you to be happy?"

"Because I can't give up hope that, someday, she's going to be ready. I just won't let myself believe that's a possibility. She's the most deserving person I know. At first, I thought I could somehow make up for her absence by doing everything we planned like nothing had changed. And I guess I wanted to honor the dreams we made. I still want those things, and I want her beside me. The scars and the emotional toll of the accident changed her, but she has grit and determination hidden away somewhere deep inside. You two are a lot alike—well, Gabby before the accident."

"I'll take that as a compliment. I liked her a lot."

I nod toward his bracelet. "I'd say it was mutual. I'm a little jealous, actually. You're the first person besides me she's ever made one for."

"Yeah?" He looks positively elated. "In that case, I'm gonna have to get a wristband so I can wear it during games."

I roll my eyes, but it makes me happy he's going to make a point to wear it even if no one else can see it.

twenty-three

Wes

"You're dragging ass, Reynolds. Shaw take Reynold's place while he rests the foot."

"Coach."

He lifts a hand. "Don't bother. You're off. I'd rather you be rested and ready."

My foot is killing me, but I keep my face neutral, not giving in to the grimace that begs me to grind down on my back molars to distract from the throbbing radiating up my leg. I sit on a chair at the end of our row, leaving a half dozen seats between me and anyone else. Cursing Coach and Shaw, I wipe my face with a towel and then toss the terrycloth onto the floor in front of me. I know it's no one's fault but my own, but I'm pissed anyway.

I'm off my game, and I don't know if I can blame it on just my foot. I'm not as focused. I spent the past two days with Blair and hardly thought about ball. I'd even put off coming back last night, convincing her to leave at the ass crack of dawn this morning to get back in time for practice. A good break before the crunch of the season was what I'd told myself when guilt crept in for not getting in my drills and daily run. Maybe I shouldn't have been so eager to have time off. I'm not where I should be, and I have only my lack of concentration to blame.

Coach takes the chair next to me as the rest of the team runs through the plays with Shaw on point.

"How many more weeks of physical therapy?"

"Two more weeks. The foot is fine, coach. It bothers me when I push too hard. They said that was to be expected."

"I'm switching up your workouts. Until further notice, I want you and Shaw working together. Everywhere you go, he goes. Everything you do in this gym, he does."

I open my mouth to object, close it, and think through my words before I say something I can't take back. "I'll be ready. I won't let my team down."

"I know. You always leave it all on the court, but your team needs you to take it easy. Even if you were at your best, we would still need a strong six man. I think Shaw can be that."

I nod. I don't like the thought of anyone taking my spot. Least of all the guy who has one foot on the court and the other on the field. What happens if he decides he just wants to play baseball? Or gets hurt? It's ironic, I realize, worrying about someone else getting hurt while my foot screams. I rationalize it away because I hurt myself playing the sport I love, not the one I'm splitting my time playing.

"All right."

"The guys look to you, and I depend on you. I've never had to ask you to do anything because you've always just done. I'm asking this for me, for your team. We need Shaw ready to go sooner than later."

Blair calls as I'm changing out of my sweaty practice jersey into a clean-ish T-shirt for weight lifting and drills.

"What's up?" I ask, my voice less grumpy than I feel.

"Heading back to Succulent Hill. I forgot my cell charger and my backpack in our rush out. Got time to entertain me while I drive?"

"Got five."

"I figured it out," she says, and I can hear the excitement in her voice. "I have you to thank, really. I can't believe it didn't occur to me on my own, but what you said about heart and talent finally hit me today while I was unpacking. The thing I'm passionate about is other people's goals."

I cock a brow. "Your dream is for other people to achieve their dreams?"

"I know that sounds like a cop out. Hell, even I thought that, which is why I've had such a hard time pinning it down. But hear me out. Think about all the people who have had an impact in your life. Those who helped you get closer to your goals. With social media and a myriad of goal-setting resources, there's an entire market out there for helping people achieve their goals. Live streams, vlogs, blogs, books, podcasts, life coaching, the list is endless. That's what I want to do."

"The lady boss that creates more lady bosses."

"Exactly." While I'd love to pretend it's all about me, I can tell she's really excited about the idea. She's a bundle of excitement that's contagious even through the phone. "I'm meeting with my advisor this week to see if there are opportunities in the career resource center."

"You're really something, you know that? You're willing to dedicate your entire life to helping others, and I'm bitter about helping one dude on my team."

She's quiet for a beat, and I picture the adorable way her brows scrunch together when she's trying to figure something out. "Why? That isn't like you."

"This guy just gets under my skin. He has talent, but I'm not sure about heart."

"What makes you say that?"

"He's a multi-sport athlete, which means he plays two sports—basketball and baseball."

"Oh yeah, Tanner Shaw. Mario mentioned him. It's kind of impressive that he's playing both sports."

I roll my eyes. "It's a giant pain in the ass for everyone."

"So, you think because he isn't solely dedicated to basketball that his heart is less than his talent?"

"How could it possibly be otherwise? I can't imagine playing another sport, trying to juggle between two different games, and then comparing that dedication to someone who only plays one. You see what it's like, how basketball takes like a thousand percent of my time."

More silence that makes me feel like a prick.

"Maybe his path is different, but I don't think it's fair to question his heart. You said yourself that the test of heart comes with how well a guy meshes with the team come game time. You're only a few games in, and he played less than six minutes of the last game."

"Keeping stats on the rookie? Should I be jealous?"

"No, I was keeping stats on you, dummy. When he was playing, you weren't."

Those words, which were meant to be reassuring, cut deep. Is that why I'm being a giant baby? I've never had a problem giving other guys the limelight. Fuck, it's what makes me a good point man. I'm not greedy. I take my shots, but I don't force it. I always do what's best for the team. Until now.

"It's my last year," I say and wonder how such a bland statement can hold so much weight. "My foot is slowing me down, and if someone is going to take my spot, I want that person to give everything for the team. Someone like . . ."

"Someone like you?"

I nod, aware that she can't see the movement but unable to speak.

"Give him a chance to prove you wrong. Maybe he just needs someone to help in his journey. Someone smarter and wiser. Someone with experience leading a team. Someone with heart and talent." Her voice is sugary sweet, and I let her words heal like a salve to the open wound of my ego.

"Someone who understands what it takes to be great."

I'm eager for more. The way she believes in me almost has me convinced I'm capable. But she doesn't say anything else.

I can do this. For my team. For myself. I can live up to the standard that Blair believes I'm capable of.

Damn, she's good.

The locker room door opens, and a few other guys stop in to change before hitting the weight room. "Gotta go. See ya later?"

"Sure, text me later. I need to do some school stuff for a few hours."

Damn, this girl spends more time studying than anyone I know.

I find Shaw in the weight room as he's finishing a set of squats. By the annoyed look he shoots me, Coach has already informed him that we're going to be working together from now on.

He moves to pull all the weight off, but I shake my head. "Another set."

Shaw glares but silently adds another ten pounds to each side of the barbell.

"You need to build up your leg strength and endurance. When you're leading the point, your legs have to be as fresh at the end of the game as the beginning. Forget about what the rest of the guys are doing," I say as he looks around the room, envy clear in his eyes. "You have to be stronger, faster, and smarter out there."

He takes the weight on his back and squats out eight reps. When he finishes and faces me, breath ragged, the glint in his eye is determined. I hide my approval.

Every exercise is the same. I push him harder than he wants, but he doesn't back down.

"All right, let's hit the gym for some ball drills and then we'll join the team for the run."

His jaw flexes. As we walk out onto the court, I grab two balls and pass one back to Shaw. "I usually start with some half court runs, switching off every turn. Left up, right back, and so on until I feel warm."

I take off, and a split second later, he's beside me, pushing me faster. I lose track of how many times we've gone up and down the court after ten.

"All right, now, suicides with the ball. Stop and touch the line with your free hand and then switch over to the other hand."

Again, we turn what should be a light warm up into a race. The only sound in the gym is the steady drumming of the ball hitting the hardwood and our sneakers squeaking as we pivot at each line on the court. We stop after each one is complete, only resting as long as the other will allow. My foot throbs, but I don't dare let him see me weak.

Sweat pours down my face, my back, my arms. After the fifth, rookie cracks a smile. After seven, I join him, my lips curling of their own accord. At ten, a laugh that is filled with tension, relief, and hope escapes from my chest, and the sound is like the first crack in a dam. It grows and builds and then is joined by Shaw until we collapse on the floor completely exhausted, probably delirious, but I've gained his respect. And him, mine.

And Blair was right.

Nathan's birthday is the following week and as much as I don't feel like going out, I can't deny the man a proper twenty-first birthday celebration. Joel elbows me and lifts a hand. I turn my attention to the door to see Blair entering The Hideout. I swear the guy has girl radar and one eye always trained on the door.

My girl couldn't make it until after she finished studying. She's starting to make me feel guilty for my big brain with all the time she spends at the library. Not that I don't ever need to open a book, but I only have to a couple of hours a week tops. Whereas it's all Blair seems to do.

I meet her halfway and pull her into a hug. "Hey, you made it."

She goes limp in my arms, leaning her head against my chest.

"So tired," she mumbles as she pulls back.

"We don't have to stay long. The birthday boy is one more shot away from passing out." I slide a hand into the back pocket of her jeans and guide us back to the bar.

Nathan is propped up on a stool, eyes glazed and wearing a drunken smile. "Blair, you made it."

He makes a move to get off the stool and stumbles, setting off a domino effect as he crashes into guys on the team, who in turn bump into the people around us.

Z helps a totally clueless Nathan back up onto the chair. "Don't move," he instructs.

Blair goes to Nathan and embraces him. "Happy birthday. Can I buy you a drink?"

He winks at me over her shoulder and sniffs her hair. Fucker is messing with me, but I'm not scared. He knows I'd kick his ass if he made a move on my girl. Still, I move closer just in case he decides to test me.

"Hell yes," Nathan responds and pulls back. That's right, dude, hands off.

She orders two shots of Fireball at his request and

Nathan slurs the same toast he's been shouting all night, "To love and basketball."

That seems to put him over the edge, thank God, and Nathan voices his desire to go home and pass the fuck out. Joel and Z help him stand, and Blair and I trail behind. We're almost to the door when someone steps in front of her.

"A word," David says, teeth clenched and jaw flexing.

My hand tenses in her back pocket, and I tug her closer. "We're on our way out."

The glare that David shoots me further pisses me off, but I feel Blair cower next to me. Instead of telling him to get lost, she pulls away from me. "Go ahead with the guys, I'm right behind you."

The fuck? I start to protest, but she leans up and presses a kiss to my lips. I relent. "Five minutes."

"Five minutes," she repeats with a nod.

I'm bristling as I walk outside.

"Something doesn't feel right." I pace behind the car as Z gets Nathan in and Joel starts the car. "Maybe I should go back in and get her. I'm gonna go back in."

No one is listening to me as I work this out aloud. David looked angry, and as tough as Blair is, and as much as I don't want to be the kind of guy who acts like a jealous asshole, this just doesn't feel right.

"I'm gonna go get her," I repeat, louder this time so the guys can hear. I get the faintest head tilt in acknowledgment.

My eyes scan the bar when I step back inside, and my pulse quickens when I don't immediately see Blair.

I push toward the back, where I found them last time,

and it seems this is David's go-to spot for cornering women. I'd only meant to check and make sure she was okay, but the tears in Blair's eyes push me to action.

"I can't keep doing this. I've barely slept all week. Do what you have to do, David, but I'm done helping you." Blair's voice quivers, but I'm damn proud of her for standing up for herself, even if I'm hella confused about what's going on.

"Blair," I say her name just loud enough to be heard but don't move to put myself between them. I get the feeling that she needs to fight this battle on her own. I'm just back up, and I want fuck face to know it.

Instead of the anger I'd expected from David at my approach, he looks downright gleeful. "Do what I have to do, huh?"

There is panic in Blair's eyes as she looks between us. He steps toward me, and she reaches for his arm. *The hell?* He rips his arm away from her and continues until we're chest to chest. He isn't a short dude, but I have him by several inches.

"Don't worry, bro, she's all yours. I got what I wanted from her, including some mementos to remember her best assets." He winks, which is the final snap to my barely contained rage. Don't know where the fuck this guy gets off, but I don't like the way he suggests he still has any ties to her.

I shove him, and he staggers back. Before I can advance, I'm being pulled backward by Z, who I hadn't realized followed me back inside. "Should get out of here, man."

Blair's crying fills the silence of the parking lot as we're ushered out to Joel's car. Z pushes us into the back with Nathan, who's already passed out.

"What the hell?" Joel asks, getting a look at our faces.

"Just drive," Z says as he slams his door shut.

I sit, stunned, as Joel takes off to the house. What the hell just happened?

"Dude." Joel's eyes find mine in the rearview mirror, and he nods toward Blair. Right, I'm meant to be comforting my girl.

"Come here," I murmur and pull Blair into my arms. She falls into my chest and sobs harder. She tries to speak, but I run a hand through her hair and tell her we'll talk later.

I need to get my emotions in check before I deal with hers. I'm pissed, and only part of my anger is at David. I'm also mad at myself for losing my cool. I mean, he totally deserved it, and I'd do it again in a heartbeat, but I've never been in a bar brawl. In fact, the only time I've ever gotten into any kind of physical altercation has been on the basketball floor. It's the only place that has ever gotten me riled up enough to want to throw a punch. Until now. Until Blair.

Her crying quiets as I lead her out of the car and up to my room. She crawls onto my bed and kicks off her shoes. "I'm so sorry."

"Hey." I slide in next to her. "What are you sorry for? You didn't do anything wrong."

That seems to set her off again, and her chest heaves with new tears. I hold her until she cries herself to sleep, and then I slip downstairs.

Joel and Z are in the living room watching television.

"She okay?" Joel asks when I plop down onto the couch.

I nod. "Yeah, I think so. Guy was a total ass to her. Never expected her to react like that, though," I admit. "She's sleeping now."

"What the hell happened in there to make you haul off and hit the guy?" Joel asks.

"I didn't hit him, just shoved a tiny bit." Okay a lot, whatever. I fill them in the best I remember and include the bits that Blair has told me about the way her relationship ended with David. At least the parts I don't think she'll mind my sharing.

"She was really shaken. It doesn't add up. You know the guy?" I ask Joel.

"Know of him. Not any more than what you told me, though. He's a Sigma, and he's a tool."

"I'm gonna text Mario. Let Vanessa know what happened and see if she knows anything."

"I'll text Mario," Joel interjects. "You need to chill out before you do something stupid."

twenty-four

Blair

I wake in the darkness, but voices carry from downstairs. My head aches from the bawl fest, and I'm filled with humiliation as I wonder what Wes must think. Or what he'll think if I tell him everything. I've played out this scenario a hundred times, how I'd tell Wes if it ever came down to it. Admittedly, I never planned on it unless my hand was forced.

Fucking David. I spent two hours waiting for him to show up at the library so I could give him the latest assignments and he blows me off then has the gall to show up at The Hideout.

What's worse than being blackmailed by your ex-boyfriend? Your new boy-whatever finding out exactly why you're being blackmailed in the first place. I have no idea how I'm going to explain myself. Wes deserves the truth, but oh God, the truth is horrifying.

I force myself out of his bed, inhaling his scent and praying it isn't the last time I'm allowed in said bed, and then I head downstairs. I know there will be questions about what went down and why I reacted the way I did, and I'm having a hard time finding the words even as I try to sort them in my mind.

"What are you doing here?" Fresh tears fall down my face as I run toward Vanessa.

She offers me a sad smile as she stands from her spot on the couch next to Mario and embraces me. "Checking on my best girl. Come sit, tell me what happened."

Wes, Mario, Joel, and Z watch us carefully. It's clear whatever I have to say, they want to hear it too. "I ran into David at The Hideout. He was an asshole, per the usual."

"Blair, honey, you need to stop giving him face time. No more letting him pull you aside. The douche canoe knows he screwed up royally, and he's trying to get you back."

"That isn't it." I look at my hands as I say the words. "He doesn't want me back."

"No guy corners a girl in a bar unless he's trying to get in her pants." As Joel speaks, I look to Wes. His expression is guarded, and I wonder how much he's already guessed. It seems laughably obvious at this point, and Wes is a smart jock.

"He cornered me tonight because we were supposed to meet up."

Wes's eyes widen slightly and then he slips the cool and collected mask back into place. I look to Vanessa, unable to watch him while I finish explaining. Vanessa raises her brows, prompting me to continue.

"I've been helping him with his classes. No, not helping. I've been doing his class work."

"Why would you do that? You hate him." V's shocked voice makes me regret the months of keeping it from her.

"Because he has pictures of me. Naked pictures. He threatened to post them online, around campus, basically ruin me." I exhale once I get it all out.

The hand that V rests on my leg squeezes. "That rat bastard."

I peek up at Wes, who has placed his head between his legs. Shame and humiliation force me to look away.

"Baby doll, every girl on campus has nude photos." Joel sits forward in his chair. "Check this out, these are just from tonight."

I cover my eyes as Joel pushes his phone in front of my face and I get an eye full of boobs.

"Jesus, that isn't helpful." Wes stands. "V, can you stay here with Blair for a bit?"

"It's fine. I can go home." My bed sounds great. A private place to hide and cry for a day or year. I can't bear to guess what Wes must think of me now.

He crosses the room and threads his hands through my hair, tilting my head up to meet his gaze. "Stay. I'll be back as soon as I can."

"Where are you going?"

"To Sigma."

"What? Why? There's nothing else to say. I told him tonight I was done. It's over."

He drops a light kiss onto my lips and pulls back, but

then he growls as he crashes his lips to mine. This kiss is hungrier. Desperate and hard and steals the air from my lungs before he steps back.

"Let's go," he says, and I watch in fascination as all the guys file out of the house.

I can't stop the anxious giggle that bubbles up and escapes from my mouth. "Did they all just march out of here like some sort of soldiers going to battle?"

Vanessa smiles. "Yep. Off to fight for your honor."

I groan.

"Sit," she orders. "Tell me how this all happened?" She holds up a hand. "Actually, let's go upstairs and wash your face. I refuse to let that ass hat be the cause of your makeup running down your face."

Leave it to V to be concerned about my smeared makeup at a time like this.

Wes

"What's the plan? We can't just waltz in there and roam the halls until we find him."

There's a group of guys outside the Sigma house, kicked back in chairs and drinking beer. I spot David as he stands and lifts his chin in a silent dare to step on to his pad.

"Not necessary," I grit out and quicken my pace.

We're welcomed by the group of guys joining David

and lining up across the small patio, puffing out their chests and pulling their hands into fists at their sides. No doubt, David's already filled them in on what happened, so our appearance doesn't seem to shock them. It doesn't make them happy either. Having four big, athletic dudes who are clearly pissed strolling up on them makes me almost feel sorry for them. Almost.

"This is private property, Reynolds. You've already given me enough ammunition to press assault charges. Get lost, or I'll have the cops here in five, and we'll add trespassing to your rap sheet."

"Maybe before you start slinging accusations you should know that blackmail and extortion are felonies. I have the Valley president on speed dial, so we could add cheating and sexual harassment to that list as well." Joel looks at David with a smirk on his face.

Joel doesn't like to use his family to fight his battles, so I acknowledge his willingness to call up dear old Dad with a nod in his direction before I step toward David. "I want every single picture you have of her, every emails, texts, or scraps of paper she wrote on gone. Delete it. Burn it. Erase her from your life."

He laughs, and I fight back the urge to pummel him. First, I need to be sure he's going to do what I ask before it comes to blows.

"And if I don't, what is it you think you're going to do about it?"

"Whatever I have to. You're a sick fucker blackmailing a girl to do your schoolwork. Tell me, are you too stupid to pass your own classes or are you just holding on to her anyway you can?"

"Holding on to Blair?" He bends at the waist as he

lets out a deep laugh. "That slut was annoying as fuck, all positive vibes and doing things for others." He rolls his eyes. "And a lousy lay on top of it."

My fist connects with his cheek, causing him to let out a grunt as his head cracks to the side. It's chaos as guys charge and punches are thrown. David's a pussy, no shocker there, and after I land a gut check, he collapses to the ground and holds up a hand for mercy. His signal breaks up the fight, but I still bend and get right in his face.

"Delete everything. Tonight. And stay the fuck away from her. You see Blair, you walk in the other direction. She's mine, and I protect what's mine." I straighten and pull out my phone. "Say cheese, asshole." I snap a picture of him lying on the ground, lip busted, and then flip him off for good measure. It isn't the same as a dick pick, but for a dude like David, I'm gonna guess a leaked photo of him looking like a pussy would be just as humiliating.

I'm still fuming when I get back to the house, but when I push open my bedroom door and see Blair curled up on my bed sleeping, it dissipates.

"Sweetheart, wake up."

Blair lets out a little groan as her eyes flutter open. I drop a kiss to her lips and pull her against me. Damn, I'd do anything for this girl. If I had any question about that before tonight, they are gone. I'm in love with her.

"Is everything okay?" Her voice is tentative.

"Everything is perfect. I'm sorry I left you alone while you were upset. You doing okay?"

"I'm so embarrassed," she says as she buries her face against my chest.

"What are you embarrassed about?"

"For all of it. Sending him the pictures to begin with, being too mortified to stand up to him, letting him use me, getting you involved. I'm especially sorry about that. Are you going to get into trouble because of this?"

"Nah, he's too much of a coward to tell anyone. Besides, it was worth it. You're worth it."

Because I freaking love you. I love you.

"The stupidest part is I didn't even want to send him the pictures. I know lots of girls do it, and that's cool. I totally respect a woman's right to sexy pictures without labeling her a slut, but I did it for all the wrong reasons. He was really possessive, and I was trying to prove that I cared for him and that there was no reason for him to play the jealous boyfriend card all the time. We were fighting a lot, and I thought, 'hey maybe this will show him.' Sounds really dumb now."

"Not dumb at all." I squeeze her a little tighter. "You were fighting for something you believed in."

"Yeah, like I said, incredibly dumb."

"Stop talking about my girl like that. She's smart, gorgeous, caring, and she didn't deserve what he did to her."

"I know."

"Do you?" I lift her chin so I can see her eyes. "You didn't deserve what he did. Even if you'd been the worst girlfriend on the planet, which we both know you weren't, you didn't deserve to be exploited and blackmailed."

The war in her eyes tugs at my emotions, which are bouncing around like a ball in a pinball machine. I want so badly to tell her how I feel about her and make her promises I have no business making. Promises to protect and love.

Tonight isn't about my feelings, though. It's about hers.

As I roll over on top of her, I kiss her tenderly, taking my time and expressing everything I can't say with gentle caresses and strokes. When I'm finally inside her, I look deep into her eyes and wonder if she can feel the shift between us or if it's just me who's careening into the unknown.

twenty-five

Blair

I slide into my seat after having pushed and clawed my way through the crowd at Ray Fieldhouse. Vanessa scoots down, making room for me, and Mario gives me a small wave from the other side of my friend.

"What took you so long? The game is about to start."

You'd think it was her boyfriend who was getting ready to play instead of mine. I'm not worried about the game. Wes has been on fire all season. He's playing amazing, the team is winning, and he's even helped bring Shaw into the group; although, he still doesn't seem thrilled about that last part.

Tonight is the last home game before Christmas break. Wes and the guys only get a week off. I'm heading to Succulent Hill to spend my break binge watching holiday movies, eating too many sugar cookies, and sleeping with no fear of missing class and no grueling study sessions keeping me up to all hours.

To be fair, the grueling study sessions usually ended with me naked in Wes's bed, so I can't really complain too much about that. And since I've been managing only my own course load, the semester had flowed along nicely.

"I was waiting for my final stat grade to be posted."

Vanessa pries her eyes away from the court where both teams are taking the floor. "Well? Did your private tutor make it worth your while?"

My face warms. Did he ever. "Grades aren't up yet."

"I'm sure you pulled an A. Even if you only studied a quarter of the time you two were together you should have been able to ace the final."

He's been insatiable this week, and I've been happy to provide stress relief in the form of letting him use my body as a distraction. It isn't as if I'm not getting mine as well. If I'm honest, it's been a good distraction for both of us. I've not seen or heard from David, but I'm still looking over my shoulder expecting him to pop up out of nowhere.

Arizona State wins the tip off and the game begins. The energy in the room is bursting. The pep band works through their material, the cheerleaders are dancing along, and the fans are on their feet. The student section, enthusiastic as ever, is overflowing with students who are burned out on classes and ready to see our team win one before we head off to see family and visit hometown friends. But the game is a back and forth, both teams playing hard and not giving an inch. As we go to halftime, the score is tied and my nerves are shot.

Determination and sweat drips off him. I stare hard at him as he follows the team off the court, willing him to somehow find me amongst the crowd. He doesn't look up. He's in whatever fog or bubble he creates to stay focused and not let the fans, the other team, or even amazingly hot girls distract him.

"I'm gonna go get some popcorn," I say to Vanessa and Mario. "Want anything?"

They shake their heads and make the exact same scrunched up face to indicate no. They're freaking adorable, but I keep that to myself. Vanessa would just roll her eyes if I said so. She's been unable to stay away from him, but I know she's still skittish, and I'm not giving her any reason to back off. Mario is good for her.

The line to the concession is long, and I slide in behind a couple of high school girls. I would say they were freshman, but even freshman know better than to wear *that* much makeup or skirts *that* short.

"Joel Moreno is definitely the hottest player," one of the girls says and fans her face. "And his family is like super rich. My sister had English with him senior year, and she said he wore a different pair of Jordan's every month."

I've seen Joel's many pairs of shoes strewn around the house and can confirm he has enough for that statement to be true.

The other girl chirps in after showing her amaze and wonder with an actual jaw drop. "Joel is hot, but Wes Reynolds is my favorite. Have you noticed he started wearing a sweatband on his right wrist?"

Her friend shakes her head, but I smile. I have to force myself from butting into their conversation to politely inform her that he started wearing the blue band to hide the bracelet Gabby made for him.

"Watch him when he shoots free throws. He kisses it before each shot for good luck or something. I wonder what it means. Think someone died or something?"

He does?

The girls keep talking. I vaguely hear them speculate between it being a death in the family or an injured teammate who passed it down, but it's background noise to the reel in my head analyzing his free throw ritual. All the guys have them. Some dribble two or three times, count to two, and a million other variations. No matter the intricacies, it's the exact same every time. Wes's ritual is burned into my memory. Breathe out, spin ball with both hands, one dribble, count to two, shoot.

I exit the line and make my way back to my seat.

"What happened to popcorn?" Vanessa asks.

"The line was too long."

The team is back on the floor, and I follow Wes's every move watching and waiting for him to step behind the line to practice free throws. He doesn't, and the coach calls them over before I can confirm the ramblings of my boyfriend's high school fan.

I pray to the basketball gods that Wes gets fouled taking a shot. Not my proudest moment, but I'm desperate to see if it's true. Has he somehow incorporated me into the ritual? What else could it mean? I'm glued to the action, holding my breath every time Wes has the ball and practically growling every time it leaves his hands.

When he's finally fouled driving to the basket, I jump

and cheer so loudly Vanessa side-eyes me. I don't pay her any mind. Wes lines up to take his shots, and the rest of the men on the court take their spots along the outside of the lane and at half court. The ref bounces the ball to Wes, who then begins his ritual.

Breathe out, spin the ball with both hands, dribble. And just as I've decided the girl in the concession line must have been mistaken, he brings the ball up to jaw level and touches the sweatband to his mouth. I could almost believe he's just wiping his mouth it's so quick. So quick and fluid that I don't know if I ever would have seen it on my own.

"Oh my God," I whisper and grin like a fool as he takes the shot and it swishes through the net. I cheer along with the rest of the home-team fans, but I'm already giddy as I wait to see it again. With the ball in his hands, ready to take the second shot, he restarts the process and just like last time, the quick kiss of his right wrist before he shoots is unmistakable.

"I think he's in love with me," I say, turning to Vanessa as the crowd cheers the point made.

Her mouth quirks up. "Duh."

"Oh, you're one to talk." I nod to Mario, and as if on cue, he turns and gives Vanessa an adoring smile.

"So we're freaking in love." She rolls her eyes, but I can read her well. She's happier than I can ever remember her being.

"Are you gonna talk to him about it?" Vanessa asks, both our eyes glued back to the court. There's a time out and the cheerleaders wave their pom poms in front of us screaming about Valley pride.

"I don't know. He's been pretty clear that whatever

we're doing isn't serious."

"He's made that clear or you're too chicken shit to ask him and assume that's what he thinks?"

"Okay, fine, I've been too chicken to ask, but his schedule is insane and is just going to get crazier. The season goes until April, if they're lucky, and then he graduates in May. After that, there's no telling where he'll end up. Meanwhile, I'm going to be here."

"You're spinning. Take a breath. Just talk to him about it. You two have managed to make it work for this long, and it's been an eventful semester."

"No kidding."

Arizona State has possession of the ball after the timeout. Wes is guarding their point man, giving me a view of the serious and determined look on his face as he provides a barrier between the opposing player and his teammates. His opponent has him on height and size, but my man is faster. The guy fakes right and passes left, but Wes gets his hand on the ball and sends it sailing toward the half court line. Both players take off as fast as they can, but Wes gets there first.

The crowd is on their feet, screaming Wes's name and jumping like the basket has already been made. But the other team isn't giving up that easy. Wes drives to the basket, power and confidence. He explodes up toward the rim, the ball safely tucked in one of those big hands of his. The defense is tight against him, a step behind, but so close that the crowd holds their breath as the ball leaves Wes's hands.

I follow the ball as it goes up and into the net. A whistle is called, and the ref signals a foul on the play, granting the basket and giving Wes an opportunity to make it a three-point play. I'm lost to the explosion of cheers around me. There's a commotion on the floor. Wes and a player in a red jersey are lying in a heap on the floor from the contact. His groan is the first signal something is wrong. Wes's face is angled down, his body curled into a ball, but he reaches for his foot and my stomach drops.

Everything happens in slow motion. The coach and some other guys wearing Valley University polos circle Wes, making it hard for me to see what's going on. I grab on to Vanessa's arm at some point, holding on to her tightly because I don't trust my legs to hold me.

There's movement, and he stands with the help of three other guys. The crowd cheers around me, but I'm silent. He's favoring his foot, holding it in a way that hurts my heart and sends a million what-if scenarios shuffling through my head. There's some back and forth between Wes and the coach, but he hobbles to the free-throw line, making it clear he's going to take his shot.

Z steps up behind Wes, and his lips move, but I can't make out what he says. Wes nods once, his mouth set into a grim line. All but two players from the opposing team move back. I hate them for even considering that he might not make the shot, even knowing they're just doing what makes sense.

Still, sensibility has nowhere to sit in the crowd of emotions pushing around inside me.

Wes has the ball. A calm sense of routine eases the hard lines of his face. Breathe out, spin the ball with both hands, dribble once . . . but the kiss of his right wrist is lost. He completes the sequence like it never changed. There's no indication in the rhythm or his features that says he's missed a step. It's as if it were never part of it at all and I just imagined it. The ball leaves his hand and bounces around the rim before slipping through the net.

Coach Daniels calls a timeout, and Joel and Z flank Wes, leading him off the court.

twenty-six

Wes

"I'm afraid the news isn't great, son."

No shit.

I don't look up at the doctor as he slaps my x-ray onto a lighted screen. From my peripheral, I can see he's pointing, but I don't need to see it to know it's broken. I knew it the second it happened.

"You've re-broken the fifth metatarsal."

"How long will I be out? Same recovery time?"

He hesitates, and I grind my teeth impatiently. "This is much more serious. The bones have displaced this time."

"How long?" I growl, not caring that I sound like an asshole.

"You'll need surgery. Three months, maybe four until you're—"

"Three months? The season will be over in three months. My college career will be *over* in three months."

His eyes are solemn. "I'm sorry, Wes. I know it's crap news."

"What if I don't have the surgery? I could wear a boot for a few weeks, finish the season and then have the surgery." It sounds crazy even to my own ears.

"You need the surgery. The bones aren't sitting properly. Even if you wanted to grin and bear it, this is just going to get worse every time you put pressure on the foot. You aren't going to be able to play competitively with this type of injury until you've had the surgery and healed properly. I'm sorry."

The doctor leaves and a nurse comes in to get my signature on a stack of papers. I sign them without reading the fine print. What the hell could it possibly say that would make this any worse?

Coach steps in as they prep me for surgery. I've taken off my jersey for the last time, and it sits awkwardly between us in a clear plastic bag. He shuffles from one foot to the other. It's obvious he has no idea what to say, but I'm glad he doesn't try to pacify me with words of hope and encouragement. We're two quiet men, each stewing with his own version of this nightmare.

"The team is out in the waiting room."

"I don't want to see anyone right now."

"I figured as much, but I wanted you to know they're here just the same. There's a pretty brunette out there pacing the floor too. That the girlfriend?"

Blair.

I nod.

"She has the stubborn look of a woman who isn't

leaving until she sees you."

"That sounds like her." A small smile cracks and then falls. "Tell her to go home. Tell all of them to go home. They aren't doing me any favors by being here. I just want to be alone."

"I'll tell them," he says and backs out of the room, stopping with one foot in and one foot out. "Won't be responsible for kicking anyone out who doesn't want to go, but I'll tell them."

As his steps echo down the hall, I lie back and close my eyes. I embrace the pain. I'd embrace it every day if it meant I could keep playing and see this season through.

I can't think about what's next or what tomorrow will bring . . . what I'll say to those people in the waiting room. My request may scare off some of my teammates, but I know when I wake up, Coach, my roommates, and Blair will be waiting for me. Waiting to reassure me and pamper me. I don't want any of it. I want to crawl into a hole and fixate until I've come up with a plan to rewind time or gain another year of college eligibility with Z.

This was our year.

It was our fucking year.

I crack one eye open, then the other. Reflexively, I close them both. The light in the room makes the fog in my head swim. There's movement beside me and then her touch. I'd recognize it anywhere—even drugged and pissed at the world, apparently.

"What are you wearing?"

"What?" Her voice is shaky and quiet like she's talking to an invalid. Guess that's me.

"I asked what are you wearing? Leather skirt maybe, halter top, sexy nurse? Give me a visual."

"Jeans and your jersey," she says with a hint of humor in her voice. "I'm sorry I'm not dressed like a puppet from your teenage wet dreams."

I peek out at her beautiful face and let my eyes wander to the jersey she wears, the one I'll never put on again. I close my eyes to squeeze away the pain. "I'm pretty sure my teenage wet dreams always included chicks wearing my jersey."

I joke with her, even though I don't feel like being funny. I'd really like to send her away and drown in misery, but I think I'm more likely to get her to leave if I pretend I'm okay instead of a man who has lost a piece of his soul.

I open both eyes slowly, letting them adjust to the light and finding her face. Looking at her heals and breaks me. I'll never be the same, and whoever I was when she met me? He's gone. Maybe she knows it, maybe she doesn't. Her eyes give nothing away as she tries a hesitant smile.

Regardless of how I've changed, I still want her. She's maybe the only thing I've ever been certain about besides basketball. But even as I realize this, I know my actions won't back up my feelings. Sometimes, we make bad decisions not because we aren't aware but because it feels good to cause pain. That's how I feel as I plan to break her heart and mine.

"Shouldn't you be in Succulent Hill by now?"

"I wanted to see you before I left."

I raise my arms to the side. "You saw me."

Her hands go to her hips. "You didn't really expect me to go without checking on you first, did you?"

I hadn't. Hoped, maybe, but I knew she'd be here.

"Go, be with your family. My parents are on their way, and I'm heading to Kansas with them."

"You are?"

I can tell she didn't anticipate this. I wasn't supposed to leave Arizona until the week of Christmas. What the hell did she think I was going to do? Ride along with the team? Roll myself in a wheelchair to the games? Sit on the fucking sidelines and have everyone look at me with pity? Yeah, no thanks.

"But what about . . ." She fidgets with the bracelet on her arm. The one that matches mine.

"I'm out for the rest of the season, Blair. I'm done." The words physically hurt. I don't feel done. I haven't finished what I set out to do. I've failed them. Failed Z. It's his last season too, and what if he doesn't get drafted because I couldn't get him the ball? I owe him my whole college career and I've failed him.

She nods. Everyone seems to be doing that a lot lately. Silent bobbleheads, unsure of what to say. "I could stay until you leave. I'm just going to be sitting around by myself. Both my parents are working next week."

She sure as shit is not making this easy.

"Nah, go. I just want to be alone. Finally catch up on sleep and all that."

She bites her lip, clearly torn between making a stand to stay and honoring my wishes. Reaching into her purse, she pulls out a box wrapped in red-and-white stripes with a huge green bow on top. "Merry Christmas, Wes."

She pushes the present into my hands and I open my mouth to speak. "I—"

She cuts me off. "It's okay. I wasn't expecting anything."

What I'd been about to say was that I'd left her present at the house where we'd planned to say goodbye before the break. I lift the box, shaking it gently like I'm trying to guess what it is. She doesn't smile. She's no longer fooled by my playful charades. She sees through me. Sees me. Always has. I wonder what she sees now, a broken man?

"Merry Christmas, Blair."

twenty-seven

Blair

I unlock my phone, checking for the hundredth—no, thousandth—time for a text or phone call that I've somehow missed.

Nothing.

Wes's texts have been few and far between and only in response to my messages, so I shouldn't be surprised. He didn't even reply back when I told him I'd gotten an A in statistics.

A man who falls short of his dream is sad. Wes is something else entirely. To call him sad is a compliment to the word and an insult to the void in his eyes. I'd been jealous of his passion, and now I realize how much that made up his identity.

It isn't as if I care about him being a ball player because of the hype around him or the jealous looks shot my way when we were together. I can admit it felt good to be on the arm of a man who sits on top of the social ladder, though. He could call me right now and tell me he was going to dedicate his life to origami, and if it filled him with as much hunger as basketball did, I'd be just as happy. It isn't the what—it is the fire that burns inside him because he is doing something he loves. He is oxygen to my own small blaze, and without him I'm afraid my flame will die out too.

It's a helpless and hopeless feeling that I remember well from Gabby's accident. The sitting around, feeling sad. The silent fury at the world. The helplessness.

Another person I love has watched their dreams slip away.

Maybe when a person's dreams are big like Gabby's and Wes's, their failures are that much more traumatic. Love lost is still love. Are dreams lost still dreams? Is there still an overarching lesson in having a dream and failing?

Dragging myself from the couch to the dining room table, I stare at the stack of books I brought home. Each title and tagline promises inspiration and steps to setting and achieving goals. How can I possibly throw myself into career planning when I've failed, twice now, to help two of the most important people in my life?

It feels like a test. I finally decide exactly what I want to do with my life, and then fate throws another bump in the road. Although, this bump is really more of a boulder in the form of a sulking man who has just had his dreams crushed. Everything he ever worked for is gone. How do I spin that into something positive and push him to make new dreams?

The Assist

They say those who can't do, teach. I never liked that. The most inspirational and knowledgeable people are those who have lived it. But maybe those who can't help the people they really want, set out to help everyone else.

I grab my purse and phone and head for the front door. After slamming it shut behind me, take that world, I walk with purpose down the street. The purpose being I need my best friend to save me from my thoughts.

I find Gabby sitting at the small desk in her room, an array of color thread laid out in front of her. I pull a chair to the side and grab the three spools closest to me, unwinding it until I have a good length for a bracelet.

I haven't done this in years, but my fingers remember, and I work at a good pace until I reach the end and tie it with a knot. It isn't perfect. In fact, the imperfections are glaring as I smooth a hand over it and place it next to the two Gabby has made in the same time.

"Can I ask you something?"

She sits back and smiles. "Sure. What do you want to know?"

"Do you ever resent the fact I'm living your dreams while you're still here in Suck Hill?"

She starts to respond, eager to tell me no way, I'm sure. I don't want whatever practiced, positive spin she's about to say.

"Honestly. I mean I know you love me and want nothing but good for me, but do you ever resent me for it? I'm doing all the things you planned for us. These were your dreams not mine. I just wanted to do whatever you did. You're the one who made me promise we'd rule the world."

"I think you're remembering that differently from how it went down."

I shake my head as I think back to all our conversations about what we wanted to do when we graduated and left Succulent Hill. "No, your dreams were always so much bigger than mine."

Gabby takes my hands. A white scar runs across the top of her hand, and I focus on the reminder of pain that has healed and hope that even in the worst of times people survive.

"You gave me permission to have those crazy dreams. My family, my teachers, even our classmates thought I was nuts. You never did."

It's true. She was, no *is*, special. I'd always known she was capable of anything.

"Your love and friendship are the reasons I dreamed big. You let me believe I could have everything I ever wished for. Even now, I don't know if I'd be able to get out of bed every day if it weren't for your voice in the back of my head telling me I can."

"Gabs." My voice breaks, and I squeeze her hand tightly. "I don't know how to be that for him. He's lost everything he ever wanted."

"Give him time. When he's ready, you'll know, and then, just be you."

"He's pushing me away."

"Don't take this the wrong way, but what do you expect him to do? His identity has changed. You still see him as the same guy, but everything he ever thought he was has been flipped upside down. He has to deal with that before he can let other people back in. I can see how much you want to run to him and fix it."

I open my mouth the deny it, but she gives me a knowing smirk. "It's written all over your face. Remember how you used to storm in here and get me out of bed? Lord, I wanted to toss you out of here some days when you'd pop in all chipper and bring me magazines or books. You're lucky we're neighbors or I'd have ghosted you too. The first time you brought the yoga mats, I thought our friendship was over for good. I could barely look at myself in the mirror and you were spouting inner peace bullshit."

I hold a hand over my mouth to suppress a giggle. "I never knew that."

"You're the strongest person I know, Blair. You don't have to hold on to my dreams, or his, but you do because you desperately want to see everyone have everything they could ever want. You're a little dream maker. You always have been. You sell yourself short for not wanting big things, but you want big things for *everyone*. Your dreams are not only bigger than mine ever were, they're more important. You're going to do amazing things. You're going to inspire and help so many people."

"Speaking of helping people." I pull out the spring semester Valley course catalog from my purse and hand it to her.

Surprise makes her eyes widen. "Blair, I can't."

"You can." I leave no room for argument. "Just think about it. It will probably be hard at first, I don't dispute that, but you can't sit up here for the rest of your life. And I promise to be right by your side."

She drops the catalog and hugs me fiercely. Her voice is quiet and shaky when she whispers, "Still letting me dream big."

twenty-eight

Wes

"You're back!" Joel stops short after he spots me lying on the couch in our living room.

"Was there some doubt about my return to school?" I ask dryly. I'm being an ass, but I want no part of all the questions and small talk now that I'm back. I've only managed to avoid it to this point because I've ignored texts and calls like it was my job.

"Classes don't start back for another week," he says by explanation.

I let out a sigh. "I couldn't handle my parents hovering over me, checking the clock like I was keeping them from their usual holiday festivities. Happy?"

Joel laughs. "No, not really, but I'm glad as shit you're back. Z has been quieter than normal. In fact, if it weren't for the shit he says on the court I'd think he'd gone mute."

As if on cue, the big man walks through the door. A smile spreads across his face and then falls. "You're back."

Before I can brace myself, I'm lifted and squeezed like a teddy bear in the desperate clutches of a child.

"Fuck, Z," I wheeze out and chuckle. "I missed you too, big guy." I pat his back a few times, and he eases me back down to the couch.

Joel plops down in the armchair with a big goofy grin on his face as if nothing has changed. Fuck, I missed being here. Even more than I hated the idea of coming back and being the only one not running off to practice. Coach told me I was always welcome in his gym and encouraged me to come be his eyes and ears, continue working with Shaw and all that. I told him hard pass.

"We going out to celebrate tonight then?"

"No," Z and I say in unison.

"Aww, come on. You don't have anything going on tomorrow." Joel points to me before swinging his attention to my right. "And, Z, we have late practice tomorrow and our next game isn't until late next week. Come on, you pansy asses. I'm texting Nathan, he'll be in."

Something about his plea or the idea that we could have a night out just like the old days touches something in both of us, I guess, because we're both nodding and making plans before I realize what's happening.

We head to The Hideout and grab a table where I can sit and prop up my leg. The pain is better every day, but too much time upright, and I'm gritting my teeth and sucking down painkillers.

The bar and grill is quiet, but then Joel has to open his mouth.

"Blair coming?" he asks as he puts a beer in front of me and takes a seat across the table.

"Think she's still in Succulent Hill."

"You think?" He pauses, beer resting on his lips.

"We haven't talked much over break. Been kinda busy," I grumble, pointing to my leg.

"Bullshit. Busy feeling sorry for yourself."

Joel takes out his phone, and I drain half the glass in front of me, thankful for once Z is quiet.

Nathan and a few more of the guys from the team trickle in, and Joel waves them over as he puts the phone to his ear.

Tables are pushed together, and pitchers are placed in the middle so we can fit everyone.

"Blair, hey, it's Joel."

My ears perk up at her name, and all the blood rushes from my head to a pit in my stomach.

"What. The. Fuck?" I grit out.

"You back in town? We're at The Hideout. Wes was just crying about how much he misses you, why don't you come down so he'll stop pouting."

I grab for the phone, but he pushes back and stands, walking out of ear shot. I pull out my own phone and open my and Blair's text history. The last thing I said to her was "Okay" in response to her asking me how I was feeling. That was two days ago. She finally got the message that I wasn't up for idle chitchat about my wellbeing and here Joel is, meddling in my shit.

He walks back to the table, a shit-eating grin on his face. "She's on her way. You're welcome."

My phone vibrates with a new text, but it's from Mario, not Blair.

Mario: Angry chick alert. Heading your way with Vanessa and Blair. Guard your good leg, V is pissed you ghosted Blair all break.

I don't respond before I tuck my phone away. Maybe I can act surprised when they arrive. Z is beside me, and I hide behind him a little. Call me a coward all you want, fucking Vanessa is scary.

Seeing Blair again after my less than warm behavior over the past three weeks makes something ache in my chest. She stays firmly planted to Vanessa's side as the trio walks up to the table and says hello. Empty space at the table and chairs scattered around the place go untouched as the girls make their excuses and head to sit at the bar. It's like she came just to make a point she didn't want to see me. Makes zero sense, but here she is, looking hot and angry and hotter because angry looks good on her. Fuck.

"Ouch," Z says, eyes watching Blair. "What the hell did you do to have Blair giving you the shrug off? Must've been something bad, it isn't like her. Girl doesn't know how to be cold."

"I was an ass all break," I admit quietly. "I haven't been returning her texts or calls."

"Why the fuck not?" It's a response I'm not prepared for. Z doesn't insert himself into relationships, and he certainly doesn't take sides when neither side is his.

"I was dealing with shit."

His expression tells me he thinks I'm in the wrong,

but he doesn't say any more.

More and more guys from the baseball and basketball teams join us as the night goes on. Blair doesn't so much as glance back at the table from her spot at the bar. Vanessa, on the other hand, glares at me every chance she gets.

Mario and Clark, a freshman baseball player, stand behind the girls at the bar. Blair laughs at something Clark says. Her shoulders shake with the movement and the strap of her dress slips off one side. My eyes dart to the bare skin at the same time Clark reaches out and pushes the strap back into place.

I see red and move faster than I thought possible. I'm pushing my way between them before rational thought has a chance to intervene.

"The fuck, man," Clark says as he catches himself on the stool next to Blair.

"Hands off if you want to keep them."

Clark steps forward, not the least bit tempted to give my punk ass a pass even if I have a gimp leg, but Mario steps between us. "Take a walk, Sinclair."

Clark doesn't budge. His nostrils flare, and his hands curl into fists.

"I said take a walk." Mario's voice is even and calm.

Clark shrugs off, his displeasure at being called down clear on his face.

"I think you should probably take a walk too."

"Don't get in my way, Mario," I warn. "I just want to talk to Blair."

He doesn't move, but I see his resolve crumble. "Just trying to look out for her. I'll move when she says it's okay, but not before."

He glances over at Vanessa, who looks at him like he's her hero.

"It's fine, you two," Blair says, hopping down from her chair and placing a hand on Mario's arm. "Can you give us a few minutes?"

Vanessa side-eyes me as Mario leads her away.

"You want to sit?" Blair reclaims her spot at the bar.

I don't know what I expected after I crossed the bar, got in some guys face for touching her, and then treated another guy that I've been cool with for years like shit, but it isn't civility from her.

"Sorry about that," I say as I sit. I'm not sorry in the least, but there's a laundry list of shit I've done in the past few weeks that needs apologizing for, so it feels like a good move to start groveling right off the bat.

"When did you get back?" A seemingly simple question made treacherous by her tone.

"Today. I was going—"

She holds up a hand. "Save it."

"You look good." At least that's the truth. She's wearing a silver dress that shows off her toned shoulders, and her hair is pulled up and away from her face in the way I like. I don't know if the effort was for me, but it doesn't go unappreciated. She looks all shiny and new, and I feel all tarnished.

"Thank you." She lets out a breath as if she's preparing for battle. "How is it being back?"

For some reason, I don't give her my rehearsed line. Maybe it's the way she asks like she cares or understands. Maybe I just want to be real with someone. Maybe it's just her.

"Tough, but it's better than watching my mom walk

around with a Kleenex in her hand, wiping her eyes like I died or something."

"Blair, we're gonna head out." V hovers off to the side.

She stands and pulls her purse strap to her shoulder. "Well, I should get going. I have work tomorrow."

"The café is open over break?"

She shakes her head. "No, I quit my job at the café. I got a job with the campus career center. I'm going in tomorrow to get things set up."

Joel appears at my side and pulls Blair into a hug. He's drunk and completely oblivious to the moment he just barged in on.

"Blair, it's so good to see you. You coming back to the house? We're having some people over for a little after party."

I grind my teeth. "We are?"

"No, sorry. I was just telling Wes I got a new job teaching workshops on goal setting and choosing a career path."

"That's a thing?" Joel asks with a confused expression on his face.

"It is. It's an optional workshop taught once a month by an upper classman. I'll also be occupying a table at the tutor center for one-on-one sessions and tips on setting and achieving goals."

"Who would go to something like that?"

I elbow him in the ribs. "Sounds"—I search for the words, any words but the ones that are coming to mind—"interesting."

"Yeah, well, let's hope others think so."

"Good to see you, Joel."

She faces off with me. "Wes."

She takes a step, and I grab her arm. The heat and spark between us surprises me, not because my feelings have changed but because I haven't felt anything in weeks. How does this girl break through my walls without even trying?

"It was good to see you, Blair."

"Take care of that foot. And maybe give your mom a pass this once. She's crying because of your loss—not hers. It is a hopeless feeling to watch the people you love go through tough times with nothing to do but hope they'll accept whatever support you offer."

She breezes past me like she didn't just cut me down at the knees.

And the fuck . . . she didn't say it was good to see me too.

twenty-nine

Blair

"It's gonna be incredible, V. I have my own little cubicle at the tutor center, and I bought this letter board so I can post inspirational sayings or quotes so everyone that comes in can get a little bit of positivity added in their day."

She chuckles but throws her arm around me. "I'm proud of you. Tossing inspiration around like confetti while your boyfriend is being an ass."

"He isn't my boyfriend," I grumble. "We were a casual thing, and now it's over I guess."

"Mm-hmm. Spin it however you want, but I saw the way he looked at you the other night."

"Well, regardless, it's been a week, and I haven't heard a peep from him."

Vanessa gives me a reassuring smile.

"It's fine." I shake off the sting of rejection. "On a happier note, Gabby is coming up next week to meet with an advisor and scope out the campus. Fingers crossed it goes well and that senior year the three of us can get an apartment off campus together."

"Now you're talking."

Her phone beeps, and she gets that look on her face that tells me it's Mario, which is confirmed when she says, "Mario says the guys are having a party tonight. What do you say we go celebrate surviving the first day of a new semester and your awesome new job?"

"I dunno."

"Come on. The basketball guys are at an away game, so you don't have to worry about running into them, and I'll tell Mario I'm spending the party hours with my best girl. I promise I will not leave your side." She sticks out her bottom lip, pouting and looking ridiculous.

"All right, all right. It's better than sitting around here feeling sorry for myself."

There are more people than I've ever seen crowded into the small space. Looks like everyone is looking for a way to celebrate the beginning of a new semester. "This is insane."

"I know, right?" Vanessa says as she pushes through the living room. "Mario is probably downstairs. Let's get a drink and say hello."

With plastic cups filled with vodka and Sprite, we move toward the music pumping downstairs. Unlike the last time I was here, the basement is so packed that I can't even tell it's a dilapidated shithole.

We skirt the edges of the dance floor, holding hands so we don't lose each other. "I see Clark and some of the other guys on the other side, maybe Mario is with them."

I sip my drink and sway to the music, following V. It feels good to be out and not to be obsessing over if or when Wes might call.

A row of couches are pushed back against the far wall and people are smushed on them, girls on laps of guys I recognize. Clark is holding on tight to a busty redhead, and another guy I recognize as one of Mario's roommates is leaning back, letting a petite blonde rape his face. She's using so much tongue that I cringe and look away.

But what I see next stops me in my tracks. His lap is currently playing host to a beautiful brunette who has her hand affectionately resting on his chest. He's drunk, that much would have been clear even if he didn't have a tequila bottle in his hand.

"What the fuck, Wes?" It's Vanessa's voice, not my own, that gets his attention.

When his eyes find mine, they're filled with regret and pain. He sits forward like he's going to get up, but I'm not interested in talking to him. Not now. Maybe not ever again.

I turn and flee the way I came, pushing through the crowd as best as I can with my eyes blurred with unshed tears.

I make it all the way to the porch before Wes catches up to me. He puts his big body in front of me. "Wait, damn it, woman. Hold up."

His breathing is labored, and he grabs ahold of the railing like he needs the support.

"What are you doing here?"

"Hanging with Mario and the guys. Nothing happened with that chick. She just sat down. I didn't do anything."

Nothing happened? God, if that isn't the guilty man's anthem, then I don't know what is. Laughter bubbles in my chest. "I meant why aren't you in California with the team?"

He shrugs. "Didn't feel like it."

He reaches out and caresses my cheek, brushing away a tear before he leans in bringing a waft of alcohol with him. I step back.

"You're free to do whatever or whomever you want. You've made it very clear that whatever we were, we aren't anymore. Just leave me alone."

He looks conflicted about my words, but I mean it. I don't want to talk to him when he's like this. I knew standing by while he dealt with his shit would be hard, but this is too much. "Please. I'm begging you. Not here. Not tonight."

He nods and tucks his hands into his front pockets before turning back to the house. I sag against the railing when he's gone and let all the tears fall. I don't even know why I'm crying. Despite the cliché, I believe that nothing happened between him and the chick downstairs. Not yet anyway. And I guess that's what wrecks me —he is going to move on, and man, does it sting to picture him with other girls.

"Aww, don't tell me the happy couple broke up?"

David's voice is like adding insult to injury. He walks out on to the porch with a beer in hand.

"I don't have anything to say to you, David. What are you even doing here?"

He shrugs. "Looks like the whole university is here tonight."

"Go away." I bite back the horrible words I want to say. "Please."

David smiles cruelly. "Reynolds cut you loose, huh? Maybe we should work out another agreement." He leans in. "You didn't really think I deleted all the pictures just because you got your boyfriend to threaten me, did you?" He laughs. "Knew that wouldn't last."

My control, and probably my sanity, snaps. Killing him with kindness seems to be a losing battle. "You know what, David? Go to hell. You're a shitty excuse for a human." I shove past him and walk all the way home, hugging myself as I ugly cry. As I crawl into bed, I promise myself that, after tonight, I won't shed one more tear over Wes Reynolds. I will cry out all the sadness to make room for hope, but the only thing I'm hoping for is to turn back to a time where Wes and I were happy.

thirty

Wes

I wake up with my cell phone resting on my chest.

Technology is awesome . . . until it's not. Having a way for someone to get a hold of you any time, any day makes it that much more painful when they don't.

I spent the past two days texting Blair, apologizing every way I could think of. I deserve to be ghosted after how I treated her, I get that, but it doesn't suck any less.

I give in to the temptation and check for missed texts that I know won't be there. My pessimism is on point, but I'm disappointed anyway.

"What the hell are you doing up?" I ask Nathan as he steps into the living room and pulls his hair back into a low ponytail.

He startles. "What the hell are you doing sleeping on the couch?"

"I'm not sleeping."

He drops onto the floor and starts repping out pushups.

"Dude, it's five in the morning."

I'm met with silence and the even exhale of his breaths.

"Fifty," he mutters quietly and jumps up. He moves to the wall and dips down into a wall squat. "You smell awful, man."

"Yep." I acknowledge the stench and the disgusting taste in my mouth from falling asleep after a night of drinking without brushing my teeth. "Feel just as awful."

Rubbing a hand over my forehead, I can practically feel the throbbing through my fingertips. I sit up slowly and grab the water I left on the coffee table, drain it, and then sit back, feeling a little more human.

"Since you're up, how about helping me with some band work?"

"Here? Now?"

"Nah, I'm meeting Shaw at the gym in five."

Lean back on the couch. "Pass."

"Come on, we need a third." He pushes off the wall. "And you know we could use the extra work. Got a lot of tough games coming up. Z's gonna need some help down low."

My better judgment hasn't had time to wake up or sober up, and he's played to my weakness—Z. "Yeah, fine. Let me shower quick."

It isn't until we're outside making our way across the street to Ray Fieldhouse that my stomach revolts and the alcohol in my system starts to seep out my pores.

Haven't been back since I was carted out to the hospital with a broken foot. In fact, it's probably the longest I've gone without stepping into a gym since I started playing all those years ago.

To my surprise, Shaw is already here, running drills. His sweat-soaked shirt and wet hair tell me he's been here a while. I bite back my approval.

"Reynolds, nice to see you." The shock in Rookie's eyes combined with the pity dissolve all good feelings.

For the next hour, I basically play ball boy. Shaw and Nathan take turns. One wraps a resistance band around his waist and the other holds the ends of the band tight and pulls backward. When I set the ball on the floor a couple of feet away, they work against each other. The point isn't to keep the guy in front from getting the ball, it's to provide just enough resistance that he has to *earn* it.

My roommate has a good flow with Rookie. There's an ease to their routine like they've done it before.

"When did you two become besties?" I ask Nathan when Shaw takes a piss break.

He lifts one shoulder and lets it fall. "He needed someone to see beyond the multi-sport athlete thing. You know I don't give a shit about that stuff."

I do know that. Not much except silence during movie night gets Nathan riled up. He's able to leave the competitive nature and intensity of being a college athlete on the floor. Outside of the gym, he's just a chill dude looking for fun.

"Taking your spot, trying to do what you do? It isn't an easy job. If we're gonna have any type of shot in the tournament, he has to start meshing with the guys. Some of the team resents him for splitting time, some are just frustrated that he isn't you, but no one feels good about where we are. It's a shitty place to be this far into the season."

I pull at my hair, hearing what he's saying and understanding the things he doesn't say. I'd been helping the rook until I realized I was done for, and now he has to find his way all on his own. Shitty for him, but I'm not in a mood to compare our tragic tales. "What do you want me to do?"

"Just show up, man. That's all anyone wants from you."

thirty-one

Blair

*V*anessa sits at her desk across our small room. "Do people actually attend these workshops?"

My shoulders slump. If my friends' reactions are any indication, the answer to that is a big fat no. "I don't know. I hope so."

"Want me to come by for moral support?"

"No, no. It's fine. I just need to help one person. Then they'll tell their friends and so on and so forth. Plus, I think the real difference will be in the one-on-one sessions at the tutoring center. Goals are personal."

"Well, I'm really proud of you no matter what. And you've inspired me. Look, I bought one of those fancy paper planners." She holds up the spiral-bound planner like a proud elementary school student with coveted new crayons.

"Impressive."

"Well, it will be if I remember to fill the thing out."

I have my doubts. An electronic planner seems way more V's style, but far be it for me to keep her from attempting organization.

"Heard from Wes since the other night?"

"Yes."

"Yes?" She turns in her chair, which I only know because it squeaks. I've turned my attention back to my desk to study my own planner carefully. I've kept this information to myself because Vanessa is currently still seeing red when it comes to Wes. He may have a boot on his foot and a basketball shaped hole in his heart, but apparently, this doesn't save him from the wrathful blowback of hurting V's friend.

I sigh. "He texted to apologize again for the other night."

"Still hasn't apologized for being an ass for the three weeks before that?"

"No. Maybe I made too big of a deal out of it. We were nothing—we never put a label on it."

"Bullshit. Uh-uh. Don't you dare let his behavior make you feel like you don't deserve to be upset. That boy was falling all over you. I get that he went through some shit, but he doesn't get a get-out-of-jail-free card just because he suddenly grew a conscious. You deserve more.

"All right, all right. Point made. You may step down from your soap box now."

V smiles. "Good. What time is Gabby getting here?"

"Her mom is dropping her by after their campus tour."

She stands and rubs her hands together. "Perfect. That gives me time to dress myself and then you."

I don't bother fighting. A little bit of V pampering and a night out with my two favorite girls sounds perfect.

"People are staring at me!" Gabby hisses and ducks her head.

"Actually, they're staring at Blair." Vanessa gives me a once over and her glossy, hot-pink lips twist into a smile. "You should let me dress you more often."

I tug at the hemline of my dress as another guy openly checks me out in a way that does not make me feel beautiful. "It's like major creep alert tonight."

"Come on, let's go to the bar. Those legs are going to get us free drinks."

"Fine. I want to check my phone anyway."

I haven't given in and texted Wes back, but I'm anxiously waiting for each one he sends. It feels good to be on the receiving end of his attention, even if it's just to clear his guilt.

"Oh no. We are not texting Wes tonight. You need to stop being available to him until he mans up and claims you. If you let him, he's going to pull you back into that weird thing that's casual but not because you spend all your time together, and its bullshit. He either wants you for real or he can take a hike."

This coming from the queen of casual. At least before Mario. "I can see what you're thinking. You aren't me.

You're in love with him, and I just don't want to see you get hurt if he decides to ghost. Again."

I look to Gabby for backup. She shakes her head. "I'm with her."

"I wasn't going to text him. I just like re-reading the ones he sent."

Okay, I've reached pathetic. I read it loud and clear on their concerned faces.

"You've made your point," I say, rolling my eyes and leaving my phone in my purse as we belly up to the bar.

"So, Gabs, are you coming to Valley next year?"

Leave it to Vanessa to cut right to the chase. I'd been hesitant to ask about how Gabby's day went. I knew this was hard for her and would be a big step.

"I'm not sure," she admits and plays with her hair, twisting and turning it around her fingers so it covers the left side of her face.

"You just need to own it. Pull that hair away from your face and hold your head up proudly. You're stunning, and people are going to stare. You show them that it doesn't bother you, and it won't bother them."

Gabby doesn't look convinced, but she does hold her head higher as the bartender comes to get our drink order.

"What can I get you ladies?" The bartender is a Valley grad student who Vanessa has dubbed the hottest guy on campus and also off limits. I can't argue with her reasoning unless I want the bartender at the most popular bar in town adding me to the no-serve list.

"Hey, don't I know you?" He points at me and narrows his eyes.

"Me?" I look around. "I don't think so. I mean . . ."

we come in occasionally. I'm Blair." I extend my hand to try to smooth over the awkward exchange.

He takes my hand and nods, recognition in his eyes. "You're one of the Valley Wild girls."

"The what?" V and I say at the same time.

"Yeah, your hair is pulled up in the photo, but I can tell it's you."

Bile coats my throat as he pulls out his phone, taps the screen a few times, and turns it toward us.

"Oh my God." V's voice is distant as I duck and push through the crowd to the bathroom. Everywhere I look, I see it now. The looks I've been getting all night aren't guys checking me out, they're guys picturing me naked in vivid detail."

Tears threaten as I close the door behind us and lock it. I pace the dingy, smelly bathroom, wishing I'd made my getaway to the car instead of here. This space does not help the downward spiral of my emotions.

"What the hell is going on?" Gabby asks, looking a bit shell shocked.

"Breathe, sweetie. It's gonna be okay. Mario is on his way. He'll get us out of here and take us home where we can figure this out."

"Figure this out? Ha! Everyone has seen me naked. Like, really naked, V."

"I know. Fucking David. I'm gonna kill him."

"David, your ex-boyfriend?" Gabby asks.

I stare up at the textured ceiling, feeling beyond humiliated as Gabby paces the floor and V scopes out the damage while filling Gabby in on the David drama from last semester.

"Why didn't you tell me?" The way Gabby looks at

me makes me feel horrible for not confiding in her.

"I guess I was afraid it'd make you even more hesitant to come to Valley if you knew how shitty people can be here."

"Are you kidding?" She laughs. "There's so much drama here I think I'll fit right in. You had me believing Valley was filled with Ken and Barbie cutouts and I was going to be the weird scar girl. No one even noticed me out there. Which is probably in part because they were picturing my best friend naked." She scrunches up her face in an apologetic frown.

V sighs and tucks her phone away. "Well, in good news, it isn't just you naked on this horrible website."

"That isn't good news."

"We'll get them taken down, honey, I promise."

"It's too late. They'll be saved and shared forever."

They flank me and link their arms in mine. "What can we do to help?"

It's a role reversal. I'm usually the one offering sympathy and comfort, or in V's case, talking her down from cutting off someone's balls.

"Nothing. I just want to go home and hang with my best girls. I'm not letting David ruin our night. I'll deal with it tomorrow. Tonight, let's just forget about it. Well . . . once we get out of here."

"I think I have an old bottle of Apple Pucker stashed in our closet."

For some reason, that sends us all into a fit of giggles, and I think maybe it might just be possible to survive this. Just as long as we're together.

thirty-two

Wes

I'm standing next to Joel's car, huddling in my hoodie freezing my nuts off while I wait for him to come out of the fieldhouse. Coming to practice was a mistake. Watching the team struggle and not being able to jump in and do it myself is torture.

By the time he appears with Z and Nathan, I could have walked home and back twice. I've taken to blowing into my hands to keep them warm.

"I'm gonna walk," Nathan says and heads off toward the house before lighting a cigarette. Coach is gonna kick his ass if he sees him smoking. Not my problem now.

"What took you so long?" I ask as Joel unlocks the car and Z and I toss our bags in before squeezing ourselves into the small sports car. He starts the engine and then let's out a long breath. "We have a problem."

He hands me the phone, and I suck in a breath. "What the fuck is this?"

"It's everywhere. Like fifty different people texted me the site."

I read the title and scroll through the Valley Wild Girls website. What the actual fuck?

I pull out my own phone and dial Blair.

"She isn't answering." Panic laced with frustration and desperation fills my voice.

Joel's phone beeps, and I read the text from Mario. "They're at The Hideout."

I scroll back through the text exchange between Joel and Mario where the latter outlines what transpired tonight. The short version: David is dead. "I'm gonna kill that fucker."

Joel's grip tightens around the steering wheel as he flips a U-turn. I tap restlessly on the dash until he screeches to a stop in front of The Hideout.

Mario and the baseball guys wait by the door.

"Where is she?"

"They're hiding in the bathroom. She hadn't seen it when they went in, and well, you can guess the rest."

Mario steps in front of me, blocking my entrance. "You need to know something else. David's in there. He was walking in as we pulled up. Thought we better wait for you."

I push past him, and Joel grabs my arm to slow me down. "Easy, killer. You have a gimp leg, and there's a bar full of people. Take a deep breath before you go in there and get yourself in trouble."

"Don't give a flying fuck, man." I pull free and keep

going.

I spot David and see red. I manage to turn to Mario. "You guys should go. Get the girls out of here."

I'm anxious to get to Blair. There's so much I want to say and so much I have to apologize for. This is all my fault. I need to make sure she knows I'll take care of it, but first, I need to deal with David. I made him a promise, after all.

Mario nods.

David has the audacity to look surprised as he watches me stalk across the bar.

My hands ball at my side, and I don't give two shits about the guys standing around him.

This asshole is gonna pay.

Before I can get to him, Vanessa flies across my vision and is up in his face. Mario and his guys flank Blair and Gabby. Gabby's here? Blair doesn't look up no matter how much I silently beg her to. I need to see her face. See that she's okay. Vanessa's voice pulls my attention back to David.

"You're a worthless piece of shit." She grabs him by the shoulders and knees him hard. So hard that my boys shrivel up and hide in fear. Damn, V is savage.

"Douche canoe," she spouts as she flips her brown hair over one shoulder and marches back to Mario's side. Mario gets the girls out of the bar just as it erupts in a collective groan. David doubles over in pain, but it isn't enough. I want him lying on the ground. Joel and Z follow me to the table David and his cronies occupy. Z crosses his arms over his chest, displaying his massive size. Glad he's on my side.

David stands upright, but he doesn't see the punch

coming, and as my knuckles meet his jaw, the pain feels fantastic. So good that I go in for another and another. My vision goes black.

"All right, all right. That's enough," Z says sternly, but I don't miss the humor in his voice. He catches my arm, and I still as awareness returns. David's buddies look torn between standing up for their friend and getting their own asses beat or letting me take my pound of flesh without their intervention. I'm almost hoping they're stupid enough to come at me. I don't have beef with them, but I'm looking for any reason to hit something else.

Z and Joel have other ideas. They pull me back and shove me down into a booth.

"Hope that was worth it." Z points outside where red and blue lights flash.

"Oh, it was worth it."

She's worth everything.

It isn't until Coach shows up that I feel even the tiniest bit of remorse. And even then, I don't regret hitting David, just getting the rest of the guys involved and making the team look bad.

He leans against the side of the cop car beside me. I've already given my statement, and so far, no one has put me in cuffs, so that's a good sign.

He's silent for a beat before he says, "What a shitty practice tonight."

Laughter shakes my chest, the sound foreign to my ears. When was the last time I laughed?

"Coming back tomorrow?"

I flex my hand. A sting of pain shoots up my arm. I search for words, an answer. Neither yes or no feels right. How can I be there? And how can I not?

Coach straightens. "Well, they aren't pressing charges, so get your ass home. See you tomorrow. Or not."

As he walks away, Joel steps up. "Come on. I'll take you to see Blair."

"Nah, somewhere else I need to go."

He raises both eyebrows, and I hold my hands up. "This stop doesn't involve the police. I promise."

Pulling up to the Morenos' estate is like pulling up to something out of the movies. The massive house sits on the side of a mountain and is lit up like an amusement park. When we finally reach our destination, Joel pulls up under the old-school carriage style covered awning in front of the house.

"Thanks," I say before we get out of the car. "I know you don't like going to your father for help."

He shrugs. "Guess there's no other way around this one. He probably already knows."

The Moreno house is organized chaos. Joel's mother brings coffee and then orders her daughters, Joel's sisters, to re-heat leftovers despite everyone's insistence they aren't hungry. Mr. Moreno sits at the head of a long dining table that looks out into the Rincon Mountains. A king on top of his mountain.

"Idiotic. This could end up splashed across every sports headline tomorrow. No respect for Coach Daniels." He mutters more to himself than us, but Joel, Z, and I stare shamefaced down at the table anyway.

Joel is the first one to speak. "Pa, the guy posted nude photos of several Valley students."

He slides his phone to his dad, who looks down at it

and then slides it back. "I've already seen it. The site was taken down thirty minutes ago."

"So, that's it?" It's my voice that yells out.

"There'll be a formal investigation, and we're sending out a reminder email tomorrow morning about the campus policy on sexual harassment."

"You can't be serious. He just gets to walk around campus while these girls are humiliated? That's bullshit."

Mr. Moreno raises his eyebrows at me as the three women in his life enter the dining room with dishes of hot food.

"Sorry," I mumble an apology to Mrs. Moreno.

"I think it's noble." She pats my shoulder. "Too many young men thinking it's okay to treat women like sex objects these days."

Mr. Moreno sighs. "Without proof, I can't do anything. Hence, the investigation."

"But we know who did it," Joel says.

"You have hearsay." He shakes his head and stands. "We're going to do everything we can to resolve it quickly. You think I want something like this going unpunished?" He looks in the direction the women disappeared. "I have two daughters who are going to be at Valley in a few years. I want others to know it won't be tolerated, but there are appropriate channels to go through when dealing with stuff like this."

All I hear is that it will be weeks or months where David goes unpunished, and it isn't enough, but I can see resolve in Mr. Moreno's face.

Mrs. Moreno insists that we stay the night, and I think we're all too exhausted to fight her. I go to bed fully clothed and watch as the minutes tick by. I really screwed things up this time. I wonder what Blair is doing right now. Is she in bed, wishing she could rewind time and erase me from her life? I've made such a mess of things. I was too busy feeling sorry for myself to protect her. As the sun rises, I'm still staring at the ceiling and trying to figure out how the hell I'm going to make this right.

No grand gestures come to mind, so I settle for persistence. I'll win her back the same way I've won at every aspect of my life—hard work and dedication. And heart.

thirty-three

Blair

My alarm wakes me at the usual time, but instead of jumping right out of bed, I lie there and play back the last year of my life like a highlight reel. Surprisingly, the most painful memories aren't of David, but of Wes. David humiliated me, but his betrayal was expected and skin deep. Wes's dismissal cuts at the very core of me.

When I finally step outside to head to class, he's the last person I expect to see sitting on the front steps. Bags under his eyes, clothes rumpled, he's still the hottest guy I've ever seen. "What are you doing here?"

"I called last night. I—"

"I heard what you did. Thank you for standing up for me, but really, I'm fine. Go home."

Of all the times I wished he'd show up for me, he picks the moment I feel the least beautiful, the least deserving of him.

"Can't do that until I apologize and make up for how I acted. I'm so sorry, Blair."

"Apology accepted. Now go home."

I take off down the sidewalk toward campus, and Wes follows beside me. Wordlessly, he walks me all the way to Stanley Hall.

"See you in fifty-five."

I sigh. "Do you even have class right now?"

"Nope. My morning is wide open."

"Go *home*, Reynolds. You aren't doing me any favors by sitting outside my class like some sort of security guard."

He challenges me with a determined set to his jaw. "You're right. I'm coming in with you."

"That's not—"

"Up for discussion." He pushes past me and holds the door open. Whatever, Wes wants to waste his day, then so be it. I have no more secrets to be used against me, and I'm more determined than ever to rock my classes.

Most people don't even look up as I take a seat in the large auditorium, and the few guys who act like maybe they want to say or do something turn away when they see Wes glowering behind me.

I slump into my seat and breathe deeply as I pull out my phone and sit back in my chair, waiting for class to start. Wes silently does the same, and as I scroll through Reddit, a text flashes on my screen.

Wes: I want names of anyone who participated in what went down last night.

I roll my eyes as I respond.

Me: I don't need you to protect me. Let it go.

Wes: Not a chance.

When class is over, Wes stands and blocks me from leaving before he's stared down every single classmate. It's so obvious he's trying to make some sort of statement that I'm not to be messed with, and as annoying as it is, it's also so ridiculous that my heart betrays my resolve. The struggle is real when it comes to hardening my heart against this man.

And so goes the rest of my day. Wes walks me to every class and even back to the sorority house. He's limping and, as frustrated as I am, I'm touched too. But this is insanity. I don't need him acting as my bodyguard. He didn't want anything to do with me before, so why act like he cares now? I get that his loyalty makes him feel somehow responsible, but I don't want him around out of loyalty alone.

"Okay, as you can see. I'm safe and sound. No one said a word to me all day. I relieve you from your duty."

"They didn't say anything because I was with you."

That's probably true.

"Seriously, Wes. You don't need to do this. I'm fine. I can take care of myself. I don't need your pity."

"Pity? You think I'm doing this because I feel sorry for you? Fuck, Blair, this whole thing is my fault. I should have stopped him. I was supposed to protect you, and I didn't."

I shake my head. "That isn't accurate, and even if it were, I'm not yours to protect anymore."

My words cause him to frown and step back. "See you tomorrow," he says and gives me a salute.

I bite my tongue as Joel's car stops in front of the house. He waves from the driver's seat. I don't miss the grimace on Wes's face as he slumps into the seat. His foot has to be killing him.

The next morning, I sneak out an hour early to avoid any possible Wes run-ins and hole up in my new cubicle at the tutor center. I'm teaching my first workshop on goal setting and career planning today and, though the timing sucks with my peers all having seen me naked recently, I'm excited.

My excitement is short lived.

"That's it. Thank you so much for coming." The words are barely out of my mouth before the three people who stumbled in run for the door. I dig around in my backpack for a stray Spree. Certainly surviving that is cause for a reward. I exit the classroom, flipping off the light and pushing the door open with a hip, and stumble into a wall of muscle and my backpack lands with a *thud* next to a black boot.

Wes leans down and scoops up my bag.

Fingers brushing as I take it from him, I manage a mumble of thanks.

"How'd it go?"

"Only three people showed up. Luckily, they seem to be the only three people on campus who haven't seen me naked."

He pulls a bag of Chewy Spree seemingly from thin air, and I salivate like a dog in one of those Pavlovian experiments. "Now, how could you rephrase that to better represent your achievements instead of focusing on the things you can't control?"

I balk, staring at him, delicious candy not forgotten but temporarily moved to second position of things of interest.

"You were listening?"

He shrugs. "We spent a lot of time together, some of what you said was bound to stick."

I quirk an eyebrow and cross my arms over my chest. "What are you doing here?"

He looks down at his shoes before meeting my eyes. "I wanted to make sure you were okay."

"I already told you, I'm fine." I move to step around him, but he's quicker and sidesteps with me.

"Also, I wanted to apologize again. Not for what happened with David. For everything before. I acted like an ass."

"Apology accepted." I take another step around him, but he cuts me off and shakes the bag of candy above my head.

I sigh. "Three people showed up today. That's three more people that I've helped and three people who might tell their friends."

"Good job." He pats my head. I'd love to be offended, but the goofy smile on his face makes him look young and carefree. Like the Wes I fell in love with.

I swipe the Sprees from his hand. We walk out of the university building together. I can feel him watching me, but he doesn't say anything.

"How'd you find me?"

He waves a hand as if it isn't a big deal, but there is a

pleased grin on his face. "I follow all the happenings of the career resource center." His expression falls. "Actually, I probably should stop in now that it's time to start thinking about what I'm going to do after graduation."

"Where are you headed next?" I ask after he goes silent.

He points to Moreno Hall. "I have macroeconomics."

I scrunch my nose.

"Eh, it'll be fine. The professor doesn't mind if I sleep through class like Professor O'Sean."

"It's infuriating that you can sleep through and still manage to get an A."

"Wasn't so infuriating when I was saving your ass from failing."

He's flirting . . . I think. It's almost like the playful banter we used to have that kept me on my toes and gave me full body tingles. My head and heart are conflicted. I do forgive him, but it's too hard to be around him like this. Wes Reynolds isn't the kind of guy you can be friends with after you've had more.

"I hear tomorrow night's game is going to be a good one."

He nods and shoves his hands into his pockets. "Utah is tough. They run a combination defense that . . ." He stops himself, and I wonder how long it's been since he's talked basketball. Is he going to practices? Has he stopped sulking and started travelling with the team again? They're questions I want to ask, but I know it would be crossing some invisible line he's drawn.

"Thank you for the candy," I say instead. "I guess I'll

see you at the game."

"Maybe. I haven't decided if I'm going to go."

"What? Why not? You have to go." I stop and stare after him. He can't be serious.

He lifts one shoulder and lets it fall. "They don't need me there."

"Maybe not in the way you want to be there, but they do need you. You're their leader. You said so yourself."

His jaw flexes. "Enjoy the candy. Congrats on your first workshop. Text me if anyone gives you any trouble."

thirty-four

Wes

I can see the steady stream of people entering Ray Fieldhouse from the window in our living room. It's weird to watch people come to a game decked out in blue and yellow. They hurry from their cars to the front door as excitement and hope that the home team will pull through radiates from them.

A contradiction to the way the bus of Utah players walked in two hours earlier. Slow, taking it all in and adjusting to being in someone else's house. They walked into my house, but it isn't really mine anymore, and it's fucking weird and awful. I consider where I should be. Do I go to the game and sit on the bench like I somehow still belong? Sitting in the bleachers isn't fucking happening. That's my team but in a completely different way than the fans think it's their team. I built that team, and spent the last four years busting my ass. Z and I crafted a team that is strong and quick and smart.

When the parking lot finally calms, I step out onto the front porch, and the sounds assault me. The rise and fall of the crowd cheering is my scoreboard, the refs whistle a shrill sound that brings silence that is more nerve wracking than the noise. I'm sweating, and my foot throbs as I pace back and forth, picturing it all.

I remove my hat, pull at my hair and then stop. Gonna make myself bald with the amount of tugging I've been doing. I put the hat back on and pull out my phone, giving in to my temptation to check the score online. I've missed two texts from Blair.

Blair: Are you here?

Blair: Where are you? Get here NOW.

Well, fuck, now I'm even more curious about what the hell is going on. Do they need me like the game is going bad or it's going well and she wants me to see the team finally meshing? I'm not even sure which would hurt less.

Or, Christ, maybe someone is messing with her. So far, people seem to have gotten the message that I'm not playing around when it comes to protecting Blair, but maybe my absence has brought out the bullies.

I cross the street and slow down as I approach.

"Wes! Wes!"

I catch a mass of brown hair in my peripheral and turn. Blair is running toward me, waving her arms.

We're the only two people out here, so it isn't like I could miss her.

"Hey. You're here." Her breaths are shallow, and she puts a hand at her waist like she has a cramp from the fifty-yard jog.

My eyes fall to her chest, where the number twelve is proudly displayed. Her eyes follow mine.

"Everything okay? Why aren't you inside?"

She's still panting as she says, "I came to find you. Why aren't *you* inside?"

"For what? I can't play." What about this is so fucking hard for her to understand?

"They need you. Z looks angrier than ever and Shaw is a mess. You may not be able to play, but they need you right now. You're still their leader."

"How bad is it?"

"Go see for yourself."

The buzzer goes off, and there is a surge of movement inside the fieldhouse.

"Halftime," she says. "I think they need a pep talk from you more than they do the coach. I can't even pretend to understand your role and how much this has to suck, but I can see they are struggling and looking for someone to step up. Go be that person."

"What the hell am I supposed to say?"

She grins widely, probably pleased I'm finally soliciting her words of wisdom. "I can't pull something from my canned inspirational quotes for this one."

"You could try," I grit out. Figures . . . the one fucking time I need her is the one fucking time she tells me she has nothing.

"How about pulling from your own material, maybe

something about heart and talent? It helped me when I needed it, maybe it'll work for them too."

She leaves me standing there gawking after her. Even in this moment, I can appreciate how damn good she looks wearing my jersey. My name plastered across her delicate shoulders and number stretching down to her tiny waist.

Well, looks like this is it. I either have to get in there or get the hell out of dodge before I'm spotted.

It's doubtful anyone is going to recognize me without my jersey, but I'm not taking any chances. I'm here for Z. The idea that he might need me, that I let him down . . . again, is more than I can take. I should be out there making sure he gets the shots he needs. Making sure the team makes it to the tournament again and ensuring Z's name is called in the first round of the draft. That was my job.

Coach's voice booms down the hallway. A set of security guards blocking off entry to the locker room look me up and down, but before I have to do something embarrassing like explain who the fuck I am, the one on the right recognizes me.

"Sorry about the foot, Reynolds. Boys sure could use you out there tonight."

I nod and open the door before I can talk myself out of it. It creaks shut, announcing my arrival just as Coach finishes his halftime yelling spree with the usual pep talk about coming back and working as a team.

"Reynolds." Coach nods and places his clipboard at his side. "You gonna join us for the second half?"

My teammates eye me with a mixture of pity and hope.

"Yes, sir."

He tosses me the clipboard. "Shaw, see Wes before you head out see if he has any notes on Utah's defense."

My hands shake as I grip the board in one hand and uncap the dry erase marker with the other. I stand in front of Shaw and make x's to represent the defense that Utah typically runs.

"Utah runs a combination. Pressure up top and zone down low. The most important thing you need to know about their style is that they're a bunch of selfish pricks. Talented, but selfish. They're aggressive and they take risks, which tends to pay off because it rattles their opponents. You can't let them rattle you. You play your game, not theirs. They want to pressure you to take the shot or make a quick pass, but that isn't our style. Our game is slow and smart. If you find yourself feeling rushed, you're giving in to their game."

Shaw nods, but he looks as good as defeated. I sigh and give in to Blair's advice.

"You can do this. We can beat them. We're just as talented, and our team has more heart. We play as a cohesive unit and get the ball to whoever has the best look—no matter what. They don't understand how not to be selfish, and that's how you're going to beat them. Take your time and move the ball around to get the best look."

"Sounds so simple."

I pat him on the back, a real smile threatening at the corners of my mouth. "It is."

Everyone clears the locker room except for Z, who hangs back, waiting for the door to close behind Shaw.

"I'm glad you came. Know it must be hard being

here."

"I think it's going to be hard either way. This way, at least I don't feel like I'm letting you down again. I'll do whatever I can to make sure Shaw plays the kind of ball that'll get you in that first round."

"Fuck the draft."

My eyebrows shoot up high enough to reach the Valley hat on my head.

"You think I care about all that more than I care about you?"

"I . . ."

Well, fuck, yeah that's what I think.

"Playing next to you these years has been an honor. God willing, I'll get picked up in the first round, but right now I just want to know my friend is okay. Whatever you need, I'm here, just say the word."

"What do you say we start with a win out there tonight?"

He smirks. "Guess that depends on the pep talk you gave rook. He ready?"

"I sure as shit hope so," I mutter as we exit the locker room together.

Sitting on the sidelines during the second half is less weird than I imagined. Or maybe I'm just too glued to the action to feel anything but anxious. I've spent very little time on this bench during my college career and never really looked around and enjoyed the view. The way the stadium is filled with blue and yellow, the way the fans are always ready to jump to their feet to defend a bad call or cheer us on. The way one particular girl wrings her hands as she watches me instead of the guys on the floor.

I smirk at her and give her a small nod. Her shoulders visibly relax. I'd give anything to be out on that floor, but the view from the sidelines definitely has its perks. I wonder what she looked like when she watched me play. Did she jump up and down and cheer for me? Did she watch me more than the other guys?

We pull ahead and win the game by two points. Too close for anyone to feel like celebrating.

"What made you decide to come?" Joel asks as we make our way back to the house. Despite Z's monologue earlier, he's back to quiet, headphones on and the bass pumping.

"Blair," I admit. "Chick's relentless."

"We owe her. Having you here made all the difference," Joel says.

And I know just how to repay her.

thirty-five

Blair

I stumble into the tutor center Monday afternoon a little defeated and a whole lot undercaffeinated. In my first week at the tutor center, I had exactly two students stop by to see me. Honestly, I think those poor souls got bad information and thought I was going to look deep into a crystal ball and uncover top-secret job opportunities with a six-figure salary on a bachelor's degree education.

I'm trying to remain positive. I know I can help people, but it's harder than I expected it to be to spread the word about what I'm doing without making it sound hokey. The students who would be up for this type of thing are either hesitant about the benefit of chatting with a peer or simply don't have time to add another to-do to their schedule. And though no one has said anything, I'm pretty sure people are avoiding me because of the nude photo ordeal. I'd expected laughter or more slimy come-ons, but it's as if I don't exist.

Every passing minute is another chance to turn it all around.

Great, now I'm thinking in Tom Cruise movie quotes. Admittedly, I binged all the ones I hadn't seen over break. It made me feel somehow closer to Wes, which makes me officially pathetic since he spent the entire break avoiding me. Sigh. And I'm now thinking my sighs aloud.

I pull open the library door and hold my head high. I can do this. It's a brand-new week.

I frown at the line that twists around the main desk and out the door of the tutor center.

Everyone in line is tall and muscular, and each and every one of them looks underwhelmed to be here.

Tanner Shaw gives me a head nod as I study the faces of the guys in line. I know it's wrong to be hostile for something out of his control, but I still bristle at the sight of him.

I find the start of the line at the doorstep of my tiny makeshift cubicle. Wes is holding the front with the look of a proud boy scout.

Merit badge definitely earned.

"What is this?"

"I owed you for the other night. For lots of things. I've given you shit about all this"—he lifts his arms—"but the other night, I guess I realized I needed it more than I knew."

"So, you brought every jock you know for what? Creative hazing?"

He covers his mouth with a fist. "Admittedly, that's

part of it, but I do think you have some things that could help each one of them. You're good at this. Better than I gave you credit for. I just wanted to show you I see it now. I get it, and I want to support you the same way you always supported me."

"Thank you." I place my backpack down beside my chair and eye the coffee cup on my desk. I pick it up and read the quote scribbled in messy penmanship. *Focus. Repetition. Heart.*

"Nice touch."

He beams back at me like a proud pupil. "That's a Coach Daniels' special."

A look around the tutor center reveals intrigued, if a bit annoyed, glances from the tutor stations. The commotion has disrupted any chance of concentration. "Well, looks like I have my work cut out for me. You gonna stick around and make sure they don't sneak out?"

"Nah. I gotta do some studying." He turns and raises his voice so the guys in line can hear him. "But I'll stop by later and get a full report on how it went."

I roll my eyes. "Get out of here, Reynolds."

Surprisingly, the guys are good sports. A few of them even take it seriously. And when the last ball player walks out the door, there's a new line that's formed. Gotta give the jocks props for that. Where they go, others follow.

Wes shows up as the tutor center is closing for the night. The last students are packing their bags and the tutors are tidying up the room. I lean back in my chair, completely spent.

Every eye in the tutor center follows his path from

door to my desk.

"Got time for one more?"

I sit forward and narrow my eyes. I can't tell if he's serious or not. One side of his mouth pulls into a smile. "Then how about dinner instead?"

"I, uh . . ." I trip over my tongue. What even are words? Did he just ask me on a date? "Sure. Let me just grab my things."

Silently, Wes leads me to University Hall. We order food and then take a table in the far corner. "Brought you something," Wes says as he slides me a small gift covered in Christmas paper. On top is a handmade origami bow made from a Chewy Spree wrapper.

Nice touch, Reynolds.

"It's a little belated. I didn't get a chance to give it to you that night . . ." His words hold a hint of sadness.

"I see you got mine." I point to his gray T-shirt, and he looks down proudly at the black bold letters: *Smart is the new jock.*

"Open yours," he says and winks.

I tear open the paper to find a flat, rectangular box. My throat goes dry. I'm not prepared for whatever is in this jewelry box. I pry open the top slowly and hold my breath as I reveal the bracelet inside. It's similar to the ones Gabby and I make out of colored embroidery thread, but there are only two colors—orange and purple. My and his favorites. My heart thumps wildly in my chest as I lift it and study the letter beads that twist around the braided thread. *BLESS*

"No way," I say in complete disbelief. "Where did you get this?"

"I, uh, may have commissioned it?"

I lift a brow.

"Gabby," he says, looking a little guilty.

"Gabby was in on this?" I inspect the bracelet and see her in the smooth braid, the neat knots at either end. I can't believe she kept this a secret. "I love it. Thank you."

"I have one other gift. Though, it isn't from me."

I narrow my gaze, intrigued. "Okay. Who's it from? Did you get Vanessa to write me a poem?"

He shakes his head. "Let's call it a gift from the university. David was expelled today."

All the air leaves my lungs as he continues.

"The campus police received several anonymous tips leading them to him, and when he was questioned, he folded. All the evidence was on his laptop anyway."

"He's gone," I whisper. I expected to feel better, but the damage is already done. I'm glad I won't have to see him, but I guess I'd already eradicated him from my life.

"You know, if you pressed charges, he could be charged with a felony. Laws in Arizona are strict about this kind of thing."

A nervous laugh escapes at the scary expression on his face. Wes is pissed and ready to see David pay. Me too. "I haven't decided what to do yet. I made an appointment with a counselor for later this week and I need to tell my parents. That's going to be hard."

His jaw flexes before he speaks. "I'm really sorry I didn't stop this from happening. I failed you in so many ways."

The loyalty of this man never ceases to amaze me. "David's crimes aren't yours. It's not on you. I just want to move on. I let him hold me back for too long.

Whatever I decide to do, it's going to be about me – what's best for me. Part of me thinks I just want to be free of him, but I don't know if I could live with myself if I don't see this through and make sure he never has the opportunity to do this to someone else."

"Obviously I'm a fan of the latter," he states dryly. "But I'll be here for you either way. Whatever you need."

Swallowing down the lump in my throat, I can only nod.

I steer the conversation to lighter topics. Between bites, we talk about classes and he tells me a little about how he's helping at practices. It's comfortable and easy to be with him, but there's the slightest tension in the way we interact. We're careful to keep our hands to ourselves, and the one time he bumps my leg under the table, I jump so high in my seat he apologizes like he's wounded me deeply.

We're us, but we aren't. This isn't Bless it's Weir—the weird, nonsensical version of our cooler couple alter ego.

"Thank you for—" I start to speak at the same time he does.

"Listen, I—"

"You first," we say at the same time and smile.

I open my palm toward him in a silent offering for him to go first.

"I owe you an explanation for the way I acted. After my injury, you were trying to be there for me and I wouldn't let you. I pushed you away. I destroyed what we had."

"You were dealing," I say simply. I always knew the

why, but his apology doesn't fix the hurt it caused or the pain he inflicted when he removed himself from my life.

"It wasn't just that." He lets out a shaky breath and meets my eyes. His blue stare is melancholy and regret. "I wanted to hurt you. You pushed your way into my life, bringing your optimism and joy, and it changed me. I made room for something in my life besides ball. But then I was laying in that hospital bed, hearing your bubbly voice tell me to flip the negativity and see the positive, and I didn't want to. I wasn't ready to do anything but be angry and bitter."

"No one expected you to see the positive in this. Least of all me."

"I know." He shakes his head. "It was petty and childish. I'm sorry it took me so long to realize it. I miss you. Fuck, I miss you. I'm just not sure who I am or what I'm doing anymore. I don't want to be this miserable guy who is pissed at the world, not when I'm with you. You deserve better than that."

"You're allowed to have bad days or months. This isn't exactly my banner year so far." I wave my hands as I speak. "Relationships are ugly sometimes." I shrug and inwardly cringe because I just used the word relationship when we never put a label on whatever we were before.

He reaches across the table and takes my hand. The warmth of his fingers soothes something that's been aching without his touch. "I'm crazy about you, but I gotta be honest that I'm still going through some shit."

"Well, I can handle your grumpiness if you can put up with my optimism and spunk."

"Deal."

My heart swells with that one word. *Deal.*

It isn't until we've said goodnight that I realize I have no idea what we just agreed to. Are we in a relationship? Are we friends?

He didn't kiss me. We said goodbye with a long hug and a promise to hang out tomorrow afternoon, but did I just agree to a friendly hang out or Netflix and chill?

I'm still wondering as I sit on his bed the following day, watching him pack for a team away game.

Joel knocks on the door and pokes his head in. "You still have that Spanish textbook from last year?"

Wes nods toward his bookshelf. "Yeah, it's on the shelf. What's up?"

"I told someone I'd help her. Just want to get an idea of how much they're covering in introductory Spanish."

"You're tutoring someone?" Wes asks, his tone as disbelieving as the thoughts running through my head.

"Shut up," Joel grumbles.

Wes crosses the room and pulls the book from the shelf. He stops in front of Joel and holds the book, obviously using it as bait for more information.

Joel mutters, "I guess I promised her I'd help with Spanish to get her to sleep with me. There, happy now?"

We laugh at his expense. "Dude, that's low even for you."

"Shut the fuck up. I don't even remember saying it . . . or doing it for that matter." He shakes his head. "She says we hung out at the baseball party last week. I was so drunk that night I crashed on Mario's couch, so anything is possible." Joel looks at me. "This is your fault. You told me chicks dig the Spanish."

I hold my hands up. "Don't put this on me. I didn't tell you to use it as a bargaining chip for sex."

"Good luck." Wes tosses the book at him and Joel walks backward out of the door already flipping through the pages.

I turn to Wes. "You know you guys are sitting on an untapped gold mine. Women would"—I pause and point after Joel—"and apparently already do, go to great lengths to have a hot, smart male tutor."

"Whatever you're suggesting, hard pass."

"Come on, the marketing alone would be fantastic." I wave my hand in front of my face like I'm seeing it on a billboard. "Smart Jocks: Get an A while enjoying eye candy too."

"That's a terrible slogan."

"It was my first attempt. Oh! I have it! Smart Jocks: Their brains are as big as their—"

"Don't finish that statement." He holds a hand up. "I want to imagine the possibilities of that last word."

I toss a pillow at him.

"How about. Smart Jocks: Figure it out your damn self. I'm busy."

I tap my chin. "*Hmmm*. I dunno, I mean it certainly sounds like something you'd say, but it's a bit grumpy."

"I thought you agreed to put up with my grumpy ass." He leans down and places a kiss at the corner of my mouth.

It's the first time his lips have touched mine in a month, and my insides turn to total mush. Instead of responding, I grab his hand and tug him closer. He lets out a throaty chuckle as he brings our lips back together. The dam has broken, and our kiss becomes frantic and needy. He places two strong hands under my ass and lifts me, bringing me upright with him. I wrap my legs around his waist as he walks us to the door, shuts, and locks it. Crossing back to the bed in two long steps, he drops us to the bed and settles on top of me. He breaks away to stare down at me. "You're so beautiful. Don't think I'll ever get enough of looking at you or kissing you."

He steals another kiss, as if proving his point. "You always taste like sugar . . . so damn sweet."

He continues his worship and praise of my body, getting us undressed in record time. We're hot and sweaty and can't keep our hands off each other. Looks as if he didn't listen to Joel this time. Or maybe he just hadn't planned for this to happen.

"Gotta head out in ten." Nathan yells and knocks from the other side as Wes tears open a condom and covers himself.

"Sadly, I'm not gonna need that long," he says around a smile, just loud enough that I can hear.

The giggle that tickles my throat is lost when he enters me, stretching me and filling me completely. He stills, braced above me, his expression fixed in exquisite torment.

"Have to make this up to you when I get back on Saturday night."

But there's nothing to make up for. I'm as needy and close as he is. Each thrust threatens to push me over the edge. His breathing is labored and sweat beads on his chest. He's holding back, delaying his pleasure to get me there. If that isn't the most deliciously sexy thing a man could do in bed, I don't know what is.

"I'm close," I rasp. It isn't a warning. It's permission for him to let go.

Still, he waits until the orgasm takes over my body before he growls out, shuddering as he gives into his release.

He rests his forehead on mine. "Last thing I want to do is get out of this bed and get on a flight with a bunch of dudes."

But he has to, and I watch him as he slides from the bed, disposing of the condom and dressing quickly. He tosses my jeans and shirt onto the bed before he shoves stuff into his duffel bag.

"I gotta run. Stay as long as you want. In fact, if you want to be in that same spot when I get back, I won't complain." He winks and drops a hurried kiss on my lips."

"Good luck," I call to his back.

When I hear the faint sound of the front door slamming closed, I pull Wes's comforter around me and inhale. I'm in deep again. No, not again. My feelings never changed. I feel like I never left, but his feelings have bounced around, and I don't want to be on the bench, waiting for more time in the game. Yep, I'm in deep. Even my thoughts have converted to basketball analogies for his sake.

I've done exactly what Vanessa warned me against. I've fallen into old habits where Wes and I spend time together without ever really discussing the depth of it. Maybe it's positive thinking or maybe it's just plain idiotic to hope things will work out on their own. Pushing away the negative and focusing on being happy is the only real choice because my heart is already his.

thirty-six

Wes

We win our game in Oregon, which has everyone in good spirits on the way back. It's a long ass flight and then an hour bus ride to get back to Valley, and every minute feels like torture. I don't know where to sit on the bus. Ridiculous as it sounds, everything has changed, and I'm no longer one of them. If I were an injured sophomore or even junior, it'd be different, but I'm never gonna be a real member of this team again.

I settle next to Z, but his silence only makes my nervous energy feel more pronounced. The tension I usually release on the floor has built up, and I can't sit still. Shaw sits across the aisle and catches my eye. "You all right? Foot bothering you?"

"What?" It takes a second for his attempt at polite conversation to register. "Nah, just feel restless."

He nods as if he could possibly understand. "Look, I know we haven't always seen eye to eye, but I'm really sorry about the way things went down. You were a good player. The guys really respect and look to you. It's tough shoes to fill. I just want you to know I don't take the job lightly."

I resist an eye roll but can't stop the disbelieving grunt that escapes.

"What is your problem with me, anyway? You've been on my ass since I arrived at Valley, so I know it isn't just that I've taken your spot."

Count to five and consider keeping my mouth shut. The consideration is rejected. "I don't like that you're dividing your time. Pick a sport. Coaches might be okay with it, but no one else is. It's damn risky, and it makes both teams feel like you aren't giving one hundred percent."

"That's such bullshit," he says and shakes his head. "I work my ass off to be a part of both teams. Twice as many practices, double the coaches and training routines."

"Why do that to yourself? Just pick one and give it your all. Save yourself and all of us a lot of heartache when you get burned out or injured."

"You just don't get it. I can't pick between the two of them like it's a choice of pizza or tacos. I love basketball. I love the sound of shoes squeaking on the floor and the echo of the ball in an empty gym. But I love baseball too."

"Yeah, sure. I loved football once upon a time, but I made the decision to put everything into one sport." Most of us played other sports as kids, but at one point or another we gave the others up and made basketball the primary focus.

"You didn't love football as much as basketball." He is adamant, and that pisses me off.

"Excuse me?"

"You couldn't have. There's no way I could pick between basketball and baseball. Come on, you know what it's like to love two things so much you can't give either up. How is my loving two sports different from you playing ball and having a girlfriend?"

"You're really comparing your situation to my dating life?"

His head bobbles like he's waiting for me to figure out the connection.

"It isn't the same," I finally say.

"Sure it is. You split your time between the two. They both consume your thoughts. Your main objective for both is to score."

I roll my eyes at his lame attempt at humor. "That is the weakest analogy I've ever heard, rook. We're done here."

I stand and move to the front next to Joel. He looks me over and nods appreciatively. "Nice work today. You have a knack for keeping Shaw and the bench ready to go. And you look damn good doing it. Getting laid agrees with you."

"Jesus H Christ," I mutter and stand again. The only other available seat is next to Coach.

He takes off his glasses and looks me over as if I've personally offended him by invading his bubble. "The guys are in rare form after that win."

"It was a good game. Shaw is finally finding his

rhythm. Thanks to you."

"Please don't thank me." I scrub a hand along my jaw and around my neck. "I resent every second of it."

He laughs. "You won't after a while."

I narrow my eyes as if that'll help me understand him better.

"I wasn't always a coach," he says

"Yeah, I know," I say. "Baylor, player of the year in 1999."

"That's right." He nods with a proud look on his face, and I see a bit of that cocky player he had to have been back then. Z and I looked up old clips once; Coach was a beast. "I played all four seasons. Four great seasons. Still hurts just the same no matter when you have to give it up."

"Why'd you become a coach if you resent not playing anymore?"

He studies me. "Why'd you decide to come back and sit with the team?"

I shrug.

"The only thing that hurts more than not playing is losing it completely. They'll have to drag me off that court kicking and screaming when I'm ninety years old."

"I guess I came back because I didn't know what else to do. Who else to be."

He shifts in his seat and studies me. "You thought about what you might want to do after you graduate?"

"My dad has offered me a junior analyst job at his company." I shrug. I haven't really allowed myself to think beyond May.

"Coach Lewis is moving on, we'll have an assistant coaching spot if you're interested. Think about it. Pay is crap and you'd have to keep working with these knuckleheads, but for what it's worth, I think you have a real talent for it. You've already made a difference in Shaw. Maybe coaching at Valley, with guys you played with, is too much, but you say the word, and I'll make some calls to other programs."

Somehow, I manage to speak through the shock. "Thank you. I'll think about it."

Be a coach? We sit in an uncomfortable silence. It's already been a night out of bizzaro land, so I ask the question that's been floating around in my head since Shaw mentioned it.

"Do you think it's possible to love two things equally?"

He regards me seriously but waits for me to say more.

"Like two different sports or two different women or anything as much as I love basketball."

"If you find a penny today, are you more or less likely to find a penny tomorrow?" He shakes his head. "I don't know what the statistical likelihood is, but I think I'd worry less about trying to quantify it and grab on to anything that can even begin to compare to your love of the game. Especially now."

I mull that over for the rest of the trip, closing my eyes and faking sleep. Maybe quantifying love is a losing man's game. It doesn't matter if I love Blair the same way I love basketball, it just matters that I love her. She's been beside me for the worst year of my life, and when I try to picture it any other way, I don't know if I would have survived. She's breathed life into me again. I might still be bitter, but I'm no longer scared of what the future holds as long as she's by my side, forcing me to look at the positives and putting up with my grumpy ass.

The bus pulls into the fieldhouse after six. Been a long ass day, but I'm not tired. Ain't that a first. I gimp home, unable to wait for my roommates to shower and drop off their jerseys.

I've already texted Blair to give her an ETA on our arrival. So many times, I've come home to her waiting for me, giving up her life to be part of mine. I'm not selfless enough to think we'd be where we are today if she hadn't. She gave, and I took. I've always known what a badass chick she is, but I wouldn't have gone out of my way for her.

Not then, but I will now. I'll follow her around campus for the next four months, tell everyone that'll listen that she's mine, prove day in and day out that I'm not going anywhere.

I'm not happy that I can't play ball. There's no positive spin I'm putting on it today or any day in the future. Going out like this sucks, and I'll always wonder what-if and wish I'd been able to savor those last games knowing it was the end.

Nah, I'm not an optimist like Blair. I'm a grumpy motherfucker, and I probably always will be, but that's why I'm not letting go of her. She evens out my dark. Makes all the dull and gray seem polished and new.

Blair

Wes: Bus just got back. Where are you?

Me: Tutor Center. Want me to head over when we close?

Wes: Got some stuff to do first. I'll text ya.

My phone rings with a video call from Vanessa. "What's up?"

Vanessa sets the phone down and steps back, turning side to side to show me her outfit.

"Mario is picking me up in fifteen minutes. Help!"

"Where's he taking you?"

"He won't say, which is why I can't figure out what to wear. All he'll say is it would be a night to remember."

"Maybe he's gonna propose."

She places a hand to her lips. "Oh my God, I think I just threw up in my mouth a little."

"You look hot, per the usual. Relax and have fun."

She picks the phone up, bringing it closer to her face. "What are you doing tonight?"

"Not sure. Wes just got back, but he said he has some things to do." Saying the words aloud makes my stomach flip—and not in a good way. I know I'm being overly sensitive, but it feels like the beginning of another brush off.

She bites at her lip and narrows her gaze. I wait for

her to give me another lecture on being too available, but her phone beeps and her expression goes serious. "Shit, he's on his way. I gotta go."

"All right. Have fun and text me later. I can't wait to hear where he takes you."

When we hang up, I look around the empty tutor center and stand. It's ten minutes until we close, but no one has walked in the door in an hour.

I shift my attention to said door, and my eyes widen when Wes fills it. His arms are full of flowers and boxes and I start to make my way to him.

We meet in the middle, and his eyes scan the room. "Where is everyone?"

"Tutor sessions are over, and I told them I'd lock up. What are you doing here? What is all this?"

He shrugs, which is all he can manage with his arms full. "I was hoping for an audience, but I guess this will have to do."

I swallow a laugh when he begins to hand me the items he carries. A dozen red roses, a box of chocolates, a giant bag of Chewy Spree, a miniature stuffed pig, and a card that I can't wait to read later.

I'm stunned speechless, but manage to say, "Thank you."

"I know it isn't much, but it's all I could come up with on short notice."

"I don't understand."

"I'm in love with you. Been in love with you, and I've done a really shitty job of showing it. I wanted to storm in here and tell you and everyone else because you deserve that and so much more. Guess just telling you will have to do for now. I never asked the first time, just assumed. I don't want to do that this time. I want to be worthy. Want to be your choice. Be my girl?"

My heart is in my throat as this amazing guy stands in front of me looking more nervous than I've ever seen him. "You're in love with me?"

He nods.

"Dumb jock fell in love with the prissy sorority girl, go figure."

He grins. The cocky swagger is back as he closes the short distance between us and bends so we are eye to eye. "The smart jock fell for the hot sorority girl."

"She fell for him too," I say as I wrap my arms around his neck.

His lips slam down over mine, and I drop the gifts so I can jump him, wrapping my legs around his waist. "Probably should get out of here. I'd been prepared for an audience. Without one I'm likely to bend you over this desk."

I consider that, but ultimately pry myself off him.

"All right, boyfriend." I test the word, loving the way it sounds. "What's next?"

He chuckles. "I have no freaking clue. What do you say we start with a double date? Mario got tickets to some ridiculous K-pop band Vanessa likes."

"BTS?"

Wes shrugs. "Don't know, but I figure my best shot at winning over V is getting on her good side while she's happy . . . and maybe drunk."

I don't tell him what I already know—that all he has to do to win Vanessa over is keep me happy. It'll be way more fun to let him sweat this one out. And I can't wait to watch it unfold.

thirty-seven

Blair

"Are you always this nervous at games?" Gabby asks, causing V to cover her mouth and suppress a laugh.

"I can't help it."

I wipe my sweaty palms on my jeans. It's the last home game of the season and Wes is taking the floor with his team one last time for warmups. Things have been great the past month. We're spending all our time together, and Wes seems to be back to his old self. I know he's still struggling to stand on the sidelines, but he's showing up. And he looks damn good doing it.

He looks over as he prepares to shoot, gives a wink, and then brings his right hand up to his mouth and kisses the blue sweatband. My heart does a pitter patter in my chest.

"Blair, why didn't you tell me how hot Wes's

teammates are? Who's number thirty-three?"

"That's Joel."

She scrunches her nose. "The one that sleeps with everything that moves."

Vanessa doesn't get her hand over her mouth in time, and she spits the soda she'd just taken a sip of.

"One and the same," I confirm. "Nathan is number twenty-four, and Zeke is wearing jersey fifty."

Zeke picks that particular moment to glance up at us. His eyes narrow, brows furrow. A look of confusion and interest crosses his face and then disappears just as quickly. Gabby ducks her head and shivers. "He's hot too in a really intimidating way."

"We could set her up with Shaw. That'd drive Wes crazy." Vanessa grins.

The game starts, and I have a blast cheering on the team with my best friends. I haven't seen Gabby this happy in years, and it makes me think about how much fun we're going to have next year. And fingers crossed that Wes will be here too. He hasn't officially been offered the job yet, but Valley would be crazy not to keep him. He's their secret weapon even from the bench.

Valley is on fire, and we pull ahead by twenty early on and UCLA never recovers. Gabby and I have stopped watching the game all together and are planning out all the awesome things we're going to do when she moves to Valley. That is why I don't see Wes until he's standing right next to me.

"Hello."

The crowd around us is patting him on the back, and I swear I can almost feel the cameras zoom in on us. I wave my hands wildly in front of me and shriek over the noise, "What are you doing here?"

"I'm trying to watch the game. Move over." He leans in front of me. "Hey, Gabby. Good to see you."

I can't stop staring at him. I've never seen him up close like this in his jersey. He smells of leather and sweat and it's giving me a contact high.

"These seats really do suck. Good thing I'm gonna get to watch from the bench again next year."

"You got the job?" I yell and draw more attention to us, but I don't care.

He nods, and I launch myself into his arms.

"Wes, that's amazing. Congratulations. You're going to be amazing.'"

The words are true. I can already picture it. Him standing on the sidelines with that confident and determined set to his jaw. Maybe I can convince him to wear a suit like Coach Daniels. I like this idea better and better.

As we pull apart, he leans down and rests his forehead against mine. "Didn't really have any other choice. This girl kept busting my balls about helping my team and being there, and turns out, I'm good at it."

"Of course you are."

I throw myself at him again and hug him tightly. The buzzer sounds, signaling the end of the game. Wes pulls back, but neither of us move as the commotion around us becomes background noise.

"I love you, Blair." He has to shout to be heard over the applause and cheers. "I thought not being able to play ball was my biggest fear. It isn't. I can live in a world where I'm not Wes Reynolds, college athlete, but I can't live without you. Or, if I can, I just don't want to. I should have locked you down the first day I met you. You're the best thing that's ever happened to me."

I lean up on my tiptoes and wrap my arms around his neck. "Stop. Just stop. You had me at hello."

"*Jerry Maguire?*"

I nod.

"That's what you're going with? In front of twenty thousand people, your friends, ESPN cameras, you're going with a cheesy Tom Cruise line?" He smiles despite his teasing.

Is this guy really busting my balls about this? And I thought he was a smart jock. "How about this? I love you, Wes Reynolds, you dumb jock."

"I can work with that. Convinced you once I wasn't dumb, I'll take that challenge again."

"Possible outcomes include convincing me and not convincing me."

"Nope. Not convincing you isn't a possibility. I have talent and heart and I know your weakness."

"Oh yeah?" I ask, wondering if he means the fact I'm absolutely insanely in love with him.

"Yep. Chewy Sprees and my reading glasses. I have both waiting for you as soon as we get out of here."

epilogue

Wes
Four Months Later

Less than one percent of college basketball players make it to the NBA. I've known the stats since I was a kid, but it didn't keep me from devoting my life to the game.

I averaged eight assists, three steals, and fourteen points per game. I ate, I slept, I balled. It wasn't enough. I'm not part of the one percent.

I prided myself on heart and dedication. I worked harder and smarter. I saw things no one else could see on the court. I made assists that not even I was sure how I pulled off. I saw through players twice as big as me. Managed to get the ball in the hands of guys before they even realized they were open.

I saw things before they happened—plain and

simple.

As I stand at the back of the room and watch my friend and former teammate hold up his Suns's jersey and wear the orange-and-purple hat his agent thrust on top of his head when his name had been announced as the third pick in the NBA draft, I have nothing but the utmost love and respect for him. He's a one percent-er, and I'm not bitter about it.

I don't begrudge him the success because he worked as hard as I did. We sacrificed a lot to be elite college athletes. Championship titles and awards have been given to both of us, and I've accepted that my road ends here. I can rest easy knowing that everything I did helped in some small way to get him where he is today.

I saw this day happening. Always knew Z would be playing professional ball.

On the court, I saw everything. But off the court? I never saw *her* coming.

One day I was minding my own business, focused on my team, and the next, I was falling ass first for her determination and optimism. Getting the ball in the hands of an open player was my forte, but it wasn't until she came into my life that I made the ultimate assist. I helped her get an A in statistics, and she gave me everything in return.

As I cross the room to her, I take in my future. I couldn't figure out what it was I was meant to do with my life without basketball, until her.

I'll coach, and she'll finish school, but after that? I have no clue what we'll do next. I hope it involves more games of PIG that I *let* her win, more Chewy Sprees, a lot more sex. Hey, I'm just being honest. More of all of

The Assist

it with her.
Bless out.

the end

Thank you for reading *The Assist!*

Please consider leaving a review!

Coming Soon

More **Smart Jocks** are coming early 2019! Next up, *The Fadeaway* (Joel's story). Sign up for my newsletter to be notified of release dates and other book news:
www.subscribepage.com/rebeccajenshaknewsletter

Playlist

- "Run the World (Girls)" by Beyoncé
- "No Brainer" by DJ Khaled ft. Justin Bieber, Chance the Rapper, Quavo
- "Wing$" by Macklemore and Ryan Lewis
- "All I do Is Win" by DJ Khaled ft. T-Pain, Ludacris, Snoop Dogg, Rick Ross
- "Born to Be Yours" by Kygo and Imagine Dragons
- "Wicked Games (cover)" by The Grateful Dead
- "All Night" by Big Boi
- "White Iverson" by Post Malone
- "Happier" by Marshmello ft. Bastille
- "Me, Myself & I" by G-Eazy and Bebe Rexha
- "Drew Barrymore" by Bryce Vine
- "God's Plan" by Drake
- "Magenta Riddim" by DJ Snake
- "My Way" by Fetty Wap ft. Monty
- "King Kong" by DeStorm Power
- "I'm a Real" 1 by YG
- "Happy Now" by Zedd and Elley Duhé
- "Never Gonna Stop" by Jay Kill and The Hustle Standard
- "My House" by Flo Rida
- "On the Low" by Logic ft.Kid Ink and Trinidad James
- "High Hopes" by Panic! At The Disco
- "Hell & Back" by Kid Ink
- "Love Lies" by Khalid and Normani
- "In the Zone" by PL

Also by Rebecca Jenshak

About the Author

Rebecca Jenshak is a self-proclaimed margarita addict, college basketball fanatic, and Hallmark channel devotee. A Midwest native transplanted to the desert, she likes being outdoors (drinking on patios) and singing (in the shower) when she isn't writing books about hot guys and the girls who love them.

Be sure not to miss new releases and sales from Rebecca – sign up to receive her newsletter
www.subscribepage.com/rebeccajenshaknewsletter

www.rebeccajenshak.com

Made in United States
Orlando, FL
03 October 2022

22960734R00172